Love Finds You in Maiden

NORTH CAROLINA

BY TAMELA HANCOCK MURRAY

D0111819

summerside
PRESS

Love Finds You in Maiden, North Carolina
© 2009 by Tamela Hancock Murray

ISBN 978-1-934770-65-8

All scripture quotations are taken from the King James Version of the Bible.

The town depicted in this book is a real place, but all characters are fictional. Any resemblances to actual people or events are purely coincidental.

Cover and Interior Design by Müllerhaus Publishing Group
www.mullerhaus.net

Published by Summerside Press, Inc., 11024 Quebec Circle, Bloomington, Minnesota 55438 | **www.summersidepress.com**

Tamela Hancock Murray is represented by Joyce Hart of Hartline Literary Agency, LLC.

Fall in love with Summerside.

Printed in the USA.

Dedication

....

To John, Jill, and Ann:

Thank you for supporting me as I wrote this book.
John, you are an extraordinary husband in every way,
especially for your willingness to read every book and novella I write.
Jill, I am so proud of you and your writing talent.
Ann, I love your flare and creative talent in music and drama.
I thank the Lord every day for all three of you.

Special Thanks

....

I would like to give a special thanks to Margaret Ikerd Moose,
born in Maiden in 1922, for her remembrances of the town's
Main Street. Her childhood memories helped me breathe life
into my descriptions, greatly supplementing my own visit to
the lovely town of Maiden this past summer.

I would also like to thank my agent, Joyce Hart of Hartline
Literary Agency. You are a special person and a dear friend.

What man of you, having an hundred sheep, if he lose one
of them, doth not leave the ninety and nine in the wilderness,
and go after that which is lost, until he find it?

LUKE 15:4

THE CHARMING TOWN OF MAIDEN is located in Catawba County amidst the rolling hills of beautiful western North Carolina. Most historians agree that the town was named for nearby Maiden Creek, but no one is certain how the creek came by its name. Local folklore says the creek was named either for some maidens who lived along its banks or for a plant called Maiden Cane that grew in abundance along its upper reaches. Regardless of the name's history, the town's origin is certain. According to historian Gary R. Freeze, Maiden was founded after a cotton mill was built near the railroad in 1881. As more people moved into town, congregations of Reformed, Baptist, and Methodist quickly formed. Churches that Booth and Hestia might have attended stand today. Born in Maiden in 1922, Margaret Ikerd Moose remembers that when she was a little girl, Main Street boasted a hardware store, a drug store, a movie theater, a service station, and an apparel shop. Today, Murray's Mill is a treasured tourist attraction. Maiden is home to the Maiden High School Blue Devils and is considered the "biggest little football town in the world."

Chapter One

....

October 1922

Hestia Myatt paused before knocking on the door of her aunt's Victorian home situated in the foothills of the Appalachians in Maiden, North Carolina. She would only be staying three weeks, helping her relative recover from a broken pelvis—and during that time, Hestia hoped to collect her thoughts and make plans for a new life after her broken engagement.

A train whistled as it passed. The familiar sound always reminded Hestia of her aunt's house. An afternoon autumn rain had left burnished leaves lying on thin grass and a musty smell in its wake. Loving this season, Hestia took a moment to invigorate herself with a breath of chilly air as a welcome respite. Aunt Louisa's friend, Mrs. Howard, had picked up Hestia at the train station in her Model T. After a harrowing ride, thanks to her inexperience with the motorcar, she had dropped Hestia at the end of the sidewalk and departed. Undaunted, Hestia handled her two brown leather bags with ease. After composing herself, she rapped twice on the front door.

"Come on in." Hestia could hear the familiar voice through the open window. Her aunt's bedroom was on the front left side of the house. "Door's open."

As Hestia entered, a faint odor of leftover vegetable soup greeted her. Evidence of lunch didn't surprise her. Aunt Tillie had left only a couple of hours before, and Hestia had stepped in to take her place. The soup's aroma didn't smell appetizing at the moment; Hestia had had a good meal on the train. She took off her wide-brimmed hat decorated with large flowers and noted that the clean but cluttered parlor looked the same as she remembered from her childhood visits. Some of the sepia-toned portraits of long-dead relatives displayed in silver frames on occasional tables brought memories to Hestia's mind. Not a speck of dust could be seen. Overstuffed chairs with doilies draped over their arms and backs, crocheted years ago from cream-colored tobacco twine, offered comfort.

Figuring she'd be assigned to the back bedroom but unwilling to make assumptions, Hestia set her luggage on the shining pine floor.

"In here, Booth! What you waiting for?" Aunt Louisa called from her sickroom.

Booth? A flicker of remembrance visited Hestia. The round little boy could be counted on to throw a frog down her back or tease her by pretending he'd take aim at the nearest innocent bird with his slingshot.

She wondered how the little squirt was doing. Only he couldn't be a little squirt anymore. Too many years had passed since her last visit.

Smiling, she made her way through the parlor and turned into the bedroom. Out of respect for her aunt's privacy, Hestia had rarely ventured into the bedroom during past visits, but it, too, appeared much as she remembered—an extension of the cluttered parlor. A cherrywood four-poster bed dominated the space. Her aunt sat propped up by many fluffy pillows and rested underneath a quilt she'd sewn years ago out of colorful fabric scraps in the pattern known as Flying Geese. As a girl, Hestia had studied the triangular patches, wondering about the history behind the different cloth remnants. When Hestia quilted with her friends at church for their annual bazaar, the women would talk about the dresses, shirts, and skirts they had sewn from the material they'd donated, so each quilt symbolized the love of friends and family.

"Oh, it's you." Aunt Louisa's voice sounded welcoming, and bright eyes regarded Hestia from behind small spectacles. "I didn't realize the time had flown by so quickly. Why, you nearly crossed paths with Tillie."

"Yes, ma'am." Hestia walked to her aunt's bedside and kissed the smooth apple of her cheek, which defied the rest of her wrinkled face. As usual, Aunt Louisa smelled of talcum powder and, more so, of menthol liniment, the combination of scents Hestia associated with her. "I can still smell the soup you two had for lunch. Am I right that you're not hungry for supper yet?"

"Not yet. Tillie left some ham biscuits in the icebox. I reckon we can eat those around six thirty this evening."

Hestia didn't find her aunt's exacting time surprising. Aunt Louisa loved to stay on top of details. "That sounds fine to me." Though not overly tired from her trip, Hestia still felt grateful that her aunt had been considerate and already made plans for the next meal. "For now, why don't you let me bring you some tea, anyway? I could use a cup myself, truth be told."

"Of course. I'd love to visit over tea. Tillie and I had the best time catching up while she tended to me, but I'm ready for fresh news from other quarters." The older woman sighed. "I hate to be such a bother. Can't believe I fell right in my own house."

"Happens to the best of us. But you'll be well soon. I'll see to that."

"Oh, and you can get settled in the back bedroom."

"Yes, ma'am."

Hestia decided her bags could wait. A pick-me-up in the form of a cup of piping hot tea sounded good. She journeyed through the dining room. A substantial table and matching oak sideboard displayed her aunt's good rose-patterned china. Aunt Louisa liked to brag that the dining room set came from nearby Hickory, which was famous for quality furniture. Smiling as she remembered the boast, Hestia entered the kitchen in the back of the house. Like the others, this room hadn't changed from Hestia's recollection. Old-fashioned appliances, the likes of which she hadn't seen since the last time she visited, remained. Aunt

Louisa never believed in replacing anything that wasn't broken. The old-fashioned room possessed charm.

Aunt Louisa had always kept a blue-and-white kettle full of hot water on the wood-burning stove, and although she now kept to her room during this convalescence, today was no exception. Hestia prepared the refreshments without delay. Spotting a cookie jar painted with blue roses on the white countertop, she lifted the top and peered inside. Empty except for a few crumbs. She'd have to bake a batch of sugar cookies so they could have a snack in the afternoons to cheer her aunt's spirits and tide them over between meals. If her aunt's bony shoulders indicated the weight on the rest of her body, a little in the way of sweet treats wouldn't hurt her.

Aunt Tillie had left a silver tray to dry in the sink, so Hestia used it for the tea. Before exiting the kitchen, she checked the stove. Using a dish towel to protect her hand from the heat, she picked up the iron handle that went with the stove, which had been fashioned to catch into the slots of the heavy circular iron lids covering the fire. With alacrity she slid the handle into the slot of the nearest lid and lifted it to take a peek inside. Bright orange flames told her the wood would be burning awhile yet. She replaced the lid and then, bending, pulled out the white enamel drawer underneath to see if the ashes needed to be emptied. They didn't. Aunt Tillie had been her usual efficient self in making sure all was taken care of before exiting—well, except for cookies. All the same, Hestia made a mental note to thank Aunt Tillie when she next wrote to her. Surely Aunt Louisa would miss seeing Tillie every day since she'd returned to her home in Shelby.

Hestia's glimpse of a corner caught a bucket overflowing with fresh cucumbers. Apparently they had been a gift from someone's second harvest. She wondered what her aunt had planned for the vegetables.

With that thought, she picked up the tray carrying the tea and entered the sickroom.

"How did Tillie leave everything?" Aunt Louisa wanted to know.

"Fine, except I couldn't bring you any cookies, but we can do without for a day. I'll bake a batch tonight if you've got flour and sugar on hand." She set the tray on the vanity table.

"Tillie said I'm a bit low on supplies, but we should have enough to get by for a while yet. Didn't you see the apple pie on the counter? I thought she said there was some left over from lunch."

"Maybe she put it in the icebox." Hestia shrugged. "I'm not hungry enough for pie, but I'll be glad to fetch you a piece." She made a motion toward the kitchen.

"No, I'll wait for dinner—or maybe even lunch tomorrow. Being on bed rest the way I am, I don't move around enough to need much to eat." Aunt Louisa appraised Hestia as though she were a newly fashioned hat she was considering buying. "You look like a slice of pie wouldn't hurt you."

"I'm not a fanatic about staying slim, but I try not to overindulge."

"That's a good idea." She studied her again. After a few seconds, an approving nod went Hestia's way. "Your mother is a beautiful woman, but I do believe you surpass her."

"Now is that the laudanum talking?" Hestia joked. "Really, you flatter me."

"I'm serious. Your father can forget a career for you. Some man will sweep you off your feet before you can shoo him away. What's all this your father says about you thinking of a career in medicine, anyhow?"

"I haven't made up my mind yet, but I do find Father's work as a doctor fascinating. Demanding but fascinating."

"Yes, you never get a good night's sleep when you're a doctor. Somebody's always sick, it seems." She chuckled. "Like me, I'm afraid."

"Maybe he sent me here so you would discourage me from being a doctor, but I do know he enjoys having me as his assistant. The truth be told, I'd be content working for him the rest of my life." Hestia picked up an old image of her parents, taken when they were newlyweds. The smiling couple had grown into contented marriage partners.

"I know he'd like to keep you close to home." Aunt Louisa's attention focused on a picture of their family at a long-ago reunion when Hestia was but a child of six and her brothers not much older. "But Roger is still close by, at least."

"Yes, and that's a comfort to all of us." She set the picture on the table.

Aunt Louisa paused. "Nothing has been the same in your family since Edwin and Roger went to the Great War, has it?"

"No, ma'am."

She hated to think about how they lost Edwin; Roger came home without a physical wound but not the carefree boy he had been when he signed up to serve in the army. Hestia had encouraged him to share his war stories, but Roger said that his commanding officer had ordered his unit to forget everything they saw. Roger, always obedient to authority, did just that. Or so he said. "Papa has always been overprotective of me, but he did get worse after my brothers went to war."

"The reality of losing a son will do that to you." Aunt Louisa paused so long that Hestia thought she might cry, but she held back her emotion with an audible swallow. Instead, she turned cheerful. "How is Roger?"

"He and Elizabeth seem happy. They're renting a little house now, near where we live."

"Good to have family around. Any babies in the near future?"

"If there are, they're keeping it a secret from all of us. I know that Papa and Mama want some babies to hug." Hestia wished for a soft new baby to arrive in their family, too. Something about a newborn had a way of bringing everyone together. Maybe the helplessness of an infant brought out the compassion in people, putting them at their best.

"They'll come soon enough." Aunt Louisa sighed wistfully, and Hestia wondered if she felt sorry she didn't have children. "Did you get a chance to investigate your room yet?"

"Not yet. I will after we have our tea."

Aunt Louisa looked at the small clock on her nightstand. "Booth should be here soon. He stops by every day and helps me out, you know. He's such a sweet boy."

Hestia held back a grimace. Booth Barrington could not be described as *sweet*, at least not by his peers. She remembered the unflattering nickname he'd given her. Perhaps he seemed more polite to older folks. He always got *their* names right. Sometimes Booth used to tease her by pronouncing her name as *Hes-TEE-ah* instead of *HES-tee-ah*, a jest that annoyed her no end. She almost let out a groan in remembrance but restrained herself.

Hestia handed her aunt a cup of tea. A second cup in hand, Hestia took a seat in the vanity chair and set her thoughts to more immediate concerns. "Well, you can tell him he won't need to stop by anymore. At least not every day. I'm here now."

A knock on the back door kept Aunt Louisa from responding.

"Does he usually come through the back?" Hestia reasoned that they enjoyed a close relationship if he took such liberties.

"It varies. He stops by after work."

"Where does he work?"

"Union Mill. He helps run the office."

The back door slammed shut and the sound of boots clacking on the hardwood floor of the enclosed porch told them that whoever it was felt free to enter without waiting for a response.

"Yoo-hoo!" A rich yet high-pitched female voice trilled. "Louisa? Tillie?"

"In here, Olive."

Hestia recalled the distinctive voice. "Miss Olive still lives next door, I take it."

Aunt Louisa nodded, which didn't surprise Hestia. She imagined the lifelong friends would always live side by side. Yet a tired sigh told Hestia that often Miss Olive's visits proved more of a trial than a pleasure.

A graying woman roughly the same age as Aunt Louisa entered the bedroom. The scent of sugar hung about her.

Hestia rose from her seat.

With sharp eyes, the visitor assessed her. "Mercy! Who is this beauty?"

"You don't recognize me?" Hestia couldn't believe she had changed so much, but perhaps she had indeed.

Miss Olive tilted her reedy figure back from the waist up and set her forefinger on thin lips. "Your voice sounds familiar. Say something again."

Hestia chose one of her favorite Bible verses. "'The Lord is my strength and my song, and he is become my salvation: he is my God, and I will prepare him an habitation; my father's God, and I will exalt him.'"

Miss Olive grinned and snapped her fingers. "I know. Hestia!"

She smiled. "Yes, ma'am. May I get you a cup of tea?"

"No, thank you. I'm fine." She eyed Aunt Louisa. "Where's Tillie?"

"She's gone back to Shelby. Has her own life to live, you know. Didn't I tell you she was going back today?"

"I reckon you did. I must have forgotten. But I see you have another nurse."

"Yes, I do. Hard to believe this is little Hestia, isn't it?"

"It sure is," Miss Olive concurred. "The last time I saw you, Hestia, you wore your hair in plaits. I'm glad to see that you haven't chopped it off like some of the young girls these days. Mercy, they look a fright."

"I agree." Aunt Louisa picked up a sepia-toned picture of Hestia's grandmother, which was in a sterling silver frame embossed with roses and leaves. "There was a day when women prided themselves on looking as members of the fairer sex should and conducting themselves in like manner. Oh, for those days once again."

"Yes, and even our generation never failed to uphold high standards." Miss Olive shook her head as she studied Hestia, her expression conveying disbelief over the passage of time. "Why, you're as beautiful as I thought you'd turn out to be. How's that handsome father of yours? I do declare, you look just like him with a wig on. And your lovely mother? Or maybe I should ask them myself. They are here, aren't they?" Miss Olive scoped the room with an eagle eye as though the mention of their existence would bring her parents leaping out of the dresser drawers.

"No, Miss Olive. I made the trip by myself."

She gasped and hit her chest with her unadorned hand. "Mercy! Whatever for?"

"I told you, Olive." Aunt Louisa's tone was prickly. "She's here to help me—and to recover from a broken engagement."

Hestia felt her face flush. Did Miss Olive also know that Luther's eye for other ladies had caused their breakup? At least Hestia had discovered the fact *before*, rather than *after*, walking down the aisle. Still, she didn't want everyone in town to know her business. Hestia tried to dodge the subject and instead encouraged the two friends to bring her up-to-date on all the news in Maiden.

Animated by conversation, the neighbor never did state the original purpose for her visit. Hestia imagined that Miss Olive had spotted her and came over to investigate.

"So, Olive, what brings you by?" Aunt Louisa's tone indicated she already knew.

The neighbor jumped. "Oh. Yes. Sugar. Why, I ran plumb out of sugar right in the middle of baking my famous jelly thumbprint cookies for the whist party tomorrow. I could have sworn I had an extra sack of sugar in the cabinet, but when I went to look for it, it wasn't there."

"That can happen," Hestia sympathized.

"I hope not at your young age," Aunt Louisa opined. "You should have a sharp enough mind that you don't mislay things."

Miss Olive didn't wait for Hestia to respond. "So, Louisa, how much longer will it be before you can come back and play whist with us?"

Aunt Louisa shook her head. "The doctor says three more weeks at least. I wish there were something I could do for my broken pelvis, but staying propped up here in bed is about it."

"Leave it to you to break something you can't easily fix. I wish you'd hurry up and get well. Ethel is such a terrible player, and I get stuck being her partner for every game. Daphne ends up winning the prize every time, and you know how competitive she is. She just waves it in my face. Not that I want the prize that badly anyway. It's the principle of the thing with me." Miss Olive stared at Hestia. "Do you know how to play whist?" The catch in her voice indicated that she hoped the answer would be yes.

The old-fashioned card game that held the country captive with fascination in years past had never caught on as wildly with Hestia's friends. "Uh, I might remember a few of the rules from my childhood."

Before either of the older women could answer, someone else knocked at the back door.

"Come in!" Aunt Louisa shouted.

Hestia wondered if her aunt should ask who might be there first but then recalled that Booth Barrington was expected. Cringing, Hestia remembered his frogs.

The sound of sprightly footfalls marked the new arrival's progress from the porch to the kitchen. In a flash, a dark-haired man entered.

"Booth, it's good to see you again." Aunt Louisa smiled.

To her shock and consternation, Hestia's heart skipped a beat. *Booth? This is Booth Barrington?*

He smiled back. "How are you today, Miss Louisa?" He looked to the neighbor. "Miss Olive."

As she watched him greet the ladies, Hestia observed Booth. All his baby fat had disappeared, revealing a strong jawline and chin. His voice had matured from a boy's medium-pitched taunt to the lower tone of a confident man. Had he grown taller? It seemed so.

Carolina blue eyes locked their gaze with hers, widening. As though he were trying to conceal surprise, he hesitated. "And…Hestia? Hestia Myatt?"

"You remember me?" Her heart beating faster, she didn't bother to conceal her shock even though that meant her mouth hung open in a most unladylike manner. She never would have recognized Booth had she not been told it was he. Not even his dark, wavy hair would have given him away. Not entirely. "Oh, I know. Aunt Louisa must have told you about my impending visit."

"As a matter of fact, I did mention it."

"Yes." A look of remembrance flickered on his face. "But of course I remember you, Pi—I—I mean, Miss Hestia."

She held back a grimace at the almost-mention of the childhood nickname he had saddled her with in honor of her plaited hair, which he called "pigtails." *Piglet.* The name still made her wince.

She wondered what he must think of her. Had she changed as much as he had? Suddenly she felt self-conscious. Many young women had given themselves over to the flapper look—short skirts, bobbed hair, lips brushed with scarlet paint. With full parental approval, she had kept her hair flowing—though confined in the daylight hours—her skirts long, her face unknown to paint. Had her former fiancé been right? Was she out-of-date, out of step with the times? For a brief moment she wished she had given in to fashion dictates so she would seem more modern to the new Booth.

Just as quickly, she chastised herself for such shameful thoughts.

What's the matter with you? The man God has planned for you to marry will love you for yourself.

Marriage? She had seen Booth for less than a minute, and the thought of marriage had entered her mind? Her thoughts muddled with confusion. She felt faint. Maybe she should ask Aunt Louisa where she kept the smelling salts.

Chapter Two

....

"Um, is there anything you need from me today, Miss Louisa?" Though he spoke to the invalid woman, Booth couldn't keep his gaze off her niece. Was this Hestia the skinny waif who'd screamed bloody murder at the mildest prank, who'd worn gingham dresses and long pigtails? He thanked the Lord he'd stopped himself in the nick of time before calling her by her old nickname.

Such a derogatory name didn't apply to Hestia now. When had she grown into a blond angel—far beyond the most beautiful model for Pears' complexion soap? He noticed her modest attire. Surely she must go to church, unlike some of the painted flappers in town. Few pristine beauties were left in this new day and age. He hoped she planned to stay awhile.

"Are you planning to stay awhile, Miss Hestia?" he blurted.

She nodded. "Until Aunt Louisa is feeling better. And, please, don't call me *Miss Hestia*. We've known each other far too long for such formalities." She tilted her head to her aunt. "If I may be so bold, by your leave, Aunt Louisa."

Miss Olive sniffed. "Young people today are much too fast and forward, I say. Why, in our day, Louisa—"

"I agree heartily, but it's no longer our day, Olive." Aunt Louisa regarded her niece with unblinking, bespectacled eyes. "Of course what you call each other is between the two of you, as long as you keep it respectable."

Booth thought he'd better change the topic. "So Miss Tillie left already?"

Aunt Louisa answered. "Yes, she left late this morning."

The nurse Miss Louisa has now is certainly much prettier, he thought.

"Staying here with my aunt for a couple of weeks will give me an idea as to whether I might want to pursue a career in medicine," Hestia spoke up.

"You mean to say as a midwife, of course." Miss Olive nodded once as though the motion would close the discussion.

"Not necessarily. Perhaps a nurse—or even a doctor."

"Mercy!" Gasping, Miss Olive seemed offended by the notion. "Whyever would you want to become a doctor? Shouldn't we women leave those difficult areas of life to the menfolk?"

"That concept seems to be up for debate." Hestia turned to Booth. "What do you think?"

What did he think? How should he respond? Standing before two generations of women in the same room owning diametrically opposing viewpoints, they could find fault no matter what he said. But with them staring at him, he had to respond. "I—I don't know any other woman who wants to be a doctor. So I guess I'd have to say I haven't given it much thought."

Miss Louisa swished her hand in Hestia's direction. "See there? That's exactly why Luther left you."

Luther? So Hestia was recovering from a broken romance. A shattered heart had brought her to Maiden, at least in part. Clearly, the man who let her go was suffering from a bad case of foolishness.

Hestia's cheeks blushed scarlet, and she looked anywhere but at him. "I am certainly not perfect, but Luther had some faults I don't care to discuss, thank you."

"Oh, so Luther is the fiancé your aunt told me about?" Miss Olive guessed.

Still blushing mightily and prettily, Hestia nodded. "Yes, ma'am."

"Mercy. If you were going on and on about being a career woman, then it's not a wonder he broke it off with you." Miss Olive's expression told everyone in the room that she believed Hestia had gotten everything she deserved. Booth didn't seek out a career woman for himself, but he didn't agree that Hestia's sentiments justified her unhappiness.

"Truth be told, I broke it off."

Miss Olive didn't seem to hear Hestia. "Now, everyone knows I worked for my father before he passed on, God rest his soul, but I never had any desire to marry. I suppose you can call me a maiden, the same as the spinster ladies who used to live by Maiden Creek."

Booth held back a smile. Miss Olive had to reach far back to remember her youth.

Miss Louisa chuckled. "Olive is right, Hestia. It's fine and good for you to help your father in his doctor's office as a diversion before marriage, but a woman of your stature should be thinking about making a good match and leave the breadwinning to the man of the house. That's what I say. Isn't that what you say, Booth?"

Why did these women insist on grilling him? He wasn't sure whether to be flattered or insulted by Miss Louisa's willingness to talk about such matters with him, even asking his opinion. Clearly she had no thought that he would consider courting Hestia. Or perhaps more to the point, that Hestia would never consider him as a suitor. The women seemed to think she was much too career-minded to marry. What type of man could change Hestia's mind?

He cleared his throat and shot his gaze to Hestia for a flicker of an instant, long enough to see her shift her slight weight from one hip to the other and take a sudden interest in a specific plank in the pine floor. Miss Olive studied him as though she planned to memorize every word of his response. What could he say that wouldn't embarrass Hestia?

He swallowed. "I think that as long as a person seeks the Lord's guidance every day and stays in His will, life will be all it's meant to be."

Miss Louisa sighed. "Such wise words. Reminds me of the kind of answer my dear departed Orvis would have given to such a question. If only he were still here among us."

"Now, now," Miss Olive consoled her friend, patting her shoulder. "He did his part, what with working such a good job at the mill. You're one of the most well-fixed widows in town, if not *the* most well-fixed."

"Yes, he was successful, but frugal living and saving your pennies does the trick every time." Pride filled her voice.

"Yes, ma'am." The sentiment reminded him of his father's wise words about money.

"Oh, Booth, we're keeping you from going home to your own dinner." Miss Louisa looked at the clock as though she had suddenly remembered Booth's presence and been tasked to remind him to go home. "I do have something I need you to do for me. Could you set a mousetrap in the cellar? Maybe Hestia can fetch a piece of cheese for you."

"We have mice?" Hestia shuddered.

Miss Louisa waved her hand at Hestia. "Honest to goodness, girl, don't tell me you've never had a mouse."

"Well, yes, I suppose, but I can't say I'm too fond of the little pests."

"I'm not either. That's why I plan to get rid of them."

"You don't need to ask Booth to set a trap. I can do that for you." Hestia stood tall and confident, as though the thought didn't bother her. He wondered if she was putting on a front for him, considering her stated aversion to mice. Did she even know how to set a trap?

"Let a girl set a mousetrap? Not under my watch." Booth couldn't imagine someone as genteel and fine as Hestia involving herself in the pursuit of rodents. "What are you trying to do, make me completely useless around here?" He didn't want to admit even to himself that that thought seemed dismal. Checking on his neighbor hadn't been an awful chore, but with Hestia's arrival, the prospect of daily visits seemed more interesting.

"You could never be useless anywhere, my boy." The way Miss Louisa smiled made her appear wise. "Now that I do have such wonderful help in Hestia, I don't want to impose on your time."

"I don't mind stopping by as long as you'll have me." Booth glimpsed at Hestia. Was that a pleased look on her face? Or did hope make him imagine it?

He didn't care. He wished he could find a better excuse to linger than setting a mousetrap, but at least he could look forward to seeing Hestia every day. He'd make sure he did.

Chapter Three

....

"Breakfast is ready, Aunt Louisa." Hestia brought a tray to her aunt the following day.

The older woman sat up in bed. Though she wore a long-sleeved nightgown, she took the pink bed jacket embroidered with a pattern of lilies of the valley from the headboard and slipped it over herself. She buttoned it to the top. "Bacon?"

"Yes, with toast, eggs, and coffee."

"I hope you didn't burn the bacon."

"No, ma'am."

Aunt Louisa put on her spectacles, which were rimmed in golden wire, and regarded the wooden tray Hestia was holding. She peered at the two plates. "You're eating with me?"

"Of course. Why would you want to eat alone?"

Aunt Louisa shrugged. "I don't. It's just that Tillie thought it was too hard for both of us to manage in here."

Hestia could understand why. The room's generous proportions disappeared, crowded as it was by Aunt Louisa's many mementos, each a testimony to a long, well-lived life. Most of the surfaces held portraits of their family. Hestia knew each one—if not by personal acquaintance, then by stories told by older relatives.

"Well, I'll eat on the vanity table, if that suits you." The vanity offered one of the few fairly clear surfaces, enough on which to hold a plate and cup of coffee. Hestia set one plate and her cup on the vanity and set the tray beside her aunt in bed.

Aunt Louisa stared at Hestia's plate on the vanity. "As long as you don't ruin it. That vanity was my sixteenth-birthday present, I'll have you know."

Hestia already knew but kept her tone as sunny as the day outside. "I'll do my best. Let's share grace, shall we?"

Aunt Louisa nodded.

Hestia took her aged hands in hers. Veiny and covered with liver spots, they were nevertheless soft to touch. After she and Aunt Louisa had prayed, Hestia had a question. "I've been meaning to ask what you plan to do with the bucket of cucumbers in the corner of the kitchen."

"Oh, those. Hugh Drum brought those. They were part of the late harvest from his garden."

"That's awfully nice of him. You two aren't sweet on each other, are you?" Hestia couldn't resist teasing as she took her seat at the vanity table.

A train whistled, and Aunt Louisa waited for it to pass before answering. "Oh, no. I'm past being sweet on anybody. Us old people just look out for each other, that's all."

"I hope God lets me live long enough to understand." Hestia wondered what life would be like living as an elder. Slower, for certain. She wanted to live in such a way that her memories would comfort her, much as Aunt Louisa treasured the memories of her life. Hestia's musings returned to present tasks. "That's a mighty heap of produce you've got out there."

"Yes, and Tillie didn't have time to pickle them before she left. She did get a few tomatoes and string beans canned."

"That's wonderful of her, but what about her family?" Hestia consumed a bite of egg.

"Oh, her daughters took care of her."

Hestia could only imagine having to preserve the substantial crops from two family gardens along with neighbors' bounty, but it couldn't be helped.

Aunt Louisa lifted a forkful of egg. "So, are you planning on making pickles for me? We sure can't eat all those fresh cucumbers by ourselves before they go bad."

Pickling cucumbers took effort, but in good conscience they couldn't waste food. "Of course I'll pickle them for you."

"That's what I hoped you'd say. You'll find my recipe box on the counter. It's not so very hard. It's the same one your mother uses."

"Oh, the sweet pickle recipe?"

"That's the one. You need to make a batch to get in practice for your own home someday, you know."

Hestia wondered if during her entire visit her aunt would keep reminding her that she should be seeking a suitor. She nodded out of respect.

"And you need to pick the October beans in the garden. I'm sure they're ready. I was going to have Booth pick them for me and take some to his mother, but I think you're quite capable. We can still send some to them."

"Of course." Hestia spread grape jelly on her toast, being careful not to spill crumbs.

"Oh, and there's some fall cabbage on the back stoop."

"I do declare, Aunt Louisa, I believe you're perfectly well and just wanted me to put up your vegetables."

"How did you know?" she teased.

"I can put up a few vegetables for you. I'm sure mine won't be nearly as good as yours, but maybe they'll be edible."

"Goodness' sakes, child. I'm sure they'll be fine. Even from here in bed, I can give you some pointers since you'll be using my recipes. I'd like you to make some fresh coleslaw out of the cabbage for us to eat now and make up a batch of sauerkraut for later. I didn't think to tell Tillie about this yesterday, so you can put in an order from the grocer to get any ingredients I might not have on hand."

Hestia had an idea. A sneaky one, but an idea all the same. "I wouldn't mind if Booth took me uptown next week to provision us fully. Do you think he'd mind? Then I can shop at the mercantile for myself and I'll have a way to bring home all the goods in one trip."

"That's a thought. Booth is a mighty nice fellow. I hate to keep on imposing on his generous spirit, though. Maybe we'd be best off with delivery."

"Or maybe I can just tag along when he's out and about anyway. It will give me the chance for a little change of scenery while not leaving you alone too terribly long."

Aunt Louisa shrugged. "Suit yourself, child."

* * * * *

When Hestia dropped a hint that she could use a ride to the mercantile the next Saturday, Booth agreed without pause. She hoped he didn't think her too bold. Aunt Louisa seemed amenable to the idea and didn't suggest that Hestia had hatched the plan so she could see more of Booth. If either of them thought her request sounded out of the ordinary, they didn't let her know.

On Saturday, what should have been an everyday trip to the mercantile turned into an event for Hestia. She found herself agonizing over her appearance as though they had planned an evening at the opera. Usually self-assured and decisive, that day she couldn't make up her mind what dress to wear. When she tried to twist her hair, the locks wouldn't cooperate. "What is wrong with me?" Exasperated, she set a wayward strand in place with a bobby pin, hoping it wouldn't show.

"Hestia?" Aunt Louisa called.

She spritzed tuberose fragrance on her wrist from a special crystal perfume bottle before making haste to go into the bedroom. "Yes, ma'am?"

"You've got your list, haven't you?"

She patted her skirt pocket and felt the folded paper. "Yes, ma'am."

"Please add kitchen matches to it. I'd sure hate for us to run out now with winter fast approaching."

"Yes, ma'am."

Aunt Louisa studied her. "Is that a Sunday dress you've got on?"

"No, ma'am." Her answer was truthful, but she had chosen one of her best everyday dresses. She'd been told—by Luther, even—that the rose color flattered her. "Does it look okay?"

"Better than okay." She pursed her lips. "You aren't getting all spiffed up for Booth, are you?"

She felt heat rise to her cheeks. "Uh—"

"Now, you should remember that I'll be well soon and you'll be back on your way to Haw River. It's best, for your own good, mind you, not to get attached to anyone here."

At that moment Booth knocked, and Hestia hastened to answer. He met her with a grin. "I'm ready if you are."

"Then don't let me hold you up." She reached for the handbag she'd left in a chair.

"You look especially pretty today, Hestia. Much too pretty to go to the store."

"I wouldn't say that, but thank you. I appreciate your help."

"Now don't you forget anything," Aunt Louisa called from her room. "Booth doesn't want to have to go back out because of foolishness."

"Yes, ma'am," she called back. "We'll be back as soon as we can."

After they ventured outdoors, Booth helped her into the Model T touring car. After she was situated in the passenger seat, he ran around to the driver's seat and set the switch then stepped to the front and cranked the engine. Once the motor got running, he rushed back and jumped into his seat. "Sorry to hurry you. Next time I buy an automobile, I hope it will have an electric starter."

She laughed. "I was ready anyway. Thanks again for taking me to the store."

"My pleasure. Mother needed a few things, so she'd planned to send me, anyway. Having company is much better."

"Good. I wouldn't want to impose."

"Is the Murray's Mill mercantile okay by you?"

"Sure."

Booth released the brake, and the car lurched as they began their journey. Hestia adjusted her driving hat and breathed in the fresh air. Murray's Mill was a long drive from Maiden, but the mill was known for its freshly ground flour. The drive would take them along the rail lines, first north to Newton and then east to Catawba. Aunt Louisa and the Barringtons lived on the north side of Maiden toward Newton, so they didn't need to travel through the center of town. The quiet road they took offered a view of oak and maple trees bursting with fall colors. People sat on the porches of the bungalows, brick Georgian, and two-story clapboard houses they passed. Booth waved at them all, and they waved back as though he was a long-lost brother they hadn't seen in a decade. Most of them also gave her a cockeyed look.

"Within the hour, I think everyone in this county will know you're in town," Booth shouted over the motor. "I hope you don't mind being seen with me."

"Not if you don't mind being seen with me," she countered. "I know all about living in a small town. They'll probably have us engaged before the week's out." She wished she could clap her hand over her mouth and turn back the clock thirty seconds. What had made her say such a ridiculous thing? What must he think of her?

To her relief, he laughed. "Sorry. Guess you'll be stuck with me, then. Shall we set our wedding date now?"

She laughed with more enthusiasm than she felt, a sign of her relief that he shared her sense of humor.

He tooted the horn at a pretty young brunette planting fall flowers in her yard near Newton. She turned and waved, flashing an appealing smile. An unwelcome pang of jealousy visited Hestia, and she reminded herself of Aunt Louisa's admonition not to get too close to anyone during her visit. "That's Miss Mahoney," Booth explained, clearly oblivious to Hestia's turmoil. "She's my secretary."

"Pretty."

"What's that?" he shouted over the motor.

Hestia wished she didn't have to repeat the obvious. "I said she's pretty."

"Oh." He kept his eyes on the road. "I guess she is. We've just never seen each other that way. Matt Drum is courting her. He's considered a much better catch than I could ever be." Hestia wanted to blurt that he need not be modest, but he quickly changed the subject. "How do you think your aunt is doing?"

"She's feisty as ever, ordering me around. I'll say, I've worked harder than I ever remember. Not only does she have me canning all the vegetables people bring her"—she waved the list—"but I've been engaged in a deep fall cleaning. I'm more of a maid than a nurse."

"Do you mind so much?"

"Not since it's her, I suppose."

"Yes, we do things for family we wouldn't want to do for strangers. I'll bet she's teaching you all the tricks to canning, supervising her kitchen even though she's in bed."

"Yes." She chuckled. "Some of the tricks she is teaching me I didn't even know from Mother. I think by the time I leave here, my aunt will be set with most of her food for the winter. Plenty of pickles and sauerkraut, anyway."

"Not sure I'd want to live on those, but I suppose it's possible...."

A trip to a mercantile was always a nice diversion, even when her list held nothing more exciting than pickle lime, but the day proved especially fun with Booth. After forty minutes, they pulled up to a well-kept mill that was situated on a lovely man-made pond. Getting out of the car, Hestia couldn't resist stopping to take a look at the dam and the millrace. The waterwheel was not engaged as she surveyed the scene. She imagined what the impressive wheel might look like with water rushing over it as it made loud swishing sounds.

"Gorgeous, isn't it?" Since Booth had cut the motor, he no longer needed to yell.

She turned to him. Yes, he was gorgeous. She noticed he had indulged in shaving water that smelled of brisk spices. A perfect choice for autumn. She wondered if he had splashed on a bit more than usual for her benefit but decided not to dwell on such a vain notion. "Yes, it is gorgeous here. I love how the trees are so colorful against the water. Look at how it's catching the sunlight."

"Even the most skilled artist would have trouble capturing the wonder of God's artwork this morning. It was worth the trip just to see this, wasn't it?"

"Yes, it was."

She would have commented that she'd be happy to go all the way across the state to Carolina Beach with him but put such a shocking thought out of her head before she said anything. They lingered in silence a few more moments then he escorted her across the small street to the mercantile located in a white house with a high porch. The store was busy enough that they met others as they went up the steps to enter.

Booth didn't hesitate with his errand. He headed straight toward the candy display. Out of curiosity, Hestia followed him. "Look." Booth pointed to a row of candy bars. "I haven't seen this one before." He picked it up. "Mounds."

"Have you tried one of those yet?" The storekeeper was waiting on another customer, but he paused long enough to pose the question. "They came out not too long ago. They're coconut covered with chocolate. Pretty good."

"Okay, I'll take five." He held up all five digits of his right hand.

Hestia tried not to seem too shocked. "Five? My goodness, you must have quite a sweet tooth."

"I do, but this time I'm buying them for other people—Mother, Daddy, your aunt, me, and you. Doesn't that add up to five?"

"Yes, but really, I can't."

"Sure you can. It's just a candy bar."

The combination of chocolate and sweet coconut sounded good to her—and the novelty of a new type of candy, interesting. "Oh, all right. And I'm sure Aunt Louisa will enjoy a treat."

He nodded and added the candy to the Barringtons' order. With efficiency, he waited on Hestia as well. All too soon, Hestia and Booth were back in the Ford with several bags of flour, some cornmeal, sugar, coffee, and a bushel of apples. She had the kitchen matches in her handbag in her lap. Thinking of all the supplies, she was glad she'd asked Booth to help her. She'd gotten much accomplished in a day.

They rumbled back onto the road, waving at everyone. Hestia basked in Booth's reflected popularity. Clearly, everyone in town thought highly of her companion.

"I hate to ask," Booth yelled, "but do you mind if I stop at the service station for gas? That way I won't have to take the motorcar out again later."

"That's fine."

They drove up Main Street in Maiden. Hestia remembered the hardware store and the drugstore from summer visits. The movie theater advertised *Blood and Sand*. The ad depicted Rudolph Valentino embracing his costar for torrid effect. Since she didn't keep up with motion pictures, Hestia wasn't sure whether the lace-covered woman was Lila Lee or Nita Naldi since both of their names appeared under his.

Booth pulled into the service station. Immediately, an attendant came to their assistance. Booth greeted him by name then nodded toward the station. "Care for a bottle of Coca-Cola?"

"No thanks."

"You're quiet. What are you thinking? You didn't forget anything, did you? If you did, I'll take you back. I'd hate for Miss Louisa to fuss at you."

"No, I don't think I forgot anything. I was just looking around at the town. It's been awhile since I was up Main Street."

Booth paid the attendant and started the automobile. Soon they were back on the road. "I look forward to when they pave the street. That's supposed to happen soon."

She gave him an exaggerated nod. They passed houses in varying styles on the way home. Each house looked as unique as its individual occupants would. Treed yards and fall plantings gave the town a serene appeal. They also drove by two churches, evidence of God's presence in Maiden. Hestia took in the scenery, thinking of how she had come to visit such a lovely place.

Once again several people waved at Booth, and he returned their greetings. Soon they had pulled up in front of Aunt Louisa's. She realized she had said very little on the way home. "I didn't mean to be rude with my silence. I was just missing home a little, that's all. Although that's no reflection on present company. It's just that you have so many friends here, and so I miss mine back home."

"I'd think poorly of you if you didn't miss your friends. I'm sure you're every bit as popular in Haw River as I am here. Probably more. But I have an idea. Why don't you make friends here while you visit? If you'd be so kind, I'd appreciate it if you'd allow me to escort you to church tomorrow."

"Why, I hadn't thought much about church. With Aunt Louisa bedridden, I suppose I assumed I'd miss church. But I really would like to go to worship, especially with someone I know."

"You know me."

"That I do." She sent him her prettiest smile. "Okay, I'll ask Aunt Louisa if she'll allow it."

* * * * *

Hestia rejoiced when Aunt Louisa granted her permission to go with Booth the following day; she could hardly object to church attendance. Church began Hestia's week the right way in Haw River, and the prospect of worshiping in Maiden delighted her.

Sunday morning proved to be a beautiful, brisk fall day. Hestia donned her best dress, grateful that she had taken her mother's advice to bring all her good clothes in case she needed them. She made certain to be ready in plenty of time and met Booth at the door promptly.

He looked her up and down from head to toe, noting her appearance in a gentle manner that didn't make her feel uncomfortable. "You look pretty today."

"Thank you, but you don't have to flatter me." She felt herself blush, although she had already seen in the mirror that she was indeed pretty that day.

"I'm not flattering you. I mean it."

Hestia tried to cover her surprise upon seeing his parents in the Model T. What had she been thinking? Of course they would be going with them to church. Mrs. Barrington sat in the back seat, with her husband in front.

As Booth helped Hestia board the car, seating her in back with his mother, Hestia caught a pleasing whiff of Bay Rum scent. Perhaps he saved Bay Rum for Sundays. Like the day before, his masculine fragrance reminded her that she missed being close to a man. He smelled good enough that she had to restrain herself from drawing closer to him as he passed.

Mrs. Barrington greeted Hestia. The older woman looked much as Hestia remembered. She had grown plumper, her figure suiting her round face framed by dark hair. The loud motor and brief trip didn't give them much chance for conversation beyond a casual greeting, but Booth's parents were as pleasant as she remembered.

Before she knew it, Booth and Hestia were walking through the doors of his church. Hestia wasn't surprised that people turned to stare when she entered with him. Two attractive women near Hestia's age gave her envious looks and then turned and whispered to each other. A couple of men noticed her and then pretended they hadn't. She tried not to appear ill at ease, and she studied Booth with her peripheral vision. He didn't seem embarrassed and held his head high as they made their way to a pew near the front.

Not until she sat did she realize that beside her was an auburn-haired beauty. The woman turned and whispered, "I'm Judith Unsworth. Welcome." When she smiled, Hestia saw no trace of resentment. "Are you a friend of Booth's?"

"Yes, I suppose you could say that. My aunt lives next door to him, and I'm visiting while I take care of her."

"Oh, you must mean Louisa Evans."

"Yes."

"I'm so sorry. My grandmother thinks highly of your aunt."

"Thank you," Hestia managed before the service began.

Hestia shared a hymnal with Booth, but Judith and she exchanged smiles from time to time. Hestia had a feeling that if she were staying in town longer, Judith would prove to be a good friend.

* * * * *

Over the next week when Booth visited, Hestia couldn't resist making sure her housedresses, plain though they were, sparkled with cleanliness. She noticed that his face lit up whenever she wore the dark blue one, so she appeared in that one the most, but not too much. The gray one seldom left the wardrobe closet.

Booth showed himself prompt, always stopping by between closing time at the cotton mill and dinner with his parents. Each day when Hestia saw him approaching the walk, she stole into her bedroom to peer into the mirror, hoping to escape her aunt's notice, and pinched her cheeks a few times to bring up the color. Tuberose toilette water, a Christmas gift from her parents, added a pleasant fragrance behind her ears. Her hair received special attention, as well.

She felt her efforts were rewarded. Booth never seemed disappointed to see her, always lingering for hot coffee with three lumps of sugar and plenty of cream or breakfast tea laced with honey. Their shared talk about family, past events, and funny stories made Hestia feel comfortable in his presence and, at the end of each afternoon, left her wanting to see him again. By that time of day, Aunt Louisa had awakened from her afternoon nap, ready to greet Booth. Hestia could see that his visits offered a bright spot in her aunt's day, too. Despite Hestia's initial reticence about being banished to Maiden, she now wished it would never end.

* * * * *

"It's almost time for Booth again."

Hestia's heart did a little jump whenever Aunt Louisa made the pronouncement. Hestia never pointed out the time herself, as she didn't want her aunt to suspect that her thoughts dwelled too much on their handsome neighbor. "Have you put on the coffee? It's so chilly I imagine he'll want a hot drink today. I know I could use something to warm my old bones."

"Yes, coffee's almost ready." Hestia tried not to appear breathless, having emerged from her bedroom after a cheek-pinching session. Thankfully, her aunt never seemed to notice Hestia's smoothed hair and reddened complexion. Or if she did, she never commented.

"I'm assuming Booth will be escorting you to preaching again this Sunday."

"Yes, ma'am. I really like the people in church. I especially get on well with Judith Unsworth."

"Yes, she comes from a fine family. I can't object to any friendship with her."

"I appreciate your being willing to be left alone long enough for me to go to church. Attending makes my week complete."

Aunt Louisa sighed. "I miss going to church myself."

"And they miss you, too. They're always asking after you. I'm sure Doctor Lattimore will give you release soon."

"One can only hope."

"Miss Louisa? Hestia?" They heard Booth call from the entrance.

"I'll greet him." Hestia strolled from the bedroom to the parlor. "Good afternoon, Booth." She saw that he carried a furry white bundle. "What have you got there?"

"Something that will help with any mice you might have. I'm assured by her previous owner that she's quite well behaved."

Hestia took the cat. "She's hardly a kitten. She must weigh fifteen pounds."

"No doubt about it, but that's all the better since you won't have to train her much. They tell me she's quite a good mouser."

"Then why would her owner want to get rid of her?"

"They just had a baby, and the two of them don't seem to get along. The owners are distressed about the whole thing. If I can't find a home for the cat, who knows what will happen to her? We already have two cats at my house as it is, and they're always walking on thin ice with Rover."

"I've watched them out in the yard. He loves to bark at the poor things." Hestia stroked the cat's head and spoke to her in a soft voice. "That's too bad about the baby. It's hard to compete with the little ones, isn't it? Well, if your owner is absolutely certain there's no room for you, then I'm sure we can find a place for you here." Hestia looked at Booth. "With Aunt Louisa's approval, of course."

"Of course. Let's hope she says it's okay."

Hestia strolled into the sickroom, still holding the cat. "Look what Booth brought us. A mouser."

Aunt Louisa looked down her nose at her neighbor. "What's the matter, Booth—tired of setting traps?"

Booth chuckled. "I haven't set a trap in days. I don't think you had more than one mouse."

Aunt Louisa crossed her arms. "Well, then, we don't need a cat. Especially one as huge as that. That animal will eat us out of house and home. Where did it come from, anyway?"

"The Nelsons. Sarah and Jonas."

Her face brightened. "How is the baby, anyway?"

"Colicky, apparently. Sarah and Jonas both look as if they haven't slept in weeks, and the baby cried the whole time I was there. They're trying goat's milk to see if that will help."

Aunt Louisa tsked. "I'd say they have their hands full."

"So that means we can keep the cat? Oh, please, Aunt Louisa?" Hestia knew she sounded like a spoiled little girl, but she couldn't help herself. "And even though our mouse is gone now, we might get another one, and we won't have to worry if we have a good mouser."

"So you say, but I don't want the bother of taking care of a cat forever."

"I'll take care of her." Hestia stroked underneath the cat's chin. The animal closed her eyes and purred.

"But who'll take care of that cat when you're gone?"

"I'll take her back with me if you haven't fallen in love with her before then."

Aunt Louisa lifted her hands in surrender. "Oh, all right. I can see my life will be miserable if I don't go along." Despite the fact she tried to sound put upon, her gentle tone told Hestia she liked the idea of owning a house cat.

"Thank you, Aunt Louisa." Hestia snuggled her nose into the cat's neck and spoke in a childlike voice to it. "So what is your name?"

Booth smiled. "Her name's Diamond."

"Well, Diamond, welcome to your new home."

Diamond purred, much to everyone's amusement.

"Thanks for adopting her." Booth rubbed the cat between the ears. "I promised them I'd find a good home, and now I can say I did."

Aunt Louisa sniffed. "I hope Selene likes cats."

"Selene?" Hestia and Booth whipped their gazes to the older woman and gasped in unison.

Aunt Louisa nodded. "I just received word she'll be visiting us. She's scheduled to arrive the morning of November twelfth. Which reminds me—Booth, could you pick her up from the train station and bring her here?"

"That's a Friday, right?"

"Yes."

"I'm sorry, but I'm almost certain I have a meeting at work I can't miss that day. Otherwise, of course I would be glad to collect her."

"That's all right. I'll ask Abe Perkins. I'm sure he'll be able to do it."

"If not, let me know and I'll find someone," Booth assured her.

Hestia only halfway listened to their plans. At least Booth wouldn't have to pick Selene up from the station. Of course, Selene would much prefer Booth over Abe, whose sixtieth birthday had long since passed. But she would become reacquainted with Booth soon enough.

Hestia tried not to pout. Selene. The cousin she'd always envied was a pretty, glamorous, extravagantly wealthy socialite. The cousin she could never match. Quickly her thoughts turned to Booth, and unwelcome jealousy raged. Hestia, with her modest looks and dress, could never compete with such a vision. She felt like the little girl called "Piglet" again. She swallowed and tried to keep anxiety from entering her voice. "Why is she coming?"

"That's hardly a charitable response." Aunt Louisa's eyebrows rose.

Embarrassed, Hestia felt her face flush. "I—I didn't mean to be uncharitable. Of course I want to see Selene. I just wondered why she's visiting at this moment in time, that's all."

"Does she have to have a reason?"

"No," Hestia answered too quickly.

"This place has gotten to be a regular hotel." Booth's voice sounded a little too bright, a sure sign he hoped to allay any tension. "It'll be nice to see her again. It's been years."

"Has it?" Hestia blurted.

Booth nodded. "She hasn't been here since before your last visit. And that was too long ago."

Hestia sent her glance to the floor and back. At least he had the good graces not to make her feel invisible now that her glamorous cousin would be by to grab all the attention. But maybe God had planned to send Selene to Maiden for a reason. If Booth wasn't the right man for Hestia, Selene would steal him away and that would be that.

Oh, how could she think such a thing? Booth wasn't hers to steal.

Chapter Four

Moments later, sitting at the kitchen table, Booth wondered about the odd exchange with Miss Louisa and Hestia. Hestia usually displayed the ultimate in Southern hospitality, so her coldness struck him as strange. Didn't she want to see her cousin? He remembered Hestia speaking about visiting Selene in New York, marveling at her penthouse in the city and her mansion in the country. No one else they knew owned two residences. Such extravagance seemed wasteful. Still, Hestia never gave the impression she was jealous of Selene's wealth and seemed to be content with a modest but comfortable upbringing in Haw River. That's why he'd always felt more of a kinship with Hestia than he ever could with Selene. Hestia's character had been formed in a place much like Maiden. Her outlook and expectations were similar to his, even if she did toy with the idea of pursuing a career in medicine. Most women he knew didn't harbor such ambition, but Booth admired Hestia's lofty goals. Selene's lifestyle seemed frivolous to him. He didn't think someone such as Selene could ever be happy in Maiden. Even Raleigh would no doubt seem small and dull to her.

"I made marshmallows yesterday." Hestia interrupted his musings. "Care for a couple in your cocoa?"

"Keen. How about I take that tray from you?"

Hestia nodded. "I'll carry this plate of cookies separately." They returned to the sickroom.

"Oh, thank you both. My, that cocoa looks good. It's so chilly today." Aunt Louisa shivered.

Hestia set the beverage on Miss Louisa's night table. "Yes, this should hit the spot. I think I'm in the mood for chocolate. I could use something to warm me inside, too."

For a flash of an instant, Booth wished he could suggest that an embrace might do more to warm her than cocoa but decided against making such a suggestion, especially with Miss Louisa watching.

Since Hestia had returned to Maiden, they'd renewed their acquaintance, but on a much deeper level this time. He discovered he loved being around Hestia, not only for her spirit but for her beauty. She never failed to make even the plainest dress—the kind his mother would wear on laundry day—look like a ball gown. If he didn't know better, he'd swear a photographer must be hovering in the background, waiting to take her picture for a commercial in a periodical. He wondered if anyone had ever suggested she might consider modeling instead of medicine, but he sensed she'd be much too modest to pursue such a career. Not that his opinion would ever matter. Soon she'd return to Haw River and he'd have to say good-bye. He missed her already.

* * * * *

"Do you hear a motorcar, Hestia?" Aunt Louisa asked a few days later. Skipping her afternoon nap, she had put on her best bed jacket—a pretty garment fashioned of cotton the color of coral, with a floral design embroidered in a thread of deep orange. Much as the belle of the ball, she'd been waiting over an hour for Selene to arrive.

Selene's tardiness didn't surprise Hestia. Selene liked to arrive late to every event so she could make an entrance. No doubt this time, the train would be blamed for the delay. Hestia peeked through the chintz curtain. "Yes, it's them."

"Wonderful. It will be lovely for you to have someone your own age to talk to now and again."

Hestia wished she could smile. If only she weren't jealous of her gorgeous cousin...but she couldn't help herself. Why did Selene have to come here and ruin everything just when Hestia's daily visits with Booth were going so well? She remembered his reaction to the news about Selene's impending visit. Always the gentleman, Booth had tried to hide his anticipation, but Hestia sensed it. And no wonder. Beside such a vivid pink orchid, Hestia looked like a wilted and faded white pansy. Still, she couldn't let herself forget her manners. "I'll greet her."

From the parlor window, Hestia stood and watched her cousin. Her lightweight traveling coat looked as though it would stand out as extraordinary even on the most fashionable Paris street. A close-fitting hat with a small brim boasted no decoration on its emerald green ribbon. Heels unmarked from wear shod tiny feet.

With a confident wave of her hand, she ordered Abe to transfer her trunks to the veranda, as though he were a paid driver instead of her aunt's acquaintance. Hestia felt sorry for him. He showed more patience than she would have. Hestia could see by her cousin's carriage and attitude that the passage of time had not humbled her. Still, Hestia imagined that in other circumstances, she might have enjoyed being friends with such a vibrant cousin—but their fathers' youthful paths had set them a universe apart from each other.

Hestia's father, Milton, loved the small-town life of his native Haw River. He married a local girl and enjoyed his position as a respected physician. His dashing brother, Ralph, took the opposite way by attending a college up north and marrying an heiress. Selene's visits to the country were few, as her mother never developed a fondness for the South, small towns, or the rest of the Myatt family. After Selene's mother lost her life when a horse threw her, a grieving Ralph took to his business, traveling, while Selene's nannies and governesses tended to her. Hestia's mother considered the situation disgraceful. Though Hestia loved her own attentive parents, she had envied Selene's freedom.

Selene strode through the door then stopped. Hestia expected an embrace. Instead, Selene surveyed the parlor as though she were inspecting a rental property and hadn't quite made up her mind. Aunt Louisa's home emanated warmth and comfort, but Hestia had the feeling Selene held back a disapproving sniff.

When her gaze met Hestia's, Selene's mouth dropped. "Hestia?"

"Yes." Hestia responded to Selene's surprise.

"Didn't you know I'd be here?"

"Why, no."

"I guess Aunt Louisa didn't have a chance to tell you. Well, won't we have lots of fun." Selene's voice sounded flat. She turned to Abe, standing beyond the entrance. "Don't leave those trunks there on the porch. Take them to my room."

Instead of seeming offended, Abe smiled like a love-struck schoolboy. "Of course, Miss Selene."

Selene's expression as she turned back toward Hestia made her feel as though she were a bother. "Where is my room, now that you're here?"

"We'll be sharing the downstairs guest room."

"Share a room? But there is a whole upstairs. Why can't I stay there?"

Hestia had anticipated the question. "I suggested it, but Aunt Louisa wants to keep the upstairs shut off now that the nights are getting chilly."

"Applesauce! She always was a tightwad."

Hestia shot her a warning look since she'd expressed such a bold opinion in front of an acquaintance. "Frugality is a virtue. Besides, do you want to do all the work it takes to keep the extra rooms warm?"

Selene grimaced and waved her hand in the direction of the back bedroom. "In there, Mr. Perkins."

Having settled that, Selene whisked off her coat to reveal a short, linear dress. Hestia almost wondered if a Paris designer had stitched the last piece of hem minutes before the cream-colored garment adorned her body. And flesh-toned stockings! Silk, no doubt. Hestia's traditional black wool stockings made her feel a hundred years old.

Hestia tried to appear confident and in control. "Let's go greet Aunt Louisa."

Selene's eyebrows shot up as high as they could. "She still can't get out of bed?"

"Not yet. Soon, we hope. Dr. Lattimore made a house call yesterday and said she's coming along nicely."

"Good. I have no desire to tend to an invalid." Selene cocked her head at Hestia. "Do you still want to be a nurse or something?"

"Yes, and Papa thought I could gain experience here with Aunt Louisa. But I've really been more occupied with housework than medicine."

"Figures. That's our Aunt Lou."

"I wouldn't let her hear you call her that if I were you." Wanting to deflect an argument, Hestia hastened to add, "I might be occupied with chores, but at least I'm helping. And, really, that's what I want to do with my life. Help others."

"You don't want to get married?"

"Yes, I do." But she didn't want to discuss Luther. "Now let's go see Aunt Louisa. She's waiting." Hestia escorted her to the bedroom. Selene entered as though she were a silent picture star and dropped her wrap on the end of the bed, placing her hat on top.

Aunt Louisa glared at Selene. "We do have a place for those in the coat closet."

"Oh. Sure." At that moment, Selene seemed to remember that Aunt Louisa didn't employ a maid. Dismissing her aunt's implied request to hang up her own belongings, Selene smiled and extended both arms. "Aunt Louisa, you do look marvelous!" Paying no mind to Hestia, Selene ran to their aunt and kissed each cheek.

Hestia wasn't sure if Aunt Louisa could return the compliment. With her hat off, the fact that Selene had dyed her short bob to an unbelievable shade of platinum became more apparent, shocking Hestia. Ever-so-slight root growth looked as though a prankster had drawn a line right in the middle of her scalp where her hair parted. Bangs framed her heart-shaped face, and she had used Ox Blood red lip paint to draw her mouth into an artificial shape Hestia knew was termed a "Cupid's bow" by starlets and those who adored them. Words about fashion edicts got around, even to those whose fathers didn't allow them to attend moving pictures.

If Aunt Louisa found Selene's appearance surprising, she concealed her thoughts behind a maternal smile as she broke the embrace. "How are you, my dear? Did you have a good trip?"

"It was hideous." Selene let out a dramatic sigh sure to lead to an extended monologue. Aunt Louisa widened her eyes, listening. Hestia sat in the vanity chair. As though she were a performer on a stage, Selene remained standing. "Yesterday I sat by a flat tire who did nothing the whole trip but point out this and that landmark. I do believe he had something to point out every five miles. Who cares about the Mason-Dixon Line? I had to listen to a whole lecture on how these two men… oh, I can't remember their names."

"Charles Mason and Jeremiah Dixon," Hestia offered. "They drew the line to settle a border dispute in the 1760s."

"Show-off." Selene wrinkled her nose at Hestia. "Aw, dry up!"

Aunt Louisa gasped. "Selene! I'm not entirely sure what that means, but it sounds very unladylike. I will not allow such idle words to be spoken in my home."

"I'm sorry, sweet Aunt Louisa." She eyed Hestia. "And I'm sorry, my dearest cousin. But you sound just like that man on the train. Please don't subject me to history lessons while I'm here. Except for parties with my friends, I hated school and I don't want to go back now."

"Sorry." An excellent student, Hestia resolved to be careful not to seem prideful around Selene.

Selene didn't acknowledge Hestia's apology but raced to tell her story. "I managed to ditch him only to sit by a dumb Dora today who did nothing but ply me with questions about this and that when I wanted to be left alone. What is it about trains that makes everybody want to jabber?"

"I'd say boredom and loneliness," Aunt Louisa speculated.

"Or maybe the prospect of meeting someone new and exciting." Hestia observed her cousin's attire. "With your sense of fashion, I'm sure you appeared exotic to a normal girl."

Selene looked down at her traveling suit. "I suppose." She sighed. "Then in the dining car they were out of filet mignon, and I had to make do with an inferior cut of beef—overcooked at that. And my tea wasn't hot enough. The entire experience was horrific, I tell you. Absolutely horrific. I'm so glad to be among my devoted family, people who care about how I feel."

Abe appeared, hovering in the doorway. "All set, Miss Myatt."

"Thank you," Selene answered.

"How are you feeling today, Louisa?"

"As usual, thank you, Abe. Won't you stay awhile?" Aunt Louisa posed the question in the polite way that sounds sincere, but Hestia had her doubts. "Hestia might be able to find a few cookies in the jar out in the kitchen."

"Sounds delicious, but I promised the missus I'd be back in time to take Ellen home. All the church ladies met at the house to do some quilting, you know."

"Yes, how is it coming along? I wish I weren't stuck here so I could help sew this year."

"I wish that for you, too, Louisa." Abe's voice sounded as warm as roasting chestnuts. "They're almost done. I think they'll get a good price this year."

"Our church will auction off the quilt at our annual bazaar next month," Aunt Louisa informed her new charges.

"Yes, I recall you mentioning the bazaar in your letters," Hestia chimed in. Aunt Louisa always wrote newsy missives enjoyed by the entire household. Her lively accounts of church life were a highlight.

Selene looked absent. Hestia wondered if she even read her aunt's letters. Surely Aunt Louisa wrote to Selene's family, too.

"Our overseas missionaries will be grateful for every penny."

Hestia agreed wholeheartedly with Aunt Louisa's statement. "What pattern are they using this year?" Hestia envisioned several quilts she remembered from years past. "What colors?"

"Ethel tells me it's the double wedding ring pattern. Mainly blue and white," Aunt Louisa answered.

"Too bad I won't be here long, or else I could offer to help," Hestia said. Thinking of her intriguing neighbor, Hestia did wish she could stay longer. "And Selene, too."

Selene shook her head and looked to the ceiling and back. When she did, Hestia realized that Selene probably hadn't picked up a quilting needle in her life. She reached for her black alligator pocketbook she had tossed by the bed and whipped out a beige ostrich-skin wallet. "Let me give you a little something for your trouble, Mr. Perkins."

Abe came as close to blushing as Hestia imagined possible for a man. "I brought you home as a favor to your aunt, Miss Myatt."

"Thanks." She returned the wallet to the purse and swished her scandalously short bob. Hestia felt dowdy wearing her hair long and wavy.

"Remember me to Lavinia. Y'all come on by and see me sometime when you can stay awhile." Aunt Louisa sent him a little wave.

The door had just shut behind Abe when Selene spoke. "I see nothing's changed in here. Except for that smell." She waved her hand in front of her nose.

"I don't imagine your father needs liniment." Aunt Louisa touched the bottle on her night table. "I hope you won't need it for a long time, either."

"Or at least if I do, it will smell better than that." Selene studied the room.

Hestia noticed her gaze taking in the chintz curtains, old images of family members, and braided blue-and-white rug beside Aunt Louisa's bed. Hestia could read Selene's mind; the modest but sentimental surroundings were not up to snuff for her.

Selene touched her forehead. "What's for dinner? I'm so famished I'm on the verge of getting a headache."

"Shall I get you an aspirin?" Hestia remembered the bottle of tablets in the kitchen drawer.

"I'd rather have a bottle of Coca-Cola."

"I wish we had some on hand." Hestia made a mental note to put the soft drink on her shopping list.

"Will you send for a case? I like to drink one every day. And what about dinner? Please say it's beef. Ever since I ate that terrible steak on the train, I've had a craving for a good cut of beef prepared correctly."

"Overcooked or rare, you won't be getting filet mignon here." Aunt Louisa frowned at Selene.

"Oh. You don't have a cook?"

"I didn't have one the last time you were here, so why would I have one now? And even if I did, I wouldn't waste money on such an expensive cut of beef."

Selene sent a pleading look Hestia's way. "What about you, Hestia? Don't you like good food?"

"Yes, but I agree there's no need to overspend."

Selene grimaced and put her gaze on her cousin. "You and your frugal ways. Haven't changed a bit, have you? You even look the same."

"I'll take that as a compliment." Then Hestia remembered that Selene hadn't seen her since she was in pigtails. "I think."

Selene drew close to Hestia and placed a consoling hand on her shoulder. As she did, the movement caused a sugary, peachy scent of quality perfume to escape from the folds of her dress. "Oh, darling, you look hotsy-totsy for someone who comes from where you do."

"Hotsy-totsy?" Aunt Louisa questioned. "That doesn't sound respectable to me. That's another phrase I'll ban from my house."

"It just means copacetic, Auntie."

"Copacetic?"

"That's the latest word for *wonderful*." Selene sent an amused look her aunt's way then regarded Hestia. "Now, wonderful cousin, could you be so kind as to get me a cup of tea? Piping hot, please." She dug a silver cigarette case engraved with her initials from her handbag and eyed the surface of each table. "And what must one do to find an ashtray around here?"

"There will be no tobacco of any kind in my house, especially consumed by a woman."

Hestia tried not to show her relief at Aunt Louisa's proclamation.

"And while I'm laying down the rules, you need to know that as long as you're living with me, there will be no face paint. Let the woman the good Lord made shine. You don't need to make yourself up like a clown."

"But—"

"And another thing. You'll be growing out that hair of yours. I can see by your roots that it's a perfectly fine shade of dark blond. By the time you leave here, I speculate you'll look quite lovely with your natural color."

"No!"

"I'm the one who says no. Unless you really think you can go back home now."

Selene's tone of voice changed from defiant to begging. "Applesauce! You're such a Mrs. Grundy, Auntie. I've been here two seconds, and already you've set enough rules on me to fill a book. I know you're old, but do you have to be priggish?"

"Now see here, girlie, I will not be spoken to like that. Do you speak that way to your elders at home?"

"Yes, but I'm sorry I offended you." She pouted in a manner that told Hestia she often used this facial expression to get her way, but Aunt Louisa was having none of it. "It's so hard to be away from home, from all my friends. Can't you please make an exception for poor little me?"

"I think not. Rest and relaxation would be much more beneficial to a young woman in your cond—"

"Now, now, Auntie, I promise not to do anything to which you might object." She shot a look at Hestia. "Just how long will you be with us, dear cousin?"

"Oh, as long as I'm needed."

"I see."

"Let me get you a chair from the parlor so we can all sit in comfort." Hestia thought Selene might offer to fetch her own chair, but she stood in place as though Hestia's waiting on her was the most natural event in the world. Considering her attitude as she brought a lightweight rocker into the sickroom, Hestia wondered why her cousin didn't seem happy about her presence. Surely such a spoiled beauty would welcome someone she considered of lower stature to cater to her every whim.

Something was amiss. But what? Perhaps she would find out later. For the time being, Selene sat in the rocker and chatted with Aunt Louisa. Always one to hold attention, Selene gave several monologues and then played with the crocheted doilies on the chair arms while Aunt Louisa spoke. Her cousin also made no offer, either with a motion or verbally, to help Hestia prepare tea. How long would Selene be treated as though she were Mrs. Warren G. Harding on vacation from the White House? Hopefully no longer than this afternoon.

Hours passed as they drank tea and Selene caught them up on New York. The flapper's life sounded fast-paced and fascinating. Money was no object for Selene's father, so she slept until noon and then spent the rest of her days in beauty salons and elegant restaurants. Her favorite seemed to be the Algonquin. Parties abounded at night. In some ways, Hestia found her cousin's situation enviable. On the other hand, her life sounded as though it would be fascinating for about a week and then quite tiring. Hestia didn't want to judge Selene, but to her ears, her cousin's life didn't hold purpose or meaning.

After a time, Aunt Louisa's posture slackened and her eyes appeared tired. The cousins took leave of their aunt and exited to the parlor.

Selene regarded her surroundings. "Can't say anything's changed much. Look at this old furniture and outdated wallpaper and draperies. She hasn't redecorated since the Grant administration."

Hestia noted a nearby gilded mirror. "You exaggerate. Besides, I find her home charming."

Selene shrugged. "I like newer styles better. More modern, less cluttered." She leaned closer to Hestia. "I left my purse in the other room. Butt me?"

"Butt me?" An image of two billy-goat kids locking horns crossed her mind.

"Yeah, you know. Let me borrow a cigarette. We can sneak a smoke while she's asleep."

Hestia gasped. "Of course not!"

"So how do you get a smoke around here? Aren't you about to go crazy for one?"

"I don't smoke."

Selene shook her head. "Tell it to Sweeney."

"No, I'm telling you the truth. I don't smoke."

"So now I'm living with two Mrs. Grundys?" Selene lifted her hands and blew out her breath so hard that her bangs flew up in the air. "What next?"

"Let me see. How about if we tell you there'll be no 'hooch'?"

"Yeah." Selene sent her a half grin. "Maybe that liquid poison gets a girl in trouble, wouldn't you say?"

"I wouldn't know." Uncomfortable with the prospect of discussing a fast life she would never lead, Hestia decided to focus on reality. "Now that we've finished our tea, why don't we investigate our quarters? You must be exhausted from your trip. Maybe you'd like to take a nap while I fix supper."

"For once you've got a good idea."

Hestia led her into the front bedroom. That morning she'd spent considerable effort readying the sleeping quarters for Selene, so even in unforgiving daylight, no specks of dust showed themselves. Lingering scents of lemon and ammonia also indicated the room's cleanliness.

Selene gave the room a disapproving study. "I see this one hasn't been redone since Lincoln was in office."

"Silly goose. It's comfortable. I took the bed by the window, if it's all the same to you."

Selene shrugged. "That's fine."

"You'll find the left side of the wardrobe clear and the first two drawers of the dresser empty for you. And I left you space on the vanity for your toiletries."

"Guess they mean what they say about Southern hospitality." Selene's smile seemed genuine. She headed to the oak vanity, picked up Hestia's bottle of tuberose water, and sniffed at its contents. "Nice scent."

Hestia sat on her quilt-covered bed. "You can borrow some if you like."

"That's okay. I brought a bottle of Mitsouko. Guerlain, you know."

Hestia hadn't known, but she wasn't surprised that her cousin wore French perfume.

"Not that I'll have occasion to wear it much. Aren't all the men around here country bumpkins?"

"Not all." Hestia's voice betrayed her caution.

"Oh? They certainly can't be as sophisticated and modern as city men."

"Maybe not, but for one, you won't believe how much Booth Barrington has changed." Hestia's voice showed even more excitement than she realized she possessed over Booth. She tried to calm her emotions. "He's nothing like we remember."

Sitting on her own bed facing Hestia, Selene didn't seem impressed. "I hope he's improved."

"Improved isn't the word. He's as handsome as a matinee idol. Even more handsome."

"Is that so? I can't believe it. You've got a crush." Selene leaned back, propping herself by her elbows.

Hestia blushed. "Of course not. Why, I–I've only been here a couple of weeks. How could I be love-struck in such a short time? Besides, I'm leaving as soon as Aunt Louisa's pelvis heals. That should be a little over a week. Then it's back to Haw River for me."

"What will you do in Haw River? It's not as though it's a jazzy town."

"How do you know? Have you ever been there?" Hestia couldn't resist asking.

"Okay, so I've never been there. Tell me, is what you're wearing in style there?"

Feeling self-conscious, Hestia tapped her wavy hair. "I—I…"

"Don't worry. It's still there. All five feet of it."

"You exaggerate."

"Do I? And look at your clothes."

Hestia wanted to ask what was wrong with her clothes but she knew better. Her conservative blouse and long skirt were no match for the linear, short dress that looked so stylish on Selene. "My mode of dress is perfectly acceptable in my group." On purpose, Hestia failed to mention that one of her closest friends bought a dress in the new style on a recent shopping jaunt to Raleigh.

"Does Booth like it? The way you dress, I mean."

"I haven't asked him, but he doesn't seem to mind taking me to church every Sunday."

"Church. Well. That's not exactly Paris, is it?"

"And is your beau planning to take you to Paris?"

"Maybe one day I'll find a beau who will. I understand through the grapevine you're between beaux."

Hestia let out a resigned sigh. "Is there anybody between here and the Mississippi River who doesn't know about my broken engagement?"

"I'm not just anyone, cousin dear."

"True. I suppose since we'll be together for the a while yet, you might as well hear it from me instead of a stranger." She conveyed the sorry story of her breakup with Luther.

"Men are rats, aren't they? Well, since you were honest with me, I'll be honest with you. I'm between beaux, too."

"You, without a beau? I can't imagine."

"You don't have to be sarcastic."

"I'm not. I—I just thought with you being able to go to so many parties, you'd meet lots of men."

"Meeting is one thing. Having a nice beau is another." She pouted. "My last one turned out not to be so nice."

"So you're here to recover from a broken romance, too?"

She hesitated, arousing suspicion in Hestia. "In a manner of speaking. So are you in the market again?"

Hestia hesitated herself. "Not actively."

"Then it sounds as though you have no claim on Booth."

"No, I don't believe so." Hestia tried not to show her distress. After all, she didn't have a claim on him. "He just comes by to escort me to church each week, that's all."

"Sounds like the bee's knees." Selene's mouth twisted.

"It might not be your idea of fun, but I'm sure Aunt Louisa will expect you to go."

"I doubt it."

Hestia opened her lips to ask why she expected to skip church, but Selene spoke first. "Oh, I meant to ask, do you have any periodicals? I've only been here minutes and I can tell it's a crashing bore here. Not only has our aunt put impossible rules on us, but there's nothing to do for entertainment. I don't see a thing to read. I absolutely must get my hands on something to take my mind off this dreary place."

"I think I have a *National Geographic* somewhere." Hestia rose to find it.

Selene turned up her nose. "Is that all?"

"Why, that's a fine magazine. I learn so much about the world in each issue." Hestia clasped her hands. "Cathedrals in Europe, Greece, Rome…" She sighed.

"Thanks but no thanks."

Images of faraway places drifted from her mind. "What do you find entertaining?"

Selene shrugged. "The same things every other normal girl likes. Stories about famous moving picture stars, the newest dance crazes, fashion trends from Paris. You know."

"Obviously I don't."

"Maybe it's time you learned."

A shrill voice interrupted. "Oh, Hestia? Louisa? Yoo-hoo!"

Selene put her fingers in her ears. "What is that? A siren? And I don't mean the ones in mythology."

Hestia giggled. "It's just the neighbor. Don't you remember Olive Kalb?"

"Can't say that I do."

"Come on and meet her. That's the reason she's stopped by, you know. Every time it looks as though something exciting's happening here, she finds a reason to drop in."

"So much for a nap, but I'm too vexed to sleep, anyway." Selene followed Hestia into the parlor.

"Oh, there you are—" Miss Olive stopped in her tracks. "Hestia, I was looking for your aunt, but you'll do." She held up an egg. "Returning that egg I borrowed last week."

"Thank you." Hestia didn't take the egg but introduced Selene.

"My, but you are a pretty one, even with that white hair of yours." Miss Olive regarded her with the scrutiny of a doctor. "Mercy, you do look as though someone scared you out of your wits and your hair turned color."

Hestia used all her willpower to keep from laughing.

Meanwhile, Selene didn't bother to hold back a grimace even though she kept her tone sweet. "No, ma'am. As I was just saying to my dear cousin, this is the style where I come from, at least with girls in the fashionable set."

"New York, is it?" Miss Olive's tone didn't hide her derision.

"Yes, ma'am." Pride filled her voice.

"I hope your aunt informed you that such dramatic hair is not the fashion with women here. I can't name a one who dyes her hair. Although I can tell you which women take a bit of colored wax to their grays." A mischievous smile revealed that she would be only too happy to tell.

"Oh, Olive!" Aunt Louisa called from her sickroom. "Is that you I hear out there in the kitchen?"

"Yes, it is!"

The threesome went to see her and found her looking droopy as she lay back on her pillow.

"Mercy, you look a sight," Miss Olive observed. "Did I wake you?"

"Yes, you did, but I have a feeling it's for the best. Did I hear you say something about some of our local ladies covering their grays?"

For the first time, Miss Olive seemed chagrined. "Oh, I might have made a little mention of it in relation to Selene's hair. You don't approve of her hair, do you?"

"No, but she understands she'll be growing it back to its natural color while she's here. Not that Selene's hair is any of your concern. Or anyone's grays, for that matter." She sent Miss Olive a chastening look. "I can't have you encouraging the girls to gossip."

"Gossip? Why, I never! Everything I say is true." She sniffed.

"True or not, the girls have no business knowing who covers what. Maybe you're just a little bit jealous that you don't have the nerve to cover yours."

"Well!" She harrumphed

"Honestly, Olive, some days I wish I had the courage to use a bit of black wax on my hair."

"Louisa! I'm shocked! And to say such a scandalous thing in front of the girls, too." Miss Olive looked at them sideways. "Speaking of girls, clearly you have gained a visitor since I last stopped by."

Aunt Louisa looked down her nose at her neighbor. "Need a cup of sugar?"

"No, I returned an egg. I put it in the icebox for you, after Hestia didn't take it for one reason or another. So do tell, Selene, what brings you to our humble town?"

"She's here for a visit," Aunt Louisa snapped. "Can't I have visitors without everyone going into an uproar?"

"Will you be with us long, my dear?" Miss Olive cocked her head at Selene.

Aunt Louisa didn't let her respond. "She'll be here indefinitely. She's overtired from the stresses of city life and must have her rest. I do hope you won't spread news of Selene's arrival all over town. She is suffering from exhaustion and must not be overly excited. Will you promise me that?"

Miss Olive's shoulders pulled back almost indiscernibly in surprise. "Of course I will, my dear Louisa. I would never dare break a confidence. Such a shame the poor little thing doesn't have anyone to turn to in New York." Her gaze scoped Selene's luxurious style of dress. Hestia could see the neighbor thought no such thing.

"Don't you remember? Selene is the child of my brother who lives in New York. Very successful, you know." Aunt Louisa's tone took on a boastful tone.

Hestia found such a statement surprising from her usually modest aunt but declined to chime in with an opinion.

"Oh, yes."

"Selene is the apple of his eye, so of course she has all the material goods any girl could want," Aunt Louisa explained. "But you might also recall I told you he's a widower."

"Oh, yes. Very sad." Miss Olive tsked. "Young girls do need their mothers."

"So you see, she'll be with us awhile." Aunt Louisa's gaze traveled from Selene to Hestia and back to Miss Olive.

The neighbor looked at Hestia. "And Selene will help you care for your aunt?"

Aunt Louisa flitted her hand at Miss Olive. "Oh, I imagine Hestia will help us in any way she can. All the more practice if she wants to go into the medical field."

"Mmm-hmm." Miss Olive eyed Selene before turning to Hestia. "I daresay you'll have plenty of practice in caretaking with these two."

Chapter Five

....

Early Saturday morning, as he did once a month, Hugh Drum delivered firewood to his customers on Booth's street. The panel truck rumbled to a halt at their house at nine o'clock sharp. With care, Mr. Drum drove his truck over the grass in between the Barringtons' and Miss Louisa's so the wood could be left beside their respective back sheds. Booth wondered how the jalopy could hold so much wood. How Mr. Drum kept from blowing a tire, Booth didn't know.

As soon as Mr. Drum arrived, Booth and his father would help unload their order then assist with Miss Louisa's order, as well. Booth was expected to chop the wood for their family. The chore had been his since his thirteenth birthday. Then, after Miss Louisa's husband passed, Booth chopped her wood, too. Depending on his mood and the weather, Booth either anticipated or dreaded the occasion. Steamy summer days were no time to chop wood, but the stove had to be heated no matter what the weather. In the fall, Booth didn't mind chopping logs. Exercise in the brisk air made him feel alive. Physical movement gave him a challenge that no amount of office work could provide.

"Need some help, son?" Daddy asked today after Mr. Drum had been paid and was on his way.

"No, thanks. I'll get started on ours then chop enough for Miss Louisa to make it through this week."

His father's smile of gratitude was Booth's reward. Daddy hadn't been the same since arthritis struck him, and he avoided hard physical tasks as much as he could.

Booth had swung only a few strokes of the ax before he heard Eric approach. "What's the story, sport? Seems as though I came at just the wrong time. I've got my own wood to chop at home."

Booth suspended his task for a moment. "Then what are you doing out wandering the streets, old man?"

"Just getting stuff at the store." Eric withdrew a small sack from his coat pocket as though he needed to prove where he'd been. "I almost kept walking by. You didn't answer after I called you three times. If I didn't know better, I'd think you were avoiding me."

"Sorry about that. I wasn't paying attention." Booth couldn't deny it. He'd been thinking about Hestia all week, barely managing to get a passable amount of work in his office completed. He couldn't remember when any woman affected him as Hestia had. She embodied everything he wanted in a wife, but she couldn't be his. Once the doctor released Miss Louisa from her invalid status, Hestia would depart and Booth might not see her again. If only she would give him some indication that she'd like to stay longer in Maiden. Then they'd have more time to get to know each other better. Strong as his feelings were, he didn't think it wise to beg her to stay in town based on such a short courtship, childhood friendship notwithstanding.

For the first time in his life, Booth wished he were married. Gazing at the bungalow he had always called home, he saw his mother standing by the kitchen window, cleaning up after breakfast. She prepared delicious meals and the place would always hold a place in his heart, but with Hestia's arrival, he found he longed for a home of his own.

"I've never seen you as preoccupied as you've been lately."

"You've noticed at work?"

"Not so much that anybody's saying your work is suffering, but I can tell you're not yourself." He grinned. "It can only be one thing. You're stuck on a girl. You know, I've noticed you haven't been yourself since that girl came to stay with Miss Louisa."

Booth glanced at the Victorian next door. Should he tell Eric? He wanted to keep his secret to himself, but Eric's knowing look told him concealment wasn't possible. No one stood outside at Miss Louisa's, so he figured he was out of earshot. "You're right. It's Hestia Myatt."

"The Pears' Soap girl. That's what I thought. She does sound keen."

Embarrassed, Booth didn't realize he'd been babbling so much about her. He must have been more besotted than he knew. "She's going back to Haw River before too long. How I feel one way or the other doesn't matter."

"You've got it bad, sport. You'd better find a way to keep her here."

Booth had to agree. But how?

* * * * *

Though the end of her stay in Maiden was near, a letter arrived for Hestia. She opened the envelope and saw June's signature. Eager for news from her friend, Hestia read:

> *Dear Hestia:*
>
> *I hope this letter finds you well and that you are enjoying your stay in Maiden. I can't wait for you to come home. We all miss you so much. Of course, you must put your aunt first and stay as long as need be....*

As Hestia read news about their mutual friends, how much money they raised for the needy at the church dinner, and how the quilt she helped to sew brought in a record-winning bid, she missed her home. She kept reading:

The following portion of this letter is very hard for me to write. I wish I didn't have to convey this news, but I'm your pal and I don't think any other women in Haw River enjoy a friendship as close as ours. Please forgive me for the need to write such distressing news, but I must. If you're not sitting down, sit down now.

Are you ready? Luther is courting a new girl in town—Lizzie Newton. Can you believe he started seeing her so soon? Why, the smoke from your departing train had hardly cleared before he started chasing her. Gertie and I spotted him and that floozy, wearing enough face paint to cover the side of a barn, on the streetcar during our last trip to Graham. Scandalous!

I'm so very sorry. I wish I could strangle him for you. Don't be envious of Lizzie. I don't find her the least bit impressive, and neither does Gertie. I can't say I'm surprised by Luther's poor judgment. His treatment of you displayed a lack of character. You deserve better.

Hestia stopped reading. Though thankful to God for giving her such an understanding friend, she still couldn't read the rest of the letter. Until that moment, she hadn't realized she'd harbored just the tiniest bit of hope that Luther would beg her to take him back. But he had been too close with other women during their engagement, and even if he had asked, she knew for her own good she couldn't return to him. He had broken their sacred trust. If they were to marry, she would never be sure he was happy with her and not always looking out the corner of one eye for someone he thought would be better. She wondered if such distrust would be Lizzie Newton's fate.

She thought back to Nat's birthday party, where she and Lizzie had met. How could she not remember the brunette with bobbed hair? She

appeared just as her friend described. Why should Hestia be surprised
that Luther would be attracted to a flapper? Part of his dissatisfaction
with Hestia stemmed from her refusal to change her traditional look.
He'd told her so himself.

She couldn't help but visualize Selene. Why did the flappers always win?
In spite of her best efforts, Hestia couldn't stop her tears.

* * * * *

The next morning before church, sliced grapefruit peels in hand,
Hestia ventured outside to place them around the azaleas even
though they wouldn't bloom again until spring. Aunt Louisa swore by
such feeding, saying that adding acid to the ground near their roots
nourished the bushes. Hestia had to admit that her aunt could always
brag on beautiful pink azaleas with bountiful blooms every spring.
Lacking enough peels for every plant in the yard, Hestia decided to
treat the flowers in the rear of the house. She ventured to the back
stoop. To her shock, she found Selene sitting in a wrought-iron chair,
smoking a cigarette.

Hestia gasped. "Selene! What do you think you're doing?"

The girl jumped and clutched her chest then relaxed when she saw
Hestia. "Oh, good, it's you, dear cousin. For a moment I thought you
might be Aunt Louisa. I keep forgetting the old bat's bedridden." As if to
calm her vexation, Selene took a drag from her cigarette and blew smoke
high into the air.

Seeing a female smoke, especially someone who held such an
esteemed position in her family, unnerved Hestia. "I hate to sound more
like your mother than your cousin, but you really need to give Aunt
Louisa more respect. After all, you are a guest in her home, and she asked
you not to use tobacco."

"Shh! Not so loud," Selene whispered. "Do you want Aunt Lou to get wise?"

"I don't mean to be spiteful, but for your sake, I hope she does. Common sense should tell you that inhaling so much smoke can't be healthy for you."

"That's debatable, cousin dear." Selene shrugged.

"Do you think you can hide this habit from her? Since we don't smoke, we can smell tobacco a mile away. When you go back inside, you'll carry it with you on your clothes and stink up the whole house. She'll be wise whether she hears us or not."

"You've got a point." She stubbed the cigarette butt on the arm of the chair and then wiped off the black mark it left. Then, seeming to regret her quick action, she crossed her arms and looked at Hestia. Her wide eyes and pouty lips set themselves in an affectation that Hestia imagined as one that worked well on Selene's father and beaux. "Can't you defend me? Please? Smoking gives me something to look forward to during the day."

"Take up knitting, then."

"Knitting! You are a Mrs. Grundy. Almost worse than Aunt Lou."

"Let me remind you—I don't think Aunt Louisa likes being called Lou. And if I'm worse than she is, that's a compliment. You've got to give up smoking. I'll find something for you to do. Something worthwhile." She realized she still held the grapefruit rinds. "Here. You can start by feeding the azaleas."

* * * * *

Booth arrived later that morning to escort Hestia to church. He'd always enjoyed church, but with Hestia, attendance had become the highlight of his week. He straightened his tie and bounded onto the veranda then knocked on the door.

"Come in, Booth," Hestia called from inside the house. "I'm running late."

He hoped she wouldn't delay too long, but since it was the last Sunday he'd take her to church, he didn't want to complain.

"In here, in the sickroom," she called.

Booth followed the scent of menthol to the sickroom. "Good morning, Miss Louisa. Hi, Hestia." As always, Hestia looked beyond lovely. He wasn't sure if her Sunday frock was especially flattering or if the prospect of worship made her radiant, but whatever it was, it was good for her. And for him. He relished sharing a pew with such an angelic being.

Hestia's smile lit his world. "Good morning, Booth. A fine Sunday, isn't it?"

"Yes, and Mother was hoping you might stop by for dinner after church. If you do, it promises to be an even better afternoon."

Her shoulders sagged. "Oh, I wish I could. I remember your mother's fried chicken to be out of this world and the company of your family even better. But I promised Aunt Louisa I would eat lunch with Selene and her."

"It's true." Aunt Louisa nodded from her perch in the bed.

"That's right." Booth wished he didn't have to recall. "I do seem to remember you saying something about her visiting. Swell timing, huh, so you two can see each other a few days before you have to—to leave."

"Yes." Did he catch a wistful look on Hestia's face? "It's Selene's first Sunday with us, you know, and my last here in Maiden. I'm sure you'll meet again soon. She was tired from her trip and napping when you stopped by on Friday afternoon."

"That's right, but I'm not asleep now." The sound of a cheerful voice floated toward them, accompanied by a strong floral scent of some sort of exotic perfume he'd never smelled. A platinum blond vision slipped beside Hestia, easing Hestia to the side so Selene could stand out in her radiant glory. "Booth? Is this Booth Barrington? It can't possibly be!"

"Uh, yes." Why did he suddenly feel shy?

Booth couldn't help but take in Selene's appearance. It was obvious even to his untrained eye that she had applied hair dye, but it lent her an air of sophistication. She wore lots of face paint—too much to pass muster at church, but she looked beautiful with it. Yet seeing her was somehow a disappointment. She appeared much too world-weary for such a young member of the fairer sex, in comparison to the fresh-faced women of his acquaintance.

Since the two females stood side by side, he couldn't help but compare Selene to Hestia. Hestia's beauty looked classic. She didn't need face paint to appear lovely. Soft, white skin spoke for itself. He was glad she hadn't chopped off all her dark blond hair. Splendid waves were too lovely to sacrifice to fashion. He wondered what Selene would have looked like had she kept Hestia's style. Somehow, he imagined that if she had, Selene's group in New York wouldn't have liked her.

Hestia gave her cousin a stare, showing her unhappiness at Selene's appearance. "Why aren't you in bed? I thought you were feeling poorly."

"Oh, we don't need to discuss my little stomach ailments. Not when we have company. But I will say the food on the train was not up to my standards. I'm still feeling the effects."

Booth thought her statement to be a bit haughty, but he decided not to comment.

Selene looked him up and down in a fashion much bolder than most women dared. "I still don't believe it. You can't possibly be Booth. He's a pudgy little boy with frogs in his pocket."

He cringed at the reference to the boy who no longer existed. "Not anymore."

"I can see that, Handsome. You put Ivor Novello to shame."

"Who?" He tried to hide his embarrassment at not recognizing the name, since she obviously thought he should.

"You know, the star of *The Bohemian Girl.*"

"A moving picture?" Aunt Louisa's frown displayed her disapproval.

"Of course." Selene's attitude made Booth feel like a dunce. He wondered how Hestia felt.

"I'm not permitted to view moving pictures, and my guess is that Booth doesn't frequent them, either." Hestia looked to Booth for confirmation.

Booth was glad Hestia didn't mind speaking up to her cousin. A protest from him would have seemed rude. "Hestia's right."

"Then you are missing exciting stories." Selene clasped her hands as though thinking of dreamy plots. "This one is about a nobleman's daughter who is kidnapped by pirates."

Hestia visualized her father wagging his finger at her, lecturing how motion pictures corrupted the youth of America. Judging from the poster displayed at Maiden's theater for *Blood and Sand*, she could see why he came to that conclusion. "I doubt my papa approves of either pirates or kidnappers."

"I can vouch for that." Aunt Louisa's tone indicated her agreement.

At the risk of incurring Selene's poor opinion of him, Booth decided to side with Hestia. "My parents prefer that I not see moving pictures, either, Miss Selene."

"Do you listen to everything your parents tell you? Maybe you are still a little boy after all," Selene's voice caressed the insult as she placed her hand on her slim hip. He noticed that her cream-colored dress looked to be sewn from an expensive shiny material, the type the girls he knew saved for evening wear rather than Sunday morning.

He cleared his throat. "My parents wouldn't stop me if I wanted to go. But out of respect for them, I choose not to attend moving pictures."

Selene's stricken expression told him she didn't understand such a posture. He couldn't help but wonder about her home life. Maybe she didn't have parents at all. Her quick recovery amazed him. "What's with this 'Miss Selene' baloney? I'm just plain old Selene. Only our aged aunt needs such a title."

"Excuse me, but I'm right here." Aunt Louisa's voice sounded sharp even as she jested.

Selene took her hand off her hip and crossed her arms. The teasing look disappeared, replaced with a wide-eyed schoolgirl expression. Booth had the feeling she'd become so caught up in her banter she'd forgotten about their audience. Perhaps such single-mindedness—letting people think the rest of the world evaporated as she flirted—was part of the charm she showed to her New York friends. He could see why such coyness could work.

Selene turned to her aunt and spoke in an entirely different tone. "I meant no harm, Auntie. You know how I often speak before thinking."

"Often, indeed. Come here." Miss Louisa surveyed her young niece. "Look at me."

Selene stared at the floor before she obeyed with reticence.

Miss Louisa took Selene's chin in her fingers and looked straight at her. "What is that on your face?"

Selene's hand went up to her cheek. "Oh, just a little help from Paris." Speaking in a rush, she looked at Hestia. "You'll have to let me show you how to apply this rouge. You could use a little color."

"You'll show her no such thing," Miss Louisa declared. "I have already told you I forbid such display. I am ashamed of you for being so disobedient. What would your father say?"

"He doesn't mind if I wear a little paint. All us girls in New York wear it. At least those in my set. But what do you care today? I'm not going to church. Or anywhere else, for that matter."

"I may be stuck in this bed, but that doesn't mean I'll abide misbehavior. I can put you right on the first train out of here, you know."

"Yes, ma'am. But can't you please reconsider? At least let me wear enough color to keep from looking as though I fell into a flour barrel."

"You don't look that pale." Miss Louisa shook her forefinger at her wayward niece. "I told you that while you are a guest in my home, you are not to paint your face, and that's my final word."

"We can wait for Selene to remove her paint," Booth offered, noting that according to the small clock on Miss Louisa's night table, church wouldn't commence for a half hour.

"No," Miss Louisa answered Booth, "she won't be going to church with you today."

Considering how much church meant to his neighbor, such an edict shocked him. "Maybe I shouldn't ask," Booth ventured, making sure to keep his tone respectful, "but are you punishing her for wearing face paint?" If that was Miss Louisa's idea, he disagreed. Church would be the ideal place for Selene.

"No, and of course I would never consider such a thing," Miss Louisa told him. "Face paint or not, she won't be going today or any day. In fact, Booth, Selene needs her rest. I would appreciate it if you wouldn't mention her presence in this house to anyone."

Booth didn't understand such secrecy, but he had no choice other than to comply. "Yes, ma'am. I won't say a word."

Chapter Six

Moments later, Selene watched out of Aunt Louisa's bedroom window and listened as the sound of the Model T's motor grew from loud to distant. Booth and Hestia had left before she could make an impact on Booth. But what did she care? Who wanted to stay in such a small town anyway, when there was so much excitement to be found in New York?

Curiosity—and hopes of distracting her aunt from the lecture sure to follow—spurred her to nosiness. "Auntie dear, I thought Booth had a good job at the mill."

"He does have a good job. Why would you think otherwise?"

"Oh, the men I know back home buy a better motorcar than a Model T once they move up a peg or two on the ladder, that's all."

"If by 'better' you mean 'more expensive,' then that's just a waste of money, in my book. Maybe you need to put on airs in New York, but we don't take to that kind of thing here in Maiden." Aunt Louisa lifted her shoulder in pride. "And speaking of airs, why did you disobey me by wearing face paint?"

She didn't want to admit she wished for Booth to see her at her best, so she went for the second kernel of truth. "I'm so used to seeing myself wearing rouge and lip color that I think I look funny without it."

"Then you should look in the mirror again. You look funnier with it, if you ask me. Like a clown. Now consider Hestia."

Hestia. The angelic, pure-as-the-driven-snow Mrs. Grundy. Selene held back a grimace.

"Hestia is beautiful without a trace of face paint. You should follow her example."

"Shouldn't everyone, oh dear aunt of mine?" Selene bit out before remembering that her aunt wouldn't appreciate sarcasm.

"Yes, any woman would do well to be like your cousin Hestia," Aunt Louisa answered, as though Selene had posed a serious question. "Now, let me get something straight with you. If I see you with face paint one more time, I'll have Hestia find out where you've got it hidden, and I'll order her to burn it all up in the stove. You hear me, girl?"

"Yes, ma'am." Sarcasm evaporated, she resolved to hide her paint so well that not even Hestia could find it.

"Your father was too preoccupied with himself and too lenient with you. He always was on the self-centered side, and that's one reason you're in the fix you're in now. I know your situation is not entirely your fault, which is why I agreed to take you. But while you're here, you'll find that I will not be lenient."

Selene felt a cloak of darkness fall over her. "Yes, ma'am."

"Now I suggest you retire to your room and rest. And before you fall asleep, think about why you should not be so disobedient."

"Yes, ma'am." For once, she didn't mind obeying her aunt. She was in no mood to spend time in her company and looked forward to being alone.

"Maybe you can do some Bible reading while you're at it," Aunt Louisa suggested as Selene shut the door.

The thought of reading her Bible made her even more vexed. She was already depressed and didn't want to read a book with even more rules telling her she couldn't have any fun.

She sat at the vanity and gazed at her reflection, trying to fix her memory upon her current appearance. Once she used cold cream to remove her beautiful paint, she couldn't apply it again without fear of reprimand or worse. She missed New York and her dear father already. So what if Father's absences meant that she was alone with the maid and butler most of the time? Father loved her. That much she knew.

With a slow turn of her wrist, she opened the blue jar, a ritual normally reserved for the end of a long evening. Under other circumstances, the sweet smell of cold cream brought happy memories of a fun night filled with flirting and dancing. But not today. She dipped her cloth into the jar and rubbed her cheek. She wished she didn't have to stay in this wretched town, where the only boy she saw swooned over her cousin. Well, Hestia was a plain Jane compared to her, and Selene could see that Booth regarded her with interest as she acted the coquette. Maybe he wasn't immune to her charms after all. If she could convince him to seriously look her way before her secret got out, then she might stand a chance of some male companionship while she was still in Maiden. Otherwise, all she had to look forward to was a self-righteous aunt and an out-of-date cousin who seemed older than her years.

I can't bear it. I just can't.

She rubbed her face with the cream-covered facial cloth until the rouge surrendered, dissolving into a stain on the cotton. Peering into the mirror, she saw a pale face with short blond hair and brown roots growing longer each day. She needed a haircut if she planned to maintain her beautiful bob. Maybe Hestia would cut it for her since Aunt Louisa wouldn't let her out of the house even for basic beauty maintenance.

Selene pouted at her reflection, but the expression wasn't cute when her lips weren't painted into an adorable Cupid's bow. Who stared back at her from the mirror? She didn't like this girl. Who'd want to be friends with such a frump? At least now she had her blond hair, but since Aunt Louisa demanded that she grow it out, she'd look like a sow sure enough. She wrinkled her nose.

Her thoughts went back to Ned and how he had said he loved her. In stolen moments, his arms wrapped around her had made her feel worshipped. But as soon as she informed him she wanted—in fact, needed—to marry, he'd run off faster than a rat deserting a sinking ship.

"And that's what I am, too. A sinking ship." Unwanted tears rolled down her cheeks. At least now she wouldn't have to worry about them smearing any rouge.

"You all right in there?" Aunt Louisa called.

"I'm fine, Auntie."

"You got that face paint off?"

"Yes, ma'am." Selene dabbed her eyes with her handkerchief. No amount of effort restored her face, now a blotched red.

"Come in here and let me see you."

"Don't you trust me?" she called back.

"No, I don't."

Selene wanted to return the answer with a retort but thought better of it. She supposed that in her aunt's eyes, Selene had betrayed her, so any trust they might have had between one another had evaporated. And she didn't want to wait for her aunt to demand that Hestia inspect her.

Soon she proved by mere appearance before her aunt that she had wiped her face clean.

Aunt Louisa regarded Selene. "Good. You look much better now. Like a sweet, wholesome girl a man would actually want to take as a wife."

Selene wasn't sure enough to answer.

"So did that bromide I told Hestia to give you earlier work for your stomach?"

Selene hadn't thought about her queasiness of late and realized she was feeling better. "Yes, ma'am."

Aunt Louisa squinted. "You been crying?"

Not wanting to admit it, she didn't answer but looked instead at her kid-leather slippers.

"Come here."

With slow steps, Selene obeyed.

To her surprise, Aunt Louisa took Selene's hand. "Now, now, you needn't cry. As soon as the baby comes, you can go back to New York and no one will ever know." She squeezed her hand and then let go.

"Really?" Selene wasn't so sure. Her friends were wise to the ways of the world. She remembered how her friend Babs went to visit a distant relative last winter, right after she and her beau had broken off their secret engagement. Babs had come back sadder, not as willing to go out on the town and be as carefree as she once had been.

Hestia would never have to worry about any such disgrace. Sure, her fiancé had been a lout, but that wasn't the same. Not by a long shot. She never thought she'd see the day she'd envy her old-fashioned cousin, but jealousy filled her being at that moment. If only she could change places with Hestia. She looked so out-of-date and conservative, but she had one thing Selene didn't—the attention of a suitor, any suitor. She never thought she'd consider Booth Barrington a desirable suitor, he of the churchgoing ways and prudent demeanor. Sure, Selene believed in God and had accepted Jesus as her personal Savior one day long ago, back when she was a little girl. Before she lost her mother. She felt a tear threaten and sniffed it back.

Her thoughts wandered to Booth. Today when he had arrived to take Hestia to church, he looked good. Very good.

Lord, forgive me.

"I'm tired." Apparently Aunt Louisa had spent her quotient of sympathy for Selene. "I'm taking a nap, Selene, and so should you. I'll see you after Booth and Hestia get back from church."

"Yes, ma'am." Selene departed to her room and sat on the bed hugging herself. Why did she ask the Lord for anything? Ever since Mother died, He'd never been a friend of hers. If He had, He would have kept her from making such a mess of her life.

* * * * *

After sleeping a couple of hours, Selene had managed to recover by the time Booth dropped off Hestia after services. Eager for company, Selene slid out of the house and waited for them on the veranda's swing, gliding back and forth. Booth had parked the Model T at his house and walked Hestia next door. Selene thought the unnecessary gesture was a way for them to spend a few more minutes together. She wished someone cared that much about her.

She swallowed when she realized how handsome they looked as they strode together up the walk. Hestia wore a warning expression. Selene wanted to be sure Hestia didn't have time to scold her for being outside, so she didn't wait to begin questioning the couple once they reached the veranda.

"I'm sorry we got off on a bad footing today, what with Aunt Louisa lecturing me about face paint," she apologized to Booth in her sweetest voice. "Won't you sit a spell?" She patted the empty seat beside her.

"I don't have a lot of time before dinner, but I guess I can stay a few minutes."

Selene smiled, though she tried to conceal her disappointment about the fact that he took a wicker rocker rather than the seat beside her. She consoled herself by the thought that she could see him better from this vantage point. She expected Hestia to go inside to prepare their meal but had no such luck. She lingered as though she needed to watch Booth. "So how was the service?"

Booth was quick to answer. "We had a good sermon today. All about how we should be careful about the company we keep, because people are looking at us as examples of Christ."

"Oh." Selene was glad she'd been absent. If the other old people in town were anything like her aunt and Miss Olive, she imagined the

pastor pointing at her blond bob and calling her a harlot on the spot.
"I don't think people should be so judgmental. A person can make a
mistake, you know."

Booth seemed taken aback. "Sure. We all make mistakes."

She imagined his mistakes might have involved minor practical
jokes or misspoken words. He was too much of a gentleman to leave a
distressed woman all alone. She put thoughts of Ned out of her mind.
"Father wanted me to bring Aunt Louisa a few apples from New York.
I think I managed to get them here without too much damage. So I'd like
to make an apple pie for you. I'll have a slice ready for you tomorrow
afternoon when you stop by. Does that sound copacetic?"

"Yes, it does. How did you know that apple pie is one of my favorite
desserts? Funny, I hadn't imagined you to be the domestic type." He
glanced at Hestia.

Following his lead, Selene looked at her cousin and noticed her lips
had tightened. At that moment, Hestia reminded her of Aunt Louisa.

"Didn't you say Selene's family has a cook, Hestia?" Booth asked.

"Of course we do, cousin dear," Selene hastened to answer, looking
back at Booth. "But I don't mind cooking sometimes."

"I'd think with you as exhausted as you are, you wouldn't want to
cook," Hestia told Selene.

"I'm not that tired." Selene bored her gaze into Booth. "Don't pay any
attention to Hestia. She's all wet."

* * * * *

Departing from the women a few moments later, Booth noticed that
Hestia avoided making eye contact with anyone and hadn't said a word
lately. What was eating her? He didn't dare hope she was upset to be
leaving Maiden—and him. But Dr. Lattimore was scheduled to make a

house call to Miss Louisa on Tuesday. Then he'd release his patient from bed if all went well. Booth almost wished the doctor would insist she stay in bed another month. Just as quickly, he put such a selfish thought out of his mind. He knew from the start that Hestia planned to leave. If only he had saved himself from disappointment by telling his heart.

He walked toward his house thinking about the two women. Hestia was the perfect companion at church, with her natural beauty and quick wit. She knew her Bible, as evidenced by the well-informed talks she'd had with him. Every once in a while, when they thought he wasn't looking, he'd caught some of the bachelors in the congregation eyeing her. Surely they were envious that he'd seen Hestia before they had. Of course, it was much too soon for him to ask to be a serious suitor for Hestia, but the thought had crossed his mind.

Then again, there was Selene. If he hadn't known it was her, he wouldn't have recognized her from the morning. Without her face paint, she looked like a different person. More wholesome, for certain. She was a beauty even without paint, just as Miss Louisa had promised. She had filled out since he last saw her, though she couldn't be called chunky. Since Miss Louisa had cautioned her to tone down her looks, no doubt Selene would soon fit in with the other respectable women in Maiden. But why wouldn't Miss Louisa let Selene leave the house? Was that her way of encouraging Booth toward Hestia? Not that he needed encouragement. Still, if he couldn't even escort Selene to church, she'd never make friends in Maiden. Or maybe Miss Louisa didn't want Selene to make friends. But why? She hadn't indicated how long Selene planned to stay, but wouldn't they have said something if Selene also planned to leave soon?

Something smelled rotten in Denmark.

Selene was definitely interested in Booth. Why else would she bake him a pie? He couldn't help but be flattered. No woman who looked remotely as sophisticated as Selene had ever given him a second look. Not that he'd met many worldly women. No female of his acquaintance in Maiden used hair color—at least not color he could detect. Face paint hadn't caught on in popularity with his group of friends, although a few of the more adventurous girls of his casual acquaintance could be seen sporting a bit of red rouge and lip color now and again. A couple of young women who aspired to be on the edge of fashion wore shorter hair, but nothing as radical as Selene's. Even without paint, Selene looked different from the women he knew well. Her style of dress and her carriage set her apart from others. He could imagine trying to go to church with her. Though no one would be rude or unkind, they would all be surprised if Booth accompanied a woman with her appearance. Surely Selene went to church, even up in New York. Did her friends worship while looking so worldly? He concluded that they must.

He was just about to cross onto his walk when he heard a hoot coming from a few doors down the street.

"Booth!" Artie called to him.

Thinking he had enough time for a quick chat, Booth responded by waving and walking toward his neighbor. A couple of years older than Booth, Artie had moved to Maiden from Raleigh three years ago after inheriting his grandmother's home. When Artie had first moved to Maiden, Booth hadn't known him. He vaguely remembered a handsome youth visiting from the state capital once in a while, but Artie had found little time to bother with someone younger. He'd sought out a few of the older teens in town and they'd set off on their own adventures. Even now Booth didn't know him well enough to call him more than a pleasant enough work acquaintance. Otherwise, Artie kept his modest brick house well-tended and proved himself a good and helpful neighbor. Once or twice Booth wondered why Artie hadn't started courting anyone. Usually a new bachelor settling in town attracted lots of attention. Booth soon came to understand that rumors of Artie's wild past had followed him to Maiden, and many respectable families didn't want him to court their eligible daughters. As far as Booth could see, Artie had repented of any checkered past. Then again, Booth didn't have reason to dig deep since he had no daughter or sister to protect.

"Everything okay, Artie?" Booth asked as soon as he could address his neighbor without shouting.

He shook his head and Booth noticed the blond sun streaks in his straight brown hair caught the sunlight. "Yes. And no."

"How's that?"

"The jalopy's not doing so well. I don't know what's wrong with her, but she won't start." With a grimace, Artie looked in the direction of his house. Booth could see the motorcar parked in the drive, looking as dejected as possible for a machine. "Good thing my church is in walking distance, or I would have missed services this morning."

"Good thing." Booth made a guess as to why Artie had sought him. "I'd be glad to take a look and see if I can figure out what might be the problem, but I have to tell you, I'm not mechanically inclined. Now, my dad is much better with engines than I am. We can both come over after lunch and have a look-see."

"Thanks, but that's not what I need. I think I know what the problem is, and I'll try to fix it myself, but with me working at the mill and it getting dark so much earlier, I won't have much sunlight, and it will take me longer than usual. I really hate to ask this, but I was wondering if I could catch a ride with you to and from work every day until I get my jalopy repaired."

"Oh, is that all?" Booth hoped relief wasn't too evident in his voice. "Sure, I'll be glad for you to ride with me. Just come on up to the house tomorrow morning and I'll get you there."

* * * * *

The next day Selene fluttered about the kitchen, opening drawers. Where did her aunt hide the measuring spoons? She groaned. What had she been thinking when she told Booth she'd bake a pie?

Bringing in Aunt Louisa's lunch tray, Hestia furrowed her brow. "What's going on in here?"

"I'm trying to bake a pie, of course. I promised Booth." She sighed. "It says to soften the lard in winter but not in summer. But it's autumn. What do you think?" She handed a coffee cup full of lard, the amount for which the recipe called, to Hestia. "Is that soft enough?"

Hestia held the cup and looked at the lard. "How should I know?"

"Because you come from the country and you know how to cook, that's why, cousin dear."

Hestia glared at Selene.

Selene looked for an out. "I mean, you don't have a cook at your house, do you?"

"My parents do employ a cook, as a matter of fact. And a laundress and a housekeeper."

"Oh. So you can't help me, then." Selene knew disappointment colored her voice, and she hoped her raw emotion would soften Hestia's heart.

"Why should I help you? You got in this mess yourself, promising to bake a pie to impress Booth. You've never baked a pie, have you?"

Ashamed, she shook her head. "I didn't think it would be hard at all. Our cook makes it look so easy. She just cuts up the apples, rolls out the dough, throws in a few spices, and she's done." Selene tilted her head toward a basket of red apples. "I can cut apples and throw in spices, but I'm not sure about the crust. This is the third time I've tried to make it work. I just can't seem to roll out the crust and make it presentable."

Hestia glanced at a lowering sun outside the window. "And you don't have time to recover, either. The pie will need at least an hour to bake. You'd be lucky to have it ready in time for dessert after dinner, much less this afternoon."

"What will I do?" Selene wailed.

Hestia shrugged. "Just serve him a slice tomorrow afternoon instead."

"But I said it would be done today."

"I wish I could be more sympathetic, but you should have thought of that before you made such a big promise."

"Aunt Louisa would help me with it if she didn't still have to be in bed."

"Yes, she probably would, and with her help you would already have a delicious pie ready to serve. But you don't, and I can't do much without enough time. I'm sorry. You'll have to confess to Booth."

"I didn't know you'd be so mad about my little efforts in the kitchen. You must have it bad for Booth, O cousin of mine."

"I never said that." Hestia sniffed with indignation, an emotion Selene thought she must be feigning.

"You're leaving soon. Would you deprive me of company once you're gone?"

Hestia pursed her lips. "I don't suppose I have the right."

Selene tried to use the glint of guilt in Hestia's eyes to her advantage. She snapped her fingers. "I have an idea. Can you run out and buy me an apple pie? I'll give you the money."

Hestia gasped. "I wouldn't consider such a dishonest trick. Absolutely not!"

"Don't you know, my dear cousin, that desperate times call for desperate measures?"

"I do believe that expression applies to a truly desperate situation, not baking an apple pie. No. I won't consider it. And even if I were so inclined, I don't know where to find a bakery short of Hickory."

"Some friend you are."

"I'm a better friend to you than whatever friends you have in New York, apparently, because I won't let you be a deceiver. I can promise you, Booth would not look kindly on such a thing if he found out the truth."

Selene sighed. "You're right."

"Good. I promise you, Booth will easily overlook the fact the pie isn't ready yet, and he'll be back tomorrow for a slice."

"Well, will you help me bake it now?"

Hestia shook her head. "No. I don't mean to be harsh, but it's for your own good. You're on your own."

Selene was just about to tell her how mean she was when they heard a knock on the door.

"That's him now." Hestia sent her a sweet smile. "I'll greet him."

Selene wished she could strangle her cousin even though Hestia spoke the truth; she had gotten herself into this mess when she tried to take on a project she couldn't handle. She wondered how her cook in New York made everything look so easy.

Smoothing her hair, she realized she felt tired. It was just as well Hestia wouldn't help her bake a pie. Energy eluded her. She took in a deep breath to gird herself. Despite being without a pie, she could at least greet Booth and keep Hestia from monopolizing him.

She put a smile on her face and entered the modest parlor as though she were making an entrance at the year's biggest gala. Then she stopped short. There was someone else present. A man she didn't know. He wasn't the dapper type she knew back home. Dark brown hair streaked blond looked stylish but not overly fashionable, and he appeared to be dressed for a good job at the cotton mill where Booth worked. He looked at her, and their gazes locked. Green eyes conveyed kindness. Eyes such as those never went out of style. And while he wouldn't stand out in a crowd in New York, he possessed a presence she hadn't seen—an air not of sophistication, but of assurance that didn't seem to be connected to the world. She wanted to learn more.

The threesome stopped talking.

She stumbled. "I–I'm sorry. I didn't mean to interrupt."

The stranger spoke for the first time. "You didn't interrupt."

Hestia made introductions, and Selene discovered that the new man was Artie Rowland. As conversation ensued, she learned more about him. She had guessed correctly that Artie worked with Booth. She wasn't sure about the pecking order at the mill, but judging from their conservative and tidy manner of dress and their easy camaraderie, they seemed to have similar jobs in the office. She wondered what type of car he drove. Probably a Model T.

"I hope you don't care that I brought Artie with me, Selene." Booth looked over at his friend, who nodded. "I thought he'd also enjoy some pie."

"Oh." Selene set a quick gaze on Hestia, who gave her a cautious look. Selene wished Hestia had broken the news to Booth and Artie. Clearly, she wasn't planning to help her out of this one. "I'm sorry. It's not ready yet. I'm such a dumb Dora, I couldn't figure out how to make it, and Hestia here wouldn't help me." Hestia sent Selene a glare, which she ignored. "I'll try again tomorrow."

"Oh." A look of disappointment registered on Booth's face, but he recovered with aplomb. "Looks as though we'll have to stop by tomorrow, too, Artie." He grinned at his friend.

"That's fine by me." Artie smiled at Selene, and for her, the rest of the group disappeared.

Chapter Seven

....

"Louisa!" Miss Olive's shrill voice whipped through the air later that evening.

Hestia paused in the middle of wiping the table. She was in no mood to see Miss Olive, but the older woman deserved the consideration and respect due a longtime neighbor.

"In here, Miss Olive," Hestia called as cheerfully as she could.

The older woman entered, carrying a circular reed basket with a lid. "I baked you a cake." She lifted the lid and tilted her chin forward to prompt Hestia to look.

Hestia observed a dessert that would have done a bakery window proud. "Oh, my, that looks wonderful! Let's show Aunt Louisa."

Miss Olive shut the lid and followed Hestia into the bedroom.

Aunt Louisa set down the novel she was reading. "Did I hear someone say 'cake'?"

Miss Olive beamed. "Indeed you did." She took off the cover and showed Aunt Louisa the prize—a lovely three-layer cake with coconut orange icing. "Robert E. Lee cake."

Aunt Louisa feasted on the cake with her eyes and inhaled its sweet aroma. "Mmm. One of my favorites. Thank you."

"I was in the mood to bake, and I hope the cake can be part of the celebration of your release from your bedridden state." Miss Olive took the cake out of the basket and set it on the vanity table.

"That would be fine indeed. I do hope the doctor gives me release tomorrow."

Hestia tried not to swallow. She wanted her aunt to get well and stay well, but Aunt Louisa's release meant she'd have to return home. Judging from the letter she'd received, she didn't have much reason to return.

"I do hope no one is overtaxing you." Miss Olive focused on the liniment sitting on Aunt Louisa's night table. "You know, when I was tending to my yard this afternoon, I couldn't help but notice lots of commotion. Mercy! Lots of coming and going. You have more company, Louisa? I'm not sure allowing so many people to stay is a wise decision, considering your state."

"No, there's no one else. But I do appreciate the cake. Hestia, will you take it out to the kitchen? Put it in the metal cake box. You'll find it in the bottom drawer on the left-hand side of the sink."

"Yes, ma'am." Hestia made haste to obey. When she returned to the sickroom moments later, the women were still talking.

Miss Olive spoke. "I have news. I saw Dr. Lattimore yesterday."

"Dear, is everything all right?" Aunt Louisa's pained expression showed genuine concern.

"Yes, for me, considering I'm no spring chicken. I wanted to consult with him about the possibility of my going to Hot Springs for my rheumatism. Remember how Ethel went and said it helped her?"

"Yes, but I believe relief is temporary at best. You might enjoy the trip, though."

"Maybe when you feel better, you can join me." Miss Olive peered out the window.

"I won't be going anywhere for quite some time. Not until after spring." Aunt Louisa patted the quilt that covered her legs.

Miss Olive sniffed. "Suit yourself. But I do see a remarkable improvement in your condition as of late, so I'd think we could get away before then."

"I wouldn't plan on it."

"Are you sure you don't have more company?" Miss Olive looked around the room.

"No one else but my two nieces. Artie came over this afternoon," Aunt Louisa answered. "Booth is taking him back and forth to work until he fixes his car."

"Does Artie have eyes for you, Hestia?" Miss Olive's inquisitive look made Hestia squirm even though she had nothing to hide.

Still, she considered the inquiry. Artie seemed to be a fine man, but he didn't elicit sparks for Hestia, and, judging from his polite coolness, she had no romantic effect on him.

Not so with Booth. Just being near him in any way brought her happiness, more happiness than she had known with her former fiancé even at the height of their courtship. But she couldn't let on about her feelings. In the meantime, she didn't want to debate with the neighbor, especially since, indeed, she could do worse than Artie. "No, ma'am."

"She has no time for romantic inclinations for Artie or anyone else," Aunt Louisa reminded her friend. "She'll be returning to Haw River soon—I'd say in a week at most."

"Did someone mention Artie?" To Hestia's surprise, Selene emerged.

"I thought you were taking a nap. You need your rest, you know." Reprimand touched Aunt Louisa's voice.

"I was, but I'm feeling better now, so I got up. I think I might be up to making that pie now, if someone will help me." She eyed Hestia.

"Pie!" Miss Olive waved both hands. "Mercy! Why do you need a pie? I just brought you a beautiful cake."

"Oh. Well, I'm sure it is beautiful, but I still need to bake a pie." She shifted her weight from one foot to another. "I promised Artie."

"Oh, so it's Artie now. You certainly set your sights from one man to another quickly." Aunt Louisa's voice sounded a warning.

"And Artie Rowland at that!" Shock colored Miss Olive's voice. "Louisa, I wouldn't let either of your nieces near him."

"Why not?" Selene's disappointment registered in her voice.

Miss Olive sniffed. "Because he has a questionable past."

"Is that so? But he seems so nice." Selene crossed her arms.

"He may seem nice now, but I knew his grandmother. Callie Rowland." Miss Olive leaned toward them. "That woman cried herself to sleep more than one night over her wayward grandson, I'll tell you. I still can't believe she left her house to him."

"Now, now, Olive," Aunt Louisa chastised her friend, "must we gossip?"

"The girls have to understand why certain men are off limits. Or at least, they should be."

"But he doesn't live a fast life now, does he?" Hestia hoped not.

"No, I see no evidence of it," Aunt Louisa admitted. "He goes to church, and I know from Penny Sidwell and Ellie Quicke that he is well-regarded there."

Miss Olive harrumphed. "I'd be mighty afraid he'd slip back into his old ways. Drinking and gambling, you know."

"You seem awfully judgmental, Miss Olive," Selene blurted.

"Well!" Miss Olive objected.

"Selene!" Aunt Louisa gasped. "Apologize this instant."

"I'm sorry, Auntie dear." Selene pouted.

Aunt Louisa wasn't finished. "Selene, I think it's high time you started to take it easy. It won't be long before your condition will be apparent for all to see, and this is no time to encourage Artie or anyone else. You'll be leaving in a few months, and nothing can come of any love affair."

Realization struck Hestia. Realization she didn't want to contemplate. "What? What do you mean, her condition?"

Hestia took all the information and thought about what it meant—to Selene, to their family. No. It couldn't be. Her beautiful cousin, the cousin who could say the world was her oyster, couldn't be in a family way. She chastised herself for not seeing the signs. What kind of nurse would she be if she couldn't diagnose something so obvious? Then again, she hadn't suspected her own unwed cousin to be in such a predicament.

"Mercy! Are you implying what I think you are, Louisa? That your niece is...is... I won't say it." Miss Olive studied Selene as though she were seeing her for the first time. "I might have figured you were a bit plump in the belly for someone your age. Well, living like a floozy, I might have known that might have been the reason for your visit."

"Aunt Louisa!" Selene blanched. "Why did you choose this moment to tell the world about me? About my position?"

"Because Hestia lives here and Olive drops in all the time. In fact, we may need your help, Olive."

"Of course."

"But Hestia—" Selene protested.

"You can trust me." To demonstrate, Hestia made her way over to her cousin and placed her arm around her shoulders.

"Everyone close to us will know sooner or later." Aunt Louisa blew out a resigned sigh.

"I'll say people will know sooner or later." Miss Olive studied Selene. She withstood the rude scrutiny bravely. Hestia wished she could shake the neighbor for her inconsiderate behavior. "I highly disapprove."

"I don't approve of Selene's former behavior either, Olive," Aunt Louisa snapped, "but I will not allow you to insult a member of my family right here under my roof. She has learned her lesson, and my niece by marriage in Georgia has agreed to take the baby. Not that she needs another mouth to feed with four of her own, but she has a generous spirit, and my brother has offered to give her a good sum of money to get them started."

"That's a comfort." Miss Olive studied the unwed mother. "Isn't it, Selene?"

"I—I suppose."

"I didn't mean to tell you in such an abrupt manner"—Aunt Louisa's tone softened—"but since you stop by so often, it's just as well for you to know now, anyway. But I do hope for the sake of our friendship that you won't disgrace us by gossiping all over town. Selene has a hard row to hoe ahead of her, and she doesn't need more problems, even the disapproval of strangers."

"I might not be as offended if you had trusted me from the start." Miss Olive huffed. "Exhaustion, indeed. You didn't have to lie."

"I didn't lie. She is exhausted. Wouldn't you be if you were in her shoes? I'd planned to tell you soon. You have to take my word for it."

Witnessing the exchange, Hestia didn't know how to respond. If anyone should have known sooner, Hestia was that person. Why hadn't her aunt confided in her?

"This is all very sudden." Miss Olive shook her head.

"I didn't know until my brother asked me to accept Selene as my charge for the next few months."

"How could he, knowing you're bedridden?" Miss Olive placed a hand on her bony hip.

"He knew my condition wasn't permanent. And pardon me for saying so, Selene, but your father has always possessed a selfish streak."

"I—I know." Selene studied dark brown swirls in the varnished Carolina pine floor.

Aunt Louisa let out a tired sigh. "I think we'd better call it a day, Olive. Thank you for the cake. Why don't you drop in tomorrow morning for a splash of lemonade? We can talk more then."

Miss Olive nodded with the eagerness of someone invited to a social event sure to be covered in *The Hickory Daily Record*.

Selene held steady until Miss Olive exited out the back door. "Oh, I feel so terrible! Excuse me." Selene rushed to the room she shared with Hestia.

"Now look what's happened. She's all upset." Aunt Louisa crossed her arms. "I love Olive dearly, but sometimes she can be judgmental." She sighed. "I'm glad you're here, Hestia. Selene did not lead the type of life the Lord wants for a maiden, but there is hope for her future. She needs you now. She looks up to you, you know."

"Looks up to me?" Hestia chuckled. "That can't be possible."

"Oh, it is. She admires you very much. I wish you were staying with us longer. She's a handful, even for this old hen."

Not knowing what else to do, Hestia thought it best for her to see Selene. She wanted time to sort out her own shock and emotions, but at the moment, thinking of Selene seemed to be more important. Maybe she could smooth over her cousin's feelings. With a careful motion, she opened the bedroom and tiptoed inside. Selene lay on her bed on top of the covers despite the chill in the room, which had been shut off from the rest of the house all day. "Selene?"

"Twenty-three skidoo, kiddo. I don't want to talk." She turned away from Hestia.

"I'm sorry Miss Olive embarrassed you." Hestia shut the door behind her and drew closer to Selene.

"I said, twenty-three skidoo. Even a rube should know that means to dry up and skedaddle."

"This is the room I share with you, so you can't force me to leave." Hestia tried a bit of humor. Selene rewarded her with a glare. "Sorry about that. Besides, I'm going back home soon, so you won't have to put up with me much longer."

"That's just it. You never needed to know."

"Or did I?" Hestia made her way to the bed and sat at Selene's feet. "I know we're nothing alike, but that doesn't mean we can't love and support each other."

She sat up. "Oh, fine. The cat's out of the bag now and so I guess we have to talk sometime. And just so you know, I don't blame you for being mad about no one telling you. If it makes you feel better, nobody told me you'd be here and I wasn't ready to share my news." The look she sent Hestia was pleading. "I—I thought it wouldn't be so bad being here with Aunt Louisa, but now that I've been here a few days, I'm not so sure I can take living alone with her until spring."

"I don't see that you have much choice."

"Or maybe I do have a choice." Selene leaned toward her and took both of her hands. "What would happen if you stayed until spring, cousin dear?"

What would happen indeed? The thought left Hestia in turmoil. On the one hand, more time would give her a chance to know Booth better. On the other, she missed her friends in Haw River. She didn't want to be a coward and not return to face Luther. He had wronged her, not the other way around. She had no reason not to hold her head up and face everyone. Then again, Booth lived in Maiden and had no reason to leave. Once she left Maiden, she'd likely never see him again.

"You know something?" Selene continued, obviously sensing her hesitation, "I didn't want to come here, but there was no one else. Except you. At first I thought Father would send me to your house, but then Uncle Milton said you were suffering from a broken engagement and you would be going away yourself. I had no idea he meant you'd be visiting Maiden."

"Seems as though we could both use a friend."

"I don't want you to feel sorry for me or to judge me."

"I won't. I wish things had been different for you."

"Me, too. I really hate this place—and how Aunt Louisa keeps me shut in like I've got typhoid. I'm in a family way, but it's not contagious. Is it?"

Hestia laughed in spite of herself. "Knowing Aunt Louisa, she's liable to say it's contagious because you caught it at a hooch party. But I understand how you feel. I get to go to church and socialize outside the house some, but even I'm closed in compared to my life in Haw River. I had a wonderful group of friends there I'd known for years and was invited to many more events than I am here."

"Like what? I can't imagine anything fun like hooch parties or shimmy dancing going on in Haw River."

"If such things do go on, I'm not invited," Hestia admitted. "But I do know about lots of fun things. We had picnics, holiday celebrations, church suppers, talent shows, dinners, and games at each others' houses. Things like that."

"Oh, we have all that, too, only most of our celebrations are more sophisticated than yours, I'd guess."

Selene didn't have many brags, so Hestia didn't protest. "I imagine there's plenty to do right here in Maiden."

"I just wish I could get out of the house." Selene looked outdoors, to the world beyond, with longing. "The people around here must really be closed-minded if all they can do is gossip and wonder about me."

"I wouldn't say that. This may be a small town, but the people here care about each other."

"I'll have to take your word for it. So far, they haven't proved it by me."

* * * * *

Sitting at a table in the mill's break room where he ate lunch with his coworkers, Booth remembered he'd been promised a slice of apple pie later that afternoon. At first it had been obvious Selene wanted him to enjoy the pie, but when she set her eyes on Artie, all that changed. Had Booth been a womanizer, he'd have been insulted and competed with Artie for Selene's attentions whether or not he cared about her. Instead, he felt happy for Artie. His friend needed female companionship, and Selene, with her bubbling personality, might just be the woman to draw him out of his shell.

Still, Selene's flightiness left him feeling uneasy. First she seemed to like him but then Artie. What would happen when the next man came along? Would she set her sights on him, too? If Artie were tossed aside, Booth wondered if he would ever recover. He said a silent prayer for Artie and Selene. And one for beautiful Hestia, for good measure.

"Hey, aren't you listening?" Eric poked him in the ribs. "It's your turn to say grace. My stew's getting cold."

"Oh. Sorry." Bowing his head, Booth complied with a quiet and reverent prayer. Afterward the four men dug in to their food and chatted.

"Say, fellows, I thought we were supposed to get up a basketball game after work since it's sunny." Eric nudged Booth. "You've got plenty to live down after that last game."

"Oh, that's right. I'm sorry. I'll have to beg off today. Maybe Saturday afternoon, unless it's too cold."

"There goes any chance of us winning." Dan's compliment heartened Booth. "But Miss Louisa must be feeling better if she's baking. I reckon it would be wrong to disappoint her."

"I think Miss Louisa's feeling better every day, but she's not the one baking." Booth pictured a little blond rolling pie dough. "Selene is."

"Selene?" Eric shifted in his seat.

"Yes, her other niece. I told you she's there, too." A pleasing image of Hestia floated into Booth's mind. "And just in case you get any ideas, I think she's got her eye on Artie here." His tone told of a jest, but he really did want to keep the field clear for Artie.

"Aw, shucks." Artie almost blushed. "You're making me out to be quite a ladies' man, but that's hardly so."

"Don't kid yourself." Dan pointed his empty fork at Artie. "You could have your pick of any number of ladies."

"This is a bold one. He'll have his hands full if he chooses this one." Booth meant what he said even though he kept his banter light.

"You can say that again." Eric tapped his plate once with his fork.

Booth twisted his lips. "What do you mean? Do you know Selene? I don't see how, since Miss Louisa keeps her hidden away like she's Rapunzel or something."

" 'Or something' is right, according to Aunt Olive." Eric rolled his eyes at his friend. "Don't you ever talk to Aunt Olive? She lives so close to you, and she's at Miss Louisa's all the time."

"I know. They've been best friends for decades. But she doesn't talk to me especially. So I'm not in on what you mean." Booth set down his fork. "Spill the beans."

"Well, I'm not really supposed to say anything. She was actually talking to my sister, warning her not to take the same path, and I overheard. You know how Aunt Olive likes to lecture. Anyway, when she realized I'd overheard, she said to keep quiet." Eric concentrated on stirring his coffee. "So I really should."

"Not if it's something important. This could affect Artie," Booth objected.

"I don't know...."

"You might as well tell us." Dan stopped eating and primed himself to listen. "You've already said too much."

"No, I haven't." Eric stirred the coffee to the point it appeared to be a creamy tornado. "If I had, then you'd be able to guess."

Booth was starting to worry. "Miss Louisa said she's visiting to recover from exhaustion."

"Oh, I'm sure she's tired. If she'd gone home to sleep earlier a few months ago, she wouldn't be so tired now." Eric didn't look at them but tapped his spoon on the side of his cup. "And she wouldn't be here in Maiden."

"So she was a party girl," Artie scoffed. "You can look at her and tell that. She's from New York. I'll bet almost every girl up there is like that. Besides, I like blond hair."

"Then you have a wild side we haven't ever seen." Dan wore a half-smile and shook his head.

Booth didn't care about Artie's wild side. Defending Hestia's cousin interested him more. "She won't have that blond hair for long. Miss Louisa's forbidden her to dye it again. And she loves to wear lots of face paint. I've seen her with it."

"Is that so?" Eric took a swig of coffee.

"What does it look like?" Artie leaned in.

Booth shrugged. "She looked pretty. I think she looks better without it, but I doubt she thinks so."

"If she's the way you describe, I can see why Aunt Olive was fussing at my sister." Eric leaned back in his seat and crossed his arms. "Now that I think about it, I might just go home and lecture her myself."

"I think I finally get it." Booth felt foolish for being so slow. "Selene's parents sent her here to get her away from a group of flappers that want to have parties every night. Maybe they want her to settle down and study. But she doesn't seem like the bookworm type to me."

"I don't think she is, either," Artie agreed.

"I'm sure they want to get her away from her friends in New York, if they're as wild as you seem to think they are." Eric swirled the coffee in his cup. "I hate to break it to you, but to hear Aunt Olive tell it, it's worse than that. Much worse."

Booth wanted to get to the bottom of the secret right away. The men huddled as much as they could around a table. Booth made sure to speak in a conspiratorial volume. "How do you mean, worse?"

"I told you, I'm not supposed to tell."

"Then I'll guess. It's that important." Since Eric's love of spreading news rivaled his aunt's, Booth had no doubt they'd soon know the secret. "Okay, first guess. Her father wants to get her away from a certain beau."

"You could say that, but I'd think in this case the beau wants nothing to do with her." Eric looked from side to side and then back at them. "How would you say she looks? Like she's gained a little weight?"

Booth froze, and he felt Artie tense, as well. "I—I haven't seen her in quite some time. Not since she was a girl, and Artie's never met her before now. So I really can't say if she's gained any weight recently." Still, he pictured Selene and recalled noticing that she wasn't as thin as a stylish flapper preferred.

"And does she feel sick every morning?" Eric's mouth turned down in a sad line.

"Sick? I remember my sister feeling sick when she was…" Dan's mouth dropped open. "You can't be saying Miss Louisa's niece is in a family way. Not as nice as her people are."

Booth's gut tightened. "Yes, especially Hestia."

"We know you like Hestia," Artie managed to quip.

Ignoring Artie, Booth set his gaze on Eric. "Is this true about Selene?" Booth felt rage pulse through his veins. "Is that what you're telling us?" In his passion, his voice had risen more than was prudent. A couple of girls from the typing pool stared then looked away and giggled.

Eric nodded but kept his voice low. "I wish I weren't, but Aunt Olive seems to think it's true. She might be the biggest gossip in town, but she does try not to spread falsehoods."

Booth thought about Selene. From all appearances, before arriving in Maiden she had lived a fast life in New York. Hestia had mentioned that Selene had been reared in wealth but her mother had died long ago. He had also gotten the impression that Selene's father was preoccupied with business and spoiled Selene with money while giving his affections to mistresses. If Hestia spoke with accuracy, and he had no reason to believe she didn't, then it wouldn't be impossible for Selene to be in a family way.

Poor Miss Louisa! She had such a superb reputation, and now this? To be asked to take in a wayward niece, and when she was mending from illness at that. No wonder she sent for Hestia.

He felt shattered. Selene, the glamorous girl he had admired for so long, who flirted with him so boldly, was in a family way? Before marriage? Even worse, everyone in town seemed to know about the scandal. And thanks to his insistence that Eric share with them at the table, Dan and Artie knew, too.

Remorse filled him. "Listen, fellows, please don't say anything about this to anybody else."

Eric chuckled. "You were the one who forced me to make you guess until you figured it out for yourself."

"I know, and I'm sorry about that. I'm a dunce. But you're talking about my friends here, people I've known for years, and I think that gives me the right not to be kept in the dark. I'm not just an outsider looking for news to spread around town."

"And you think my aunt is?"

"No, I didn't mean that." Booth swiped his hand in a horizontal motion as if to wipe the slate clean of such a thought. "If I'd been your aunt, I probably would have run home and yelled at your sister, too. Nobody wants to see anything like that happen to her. But I don't think she's got the temperament to be a flapper, anyway."

"Me, neither." Dan pointed his fork at Eric. "I don't think you need to worry."

"Not to mention, it's a lot harder to get in trouble here in Maiden than it is in New York." Booth imagined New York as crowds of people dressed in clothes he couldn't afford, dancing wildly, holding glasses of bubbling champagne. Such a world held no appeal to him.

"Yes, a big city does offer more temptations." Artie's tone sounded with regret. "But you can find trouble anywhere if you look hard enough."

"Yes, but my sis is a good girl." Eric sounded with the conviction of a big brother. "I think Aunt Olive was looking for an excuse to talk. She was pretty upset. Even though she doesn't know Selene like she knows some of the other girls in town, she's upset for Miss Louisa's sake."

"Yes, it's a sorry situation for everyone concerned." Booth was grateful it was almost the end of the meal. He drank coffee while the others indulged in dessert then made a point of leaving with Artie.

Booth waited until the others were out of earshot before bringing his concern to Artie. "Look, sport, you've worked hard to build your reputation back up here in town, and now pretty much everybody thinks you're swell. Selene's reputation is tarnished. I won't think hard of you if you don't want to go over with me to see them anymore. I'll just drop by as usual to see if I can do anything for Miss Louisa. I'll make some excuse for you. They might figure out the score, but Selene has to realize she's not going to be well-respected after this."

Artie's eyebrows rose. "Is that how you feel? Like you don't want anything to do with her?"

Booth felt ashamed he had even spoken in a negative way, but he'd only been trying to protect Artie. "They're my neighbors and I'll help them. I don't mind, anyway. Not that I think Selene did the right thing, but I'm not her judge."

"I feel the same way." Artie's voice and the way he straightened himself showed his determination. "I'm not obligated to them the same as you, but I want to go. And I will go, as long as they'll open the door to me."

Booth gave him a singular nod. "Somehow, I have a feeling you're just what they need."

Chapter Eight

....

"Here. Like this." Rolling pin in hand, Hestia showed Selene how to form a piecrust. The doughy smell promised that the pastry would taste delicious. "Now you try."

Following Hestia's lead, Selene rubbed flour on the rolling pin and then set to work. At first, she rolled with slow motions, but as she worked, her movements became vigorous. "Say, this is kind of fun."

"Yes, it can be." Hestia smiled to herself, glad to see her cousin taking joy in a productive task. "Make it smooth, now. And you'll want a uniform thickness so it bakes evenly."

Hestia's trick of using a recipe including vinegar had served her well. Her piecrusts always rolled out with little effort and, after they baked, were flaked to perfection. Hestia didn't brag on herself, but she knew that as she'd gained practice, her pie-baking had progressed to an expert level. A pang of guilt stabbed her, but their plan wasn't totally dishonest. Selene had done most of the work, and Hestia reasoned that all women had to learn how to bake at some point.

The cousins worked on making the pie look beautiful, too. Soon they'd set it in the hot oven, and by the time Booth and Artie were due to arrive, the pie would be nice and warm, a pleasant way to divert the day's chill.

The pie would be a victory indeed. Hestia felt tempted to bake scrumptious apple tarts for Booth but knew that to do so would be competing with her cousin and would only serve to make Hestia appear childish. Let Selene have her day. Her happy hours would be numbered once Aunt Louisa clamped down on the socializing. Hestia wondered if Selene would even be permitted visitors. Perhaps this little tea promised to provide the break her cousin needed.

Placing the pastry in a ceramic pie plate, Selene glowed with a sense of accomplishment. "There. What next?"

"Do you want a lattice top or a plain top?"

Selene eyed the pie. "Lattice."

"Then we'll pinch the crust like so." Hestia showed her the technique of using her thumb and forefinger to make the edge curve into a pretty form. "Now it's your turn."

Selene tried but quickly frowned. "My half's not coming out pretty like yours."

Hestia wished she could deny it, but Selene spoke the truth. The wavy edges of her crust weren't even and looked as though they had been prepared by the beginner Selene was. "It takes practice." Hestia was tempted to finish the edge herself, but she didn't want to take away from Selene's accomplishment. "Would you rather try pressing it down with the tines of a fork? It's a little easier that way but makes a pretty pattern, too."

"No. I'll keep trying this way." Selene flattened the crust and tried once more from the beginning. Hestia watched her cousin finish the edges. Though not curved to perfection, it was pretty enough. "Looks nice."

"Do you really think so?"

"I wouldn't enter it in a contest, but it's wonderful considering this is your first try. I know Artie and Booth will think it's just fine. Besides, I imagine they'll be more interested in how it tastes, anyway."

"True."

"Now let's prepare the filling."

The two women worked to make cinnamon-laced fruit filling, complete with plenty of butter and sugar. Then, following Hestia's instructions, Selene sliced more pie dough into even strips and crisscrossed them over the filling.

Hestia leaned against the counter and admired Selene's handiwork. "That does look wonderful. You did a grand job. Looks as though you're a natural with latticework."

"Copacetic! Let's just hope I don't burn it."

"You won't. We'll watch the clock."

As the pie baked, they sat at the kitchen table. Selene patted Hestia's knee. "Thank you for helping me make the pie. I couldn't have done it without you. You know something? When I first got here, I thought you'd changed from the cousin I'd always admired to a big Mrs. Grundy. But now that I've been here awhile, I see you're not half bad. Why, I might even go so far as to call you the bee's knees."

Hestia had never been called such a thing—and doubted such a thing existed—but she realized that Selene had given her a supreme compliment. "Thank you. You thought I was terrible, did you? Well, I'm glad you got to know the real me."

"So am I. Maybe country bumpkins aren't so bad after all."

Hestia refrained from rolling her eyes. Why Selene felt she had to spoil the compliment by following it with an insult, she didn't know.

Selene sent Hestia a rueful grin. "I'm sorry you'll be leaving."

"Me, too."

"Do you mean it?"

Hestia thought for a moment before responding. "Why, yes, I do. But I have a life in Haw River. I work for my father, you know."

"Yes, your father, the doctor." Selene's voice took on a surprising degree of venom.

"Uh, yes."

Selene paused before sharing news that came as a revelation to Hestia. "My father is awfully jealous of Uncle Milton, you know."

"What? Jealous of my father? Why, we have a wonderful life, but your father lives the high life."

"I know. But I wonder sometimes if he's happy. I think he sometimes longs to come back here, to a life he thinks is simpler." Selene looked around the kitchen, at its less-than-modern appliances and creaking floor. "I can promise it's definitely simpler here."

"What's stopping him from moving back here? He'd be welcome."

Selene shrugged. "He's got too many people depending on him in New York. He's an important businessman."

"Makes sense."

"But he's not really happy. I know he's not happy with me." Selene looked down at her expanding midsection and rubbed it with the gentleness of a mother.

Hestia weighed her words. "I'm sure this isn't what he planned for you."

"You don't say?" Sarcasm penetrated her voice.

"That's my old Selene," Hestia couldn't resist joking.

"So what will you do when you go back to Haw River, other than slave away for your father? I mean, your marriage prospects have flown out the window."

Hestia winced. "Maybe I'll never wed."

"Aw, applesauce! You won't die an old maid. I've seen how you look at Booth. And how he looks at you."

So Selene *had* noticed! Booth's interest in her wasn't a figment of her imagination, after all. With Selene's competitive spirit, Hestia knew she'd never make such an admission unless she believed it. Hestia felt her face warm with the embarrassment of being discovered. "Oh, pshaw."

"No, it's true. I think he's sweet on you. And now you have to go to Haw River." Selene leaned closer to Hestia. "Do you think you really have to go back?"

"Well…Mother's last letter did indicate she's been assisting him in the office and it has worked out well so far."

Selene returned to her position in the chair. "Sounds as though you're being replaced."

The idea left Hestia feeling more lost than she imagined she would. "I—I hope not. But if I am, I'm sure that's God's plan. He always has a way of prodding us in the direction we need to go. And if my guess is right, my direction will be to go back home after today."

"When is Dr. Lattimore supposed to stop by?"

"Any time now. I hope Aunt Louisa gets a good report."

"That would be copacetic. She's certainly been a trouper. She deserves to be able to get out of bed."

"So you have some good words for our aunt after all?"

Selene flitted her hand. "Oh, she's not so bad. She's just doing the best she can. With your medical background, what's your opinion? Will the good doctor let her out of bed today?"

Hestia considered the possibility. "That will depend on how fast her bones have healed. I'll admit, she's been patient. I think I would have gone crazy hardly being able to move."

"I'll bet she won't try to hang up any more pictures."

"Or she'll at least ask Booth to help her next time." They heard a knock on the front door. "Perhaps that's Dr. Lattimore now."

Answering the door moments later, Hestia discovered that the visitor was indeed the doctor. He granted Hestia permission to accompany him into the sickroom. Anxious about her aunt, Hestia hovered near the door.

"How's the patient today?" His manner was professional yet kind. An image of her own father entered Hestia's mind.

"Ready to get up out of this bed."

"I'm sure you are. I'll give you a chance as soon as I check out a few things here." The doctor gave her a cursory examination. He reminded Hestia of her father, who had given many such examinations himself.

"Looks as though you're doing quite well. All right, you may get up and see how you do. I'll help you. Take my arm." He extended his hand.

Aunt Louisa shifted herself out of the bed and, using the doctor's arm as a crutch, set herself aright and placed both feet on the floor.

"Do you feel like walking across the room?"

"Indeed I do!"

Selene came up behind Hestia and watched.

Aunt Louisa proceeded to show them how well she could walk, if only for a few steps. As soon as she had walked six steps to the vanity chair, she took a seat. "I'm tired already."

"That's to be expected. You have done quite well." The doctor gave her a reassuring pat on the back.

"So Hestia can go home now?" Selene's voice betrayed her upset.

"As long as you can help your aunt, then yes, Hestia can go home."

Selene's body tensed. She nodded quickly then retreated to her room. Hestia knew Selene wasn't being rude. Aunt Louisa had instructed her to stay to herself whenever visitors arrived, except when she gave special permission, as when Artie visited.

"Thank you, doctor." Hestia remembered her manners. Even though the doctor wasn't making a social call, she liked to offer food. "Might I offer you a cup of coffee and cookies?"

"Thank you, but I have a few more stops to make today." Aunt Louisa and Hestia murmured farewells, and Hestia escorted him to the door.

In a manner unusual for her, Hestia paused and watched the doctor walk to his Nash motorcar. Holding her arms across her chest, she tried to fight her roiling emotions. She wanted her aunt to be well, to gain her strength. She wanted to be there for Selene. Most of all, she wanted to be near Booth. But she also wanted to return to the life she knew in Haw River. Seeing the doctor reminded her of her dream to help others through medicine. If she didn't return to Haw River, she could bid good-bye to any hope of a career. She enjoyed the day-to-day activity of her father's office and loved to witness how his healing touch helped others. True, modern medicine couldn't do everything, but science discovered something new every day, it seemed to Hestia. As time marched on, would there be any cure out of medicine's reach? She wanted to be a part of that.

But for the moment, she had to put aside any thoughts of herself. She had Aunt Louisa to consider. Straightening herself, she thought of her aunt's progress and, with a pleasant expression on her face, entered the sickroom. Now the smell of menthol liniment mingled with the faint medicinal aroma the doctor always carried with him. The remnants of the doctor's presence wouldn't linger, but Hestia guessed that the smell of menthol would remain until the house saw its last day.

Her aunt had returned to bed and sat propped up on pillows as usual. Hestia approached her. The day before, she had laundered Aunt Louisa's coral bed jacket and matching gown. The scent of soap mixed with the soft talcum powder the older woman wore.

"How are you feeling now, Aunt Louisa?"

"Better, now that I know I'm well and can start moving around again. I'm surprised by how tired I feel, I'm sorry to admit."

"As the doctor said, that's to be expected. We haven't let you move for weeks, remember? Now, I don't want you to stress yourself. You might break your bone again. We wouldn't want that to happen. Why don't you rest now, and I'll fix supper later. You can eat at the kitchen table for a change. In fact, maybe I should set the dining room table special to celebrate."

"Don't go to all that trouble. The kitchen table and everyday china are good enough for me." Still, her wistful look told Hestia she wouldn't mind the extra effort made in celebration of her doctor's good report.

Selene entered. "It's been almost an hour. Is it time to take the pie out of the oven yet?"

Hestia glanced at the nightstand clock. Where had the time gone? "Let me check on it before you do. I'll be right there."

Aunt Louisa took in an exaggerated sniff. "It smells good."

Hestia inhaled the aroma of the baking pastry, the mixture of apples, butter, sugar, cinnamon, and dough promising the unmistakable delight of hot apple pie. "Yes, it does. I'm glad I found your recipe, Aunt Louisa. I didn't remember all the details of Mother's."

"Glad to help."

"Will you try a piece with us when the men visit?"

"I'm a bit tired. I think I'll wait until dinner, if it's all the same to you."

Hestia had a feeling her aunt wasn't as tired as she claimed. Instead, she was probably being nice by not interfering in their visit. She hurried into the kitchen to check on the pie. A golden crust and bubbling cinnamon-colored filling told her that the treat was ready. Using a dish towel, she took the pie from the stove.

Selene watched. "Mmm. I hope that tastes as good as it looks."

"I think it will. It certainly smells good, too."

Thinking about how much help Selene had needed just to bake a pie, Hestia thought about all the other duties she'd taken on during her visit. She alone had been responsible for the cooking, laundry, and cleaning. From her perch in bed, Aunt Louisa had managed to keep up her correspondence. Selene made halfhearted attempts at dusting, but that was the extent of the housekeeping help she offered. Hestia couldn't imagine that her cousin, with her lack of skill and even less enthusiasm, would be successful in caring for their aunt. Besides, she would need care herself as her pregnancy progressed.

Hestia still wasn't sure she wanted to stay. Sure, Booth made the place interesting, but with his good job at the mill's front office, he had no reason to live anywhere but his home town. Maiden had its charms, but she had a life in Haw River, a life to which she planned to return. She enjoyed assisting her father in his medical practice and had hoped he'd keep her on indefinitely. But truth be told, Papa thought of her helping him as a diversion, not something to be taken seriously. He wanted marriage for her, not a career. She couldn't deny the desire to have a husband and children was appealing to her. Couldn't she have both a career and a home?

She wondered what Selene's ultimate dreams were for her life. Surely she knew she couldn't live the life of a flapper forever. Already, such a life had been interrupted by an unscrupulous man—though even Selene would admit she had to take responsibility for her own behavior. Eventually she would have to choose a path that would lead to a future beyond friends and fun. Perhaps the reality of an unplanned pregnancy would bring her to her senses. Hestia recoiled at some of the things Selene had suggested. Hooch parties could lead to nothing but trouble, especially for young people unaccustomed to strong drink and out to prove how daring and fashionable they could be. Selene had found out the hard way. Hestia wondered what Selene's options would be once she returned to New York.

Hestia thought of her cousin, buying lots of dresses and enjoying a life of leisure in New York, while Hestia had studied hard, graduating from Meredith College in Raleigh with high honors. Hestia had allowed herself to be courted by a respectable man, who only served to spurn her. All things considered, perhaps Luther could claim to be no better than Ned. At least she and Selene had broken hearts in common.

Perhaps that's why Hestia now felt a certain bond with her cousin, no matter how unlike each other they appeared to be.

But Hestia hadn't deserved how Luther treated her. Selene had invited such punishment. If she had followed God's laws instead of her own pleasures, she would be married to a respectable socialite in New York and not waiting out an unwed pregnancy in Maiden.

The indignation Hestia felt shocked her.

Lord, keep such thoughts from me.

The pie, now set on the counter in all its glory, with its sugar-and-cinnamon aroma, reminded Hestia of the sweets her mother liked to bake for church suppers. A sudden feeling of homesickness visited her. She wished she could go home, if only for a visit. Sure, Maiden wasn't all that different from Haw River in many ways, and Hestia was with people who loved her.

But it wasn't home, and responsibility for two women's health had been left to her. It was all too much.

All too much. How would she feel if she were responsible for many more people, such as a nurse or doctor? Her thoughts left her in turmoil.

Selene tapped her on the shoulder. "You look as though you're a million miles away, cousin dear. A penny for your thoughts."

"You'll want to keep your penny. I promise you that." Then, noting Selene's stricken look, she made another offer. "Why don't we sit on the back porch and enjoy this fine fall day? I'd offer to make cocoa, but with pie coming up, that's too much sugar."

"I'd agree on the sugar. But isn't it a little chilly to sit outside?" Selene peered outside the kitchen window and shivered.

Hestia followed Selene's gaze with hers. Sun beckoned, and she didn't want to miss a chance to enjoy fresh air. She had to convince her cousin to be more hale and hearty. "What do you expect for November? Bring your shawl."

"Oh, all right. I'm getting tired of being in the house all the time, anyway. Aunt Louisa treats me as though I have to hide."

Hestia wasn't sure what else Selene could expect but held back a comment.

Selene tilted her head toward the freshly baked dessert. "Don't you think we'd better put the pie away? I'd hate for Diamond to get into it."

"You have a point." Hestia opened the storage area above the stove and set the pie inside. "There. That should be safe."

Hestia called to Aunt Louisa that they'd be outside, and the older woman shouted her agreement. The younger women headed to the back, where chairs, cold to the touch from being outdoors, awaited.

As her cousin sat, Hestia couldn't help but observe Selene's abdomen. Indeed, it was growing larger by the day. Selene's dresses, all fashioned in the linear style flappers favored, had ceased to be flattering.

Hestia had a thought. "Why don't you and I buy some patterns and sew you a few new dresses? Would you like that?"

"I can't sew."

"Of course you can. I'll teach you."

Selene fiddled with the sash of her dress. "Is there anything you can't do?"

"There's lots I can't do."

"Name one thing."

Hestia didn't want to think too long lest she appear vain. "I couldn't keep my fiancé interested long enough to marry me."

"Neither could I."

"Well, we have something in common, don't we? Do you mean to say you were engaged to Ned?"

She nodded. "Secretly."

"Oh." Hestia knew that secret engagements usually served to allow the man to take advantage of the woman without consequences. "You know something? You're lucky Ned left you. If he didn't want to marry you, then he would have made a terrible husband in the long term."

"But I would have had a name for my baby."

"True, and that is important."

Selene paused and looked reticent. "Can I tell you something I've never told anybody else?"

"Of course."

"When I told Ned about the baby, he…he wanted me to see if I could…" She stopped speaking, and tears came to her eyes.

"Could what, honey?"

"It's hard to say, it's so terrible."

"Well, if he talked to you about adoption, you can't blame him. I know it's hard, but just think. Your baby will be with relatives. They'll take good care of the baby, and it will have a happy life. Then you can marry one day and have your husband's babies, knowing in good conscience that you did the right thing for this first baby."

Instead of consoling Selene, Hestia's words seemed to upset her more. Tears flowed. Hestia reached out to her cousin and put her arms around her. "I'm so sorry. I'm so, so sorry."

Selene sniffled. "I am, too. And now because of this, I will have to tell my future husband that I have already had a baby, a baby that he'll never know. And neither will I."

Hestia couldn't find any words. What could she say, when the truth hurt so much?

Selene wanted to talk, so Hestia listened. "It will be hard to give up the baby," she admitted, "but I know it's the right thing to do."

"Of course it is."

"But that's not why I was upset with Ned. You see, he thought I should try—try to…"

Hestia couldn't imagine what Selene wanted to say. "Try to what?"

She sniffled. "To—to kill the baby."

Such an idea shocked Hestia. She felt her chest tighten with outrage. "No!"

"It's true. He said he could find out where I could go to get 'the problem' taken care of."

"I can't believe it. Not even of someone like Ned."

"What do you mean, someone like Ned?"

Hestia couldn't believe she'd be defensive about an insult directed at such a rat. Yet she had loved him, and Hestia wondered if perhaps a part of Selene's heart would always be with Ned. She was only glad Luther had at least shown her the courtesy of not asking for undue affection. Not that she would have considered the idea. Getting too close to one's fiancé just wasn't done in her set.

She searched for an answer. "I mean, Ned did abandon you and his child. I'm sorry, but that doesn't speak well of his character. As I said before, you're better off without him. Maybe it doesn't seem so now, but you are. I just know it."

"I know, but it hurts. When he said he wanted me to get rid of the baby, I couldn't believe it, either."

Hestia wondered about something. "What did your father say when you told him you were expecting Ned's baby?"

She shuddered. "He hit the roof, of course. He hates Ned. Always has, always will. I'm sure that has something to do with why Ned didn't agree to marry me after the truth was out. Father doesn't think we're in the same class."

"Are you?"

"No." Selene swallowed. "But at least Ned didn't use this baby as an excuse to marry into money."

"True, but I still don't give him a lot of credit for being a good man. It's character, not class, that's important. And considering he wanted you to murder your baby, it doesn't sound as though Ned has much of a heart. So how did you become involved with someone like that, Selene? You are so pretty. You could have your pick of any man."

"I wouldn't say that." Still, a natural pink rose to Selene's cheeks, and she looked down in a manner much shyer than usual for her.

"When you first started keeping company with Ned, did you think you'd end up married to him one day?"

She didn't answer right away. "No."

"Then why did you keep seeing him? I would never consider allowing a man to court me if I didn't seriously think we could wed. And to become secretly engaged to him on top of that." Hestia knew she sounded like a shrill headmistress of a girls' school, but she couldn't help herself.

"I don't know. Ned had that certain something that attracted me to him. And I don't mean a supply of hooch." Her eyes became dreamy, and she looked over the backyard but didn't seem to take in how the autumn wind swirled leaves off the maple trees or how the squirrels were scampering, looking for fallen acorns under the tall oaks. "He was so good-looking. And charming. I fell for him the day I met him. Other girls wanted him and they were jealous, but I won out over them all."

"I'm not surprised. So winning out over the others was part of the appeal."

"I hadn't thought of it that way, but I suppose you're right."

"Maybe that's why you found Booth so fascinating when you first got here," Hestia pointed out.

"What's that supposed to mean? Have you fallen for Booth?"

Hestia felt uncomfortable. "That hardly seems likely, since I'm going back to Haw River. But I think you found him appealing because he's been my escort to church since I arrived."

"And he is quite handsome. But if you spend time with him, then according to your rules, you are thinking of marriage."

"I—I hadn't thought much about marriage," Hestia blurted in protest. Selene's logic was hard to defy, so she sought a good argument. "I have a leading to be a doctor, or at least to be involved in medicine in some way. But I do have some reservations occasionally, and the men in my life don't approve. Father is lukewarm about the notion, and I've already lost a fiancé partly because of my progressive ideas."

"Well, if your fiancé decided not to marry you for that reason, then he wasn't right for you, either."

Such words, almost identical to what she had said to Selene about Ned, didn't offer Hestia much comfort. Yet she couldn't deny that they applied to her.

"But the right man might make you change your mind," Selene ventured. "And might that right man be Booth?"

Hestia hadn't thought about such things even to herself, and hearing Selene put the idea into words made her nervous. How could Selene pass judgment on her, when she was the one who'd brought disgrace to their family by her actions? Still, her upbringing hadn't been a Christian one except in name, so she couldn't be blamed entirely for her bad decisions. "I think we've chatted enough for today. I don't know if we can ever have a full meeting of the minds and hearts, but I love you very much."

"Thanks, cousin." Selene cleared her throat. "I know Aunt Louisa loves me, too. And without a doubt, she loves you more."

"I wouldn't say that. Because I'm more traditional than you are, she may feel she can understand me better than she can you, but that doesn't mean she loves me more."

Selene shrugged. "No use arguing about it. She means well, but now that I've gotten reacquainted with you, I have to say, I'll miss you."

"I'll miss you, too." Hestia heard a motorcar in front of the house. "Sounds as though Artie and Booth are here."

Chapter Nine

....

Hestia watched Selene's hand shake as she tried to slice the pie while the men waited for them in the parlor. "Here, let me get that."

"I can do it."

Seeing that Selene wanted to do as much of the work as she could to impress Artie, Hestia did her best not to interfere. Still, she felt her cousin's nervousness. Did she already have a crush on Artie, or was this her way of carrying on a mild flirtation to pass the time? At least Artie was a mature man, able to defend himself against any false feminine wiles.

"I'll take the coffee." Hestia figured Selene's handling a hot liquid wasn't a good idea, considering her state. She took the tray with the small silver coffeepot, sugar and cream, silverware, and cups. Selene followed with another tray of four slices of pie on Aunt Louisa's good china.

After they were served, the men didn't waste time before tasting the dessert right away. Hestia suspected they must have eaten less lunch in anticipation of this treat.

Artie closed his eyes, a look of happiness on his face as he let the pie melt in his mouth. "This is even better than I expected."

"What is that supposed to mean? Were you expecting a poison ivy pie?" Selene's teasing manner and tone of voice reminded Hestia of the way her cousin had spoken to Booth when she first arrived.

Hestia shot a glance Booth's way. No trace of jealousy over Selene's coyness with Artie colored Booth's handsome features. Instead, he caught Hestia's glance. She looked down at her sliver of pie then back up, and she saw him grin. If Selene had ever presented Hestia with competition for Booth, she did no longer.

"Or something," Artie mumbled, though still having a smidgen of pie in his mouth. He swallowed and wiped his lips with a cotton napkin. "But I could eat a whole pie this good."

"Hestia did help me with it." A hint of a blush colored Selene's cheeks.

Hestia held back her surprise. She hadn't considered that a flapper as bold as Selene possessed the ability to blush, and such a confession showed how far her cousin had progressed. "With practice, you'll be able to bake anything by yourself in no time."

"I'm not sure I want to go that far." Everyone laughed at Selene's quip, but Hestia had a feeling she wasn't joking.

Booth's fork slid into his slice of pie. "So how'd the doctor's visit go with Miss Louisa?"

"Very well." Hestia felt grateful to deliver a good report. "She was able to walk a few steps to her chair. She's weak, though. I'm not encouraging her to overdo it. She still needs help."

"So you'll be staying a little longer?" Booth's eyes brightened.

Hestia noted that his voice sounded hopeful. "Yes, I think I should stay at least another week." She had a thought. "I suppose that means you'll be stuck escorting me to church, if you don't mind too terribly."

"I don't mind at all. In fact, it will be my pleasure. Not that I wish your aunt to be anything but her feisty self." He grinned as the others laughed.

"I know. But the good news is that she will be completely well soon."

"I wish I could go to church." Selene set her empty plate in front of a painted Colonial girl figurine on the nearby occasional table.

An awkward silence told Hestia they knew Selene's secret and that going to church wasn't in the picture for her anytime soon. "I wish you could go to church with us, too."

Selene looked at both men but didn't flinch. "You know, don't you?"

"Yes, we do," Artie said in just above a whisper.

With shame on her expression, she looked at her lap. Hestia felt

embarrassed for her. "How did you find out?"

"Miss Olive's nephew, Eric. We eat lunch together." Booth leaned toward her in a sympathetic manner but stopped short of patting her on the knee. "Please don't blame Eric. I was keen on him telling us because he was telling how Miss Olive was lecturing his sister. She was mighty upset when she heard about the situation."

"If a speech from her aunt is all it takes to save her from getting into the trouble I'm in, I think it's a copacetic idea." Selene's hand went to her midsection, but she took it away with a quick motion.

"As though any lecture would have kept you from your parties." Hestia didn't mean to chastise her cousin, but she spoke the truth.

Selene grimaced. "True. I didn't think anything bad would ever happen to me."

"So you're really sorry you lived like a flapper?" Artie's tone of voice told her what the answer should be.

"I regret that this happened."

"Do you want to go back to New York and live the same way you used to after all this is over?" Artie leaned toward her.

"Artie!" Booth slapped him on the knee. "What's the matter with you, asking such a thing?"

"I'm sorry."

Selene looked pensive. "No, I'll answer. I don't know what the future holds. As for my old life, I can't say I don't miss my friends. And I do like the new fashions."

"Never let it be said that Selene doesn't tell it like it is." Hestia laughed.

A regretful look entered Selene's eyes. "So the two of you knew, but you were still willing to come here and eat pie with us?"

"Yes," Artie was quick to answer. "There's nowhere else I'd rather be." He rose from his seat, holding his empty plate and fork. "Say, Selene, would you like me to help you take the dishes into the kitchen?"

"Sure." She sent him a smile and rose from her seat as well.

"Need some help?" Hestia thought she should ask, but she doubted they wanted her around.

"I think we can handle it," Artie confirmed.

Hestia and Booth handed them their dishes. Hestia watched them exit and then leaned toward Booth, keeping the volume of her voice low. "I wish she could have met someone like Artie before she met Ned."

Booth leaned in to hear her. "So that was his name? Ned?"

"Yes."

Booth looked toward the kitchen. "Selene is what some of the bold fellows would call a tomato, even now."

Such a comment would have sent waves of jealousy—and maybe even shock—through Hestia not so long ago, but she could tell by Booth's blank expression that he had no fixation on Selene. "She is lovely, especially without all that face paint."

"Maybe if Ned could see Selene, knowing the baby is his, he would change his mind. Maybe he would even marry her."

"You sound like a hopeless romantic."

"Is that so bad?"

"No. It's charming, especially from someone as manly as you are, Booth." Hestia recalled everything Selene had confided in her. "No. There's no hope for them to get back together. And after talking with her, I think it's probably for the best."

Booth shook his head. "Seems hard to believe, considering the situation."

"Yes, it's a situation I never thought I'd see happen in my family, and especially with Selene. She was always so confident, so beautiful, so carefree. I envied her." Hestia clamped her mouth shut, wishing she had never made such a confession.

"You never had reason to envy her." Hestia was glad he didn't insist that she answer, as he launched into another topic. "Since you'll be staying for another week, you can go with our friends from church tomorrow night."

Hestia tried to remember the announcements that had been made in church before formal worship started. When social issues arose, she only half listened since she never thought she'd be there long enough to be included. "Oh. The hayride at the Carpenter farm."

"Yes. And if you want to leave early enough to go to the pumpkin patch and choose a few pumpkins, we can take a picnic supper. I can raid the icebox and find something for us, I imagine. Would you like that?"

"I think Aunt Louisa will allow it. And if we go early enough for a supper, I'll prepare the food. No need to disfurnish your mother." She couldn't resist making an observation. "Do you like pumpkins, or are you just hoping for pumpkin pie?"

"A little of both." He grinned and fiddled with the change in his trousers pocket as he asked the next question. "So will you let me come along about five to pick you up for the hayride? That should give us time for pumpkin picking."

"Sure. We could choose several. I have a great recipe for pumpkin soup that makes quite a nice lunch on a fall morning." Hestia sighed. "I wish Selene could go. She and Artie make a nice couple."

"Aren't you rushing to make a match?"

"Maybe, but you have to admit they're cute together."

"Yeah. But I think Selene can forget about getting out of the house anytime soon."

"I know. I wish she'd been more protected before. Uncle Ralph shouldn't have trusted her beau. I think he would have put a stop to the relationship if he'd been home more. But truth be told, she could have been stronger in her resistance to Ned. I, for one, wouldn't allow a beau of mine to take advantage of me like that."

"I know you wouldn't."

Hestia leaned toward him and lowered the volume of her voice. "Do you really think Artie likes Selene?"

"Didn't you see the way he hung on her every word—and how he couldn't keep his eyes off her? Yeah, I'm pretty sure he's got a crush on her."

"Even with her being in the condition she's in? That can't be easy."

"I've talked to him, and I think he's more worried about her spiritual condition than her physical condition. I can't help but wonder—is she a Christian?"

"Of course." Hestia hoped her quick answer didn't seem as if she protested too much. "I mean, I know they're members of a church in New York. Not sure which one."

"Pretty much everybody is a member of a church. You can be on the roll for fifty years and still not be going to heaven."

"True. I know she believes in God, though I have to say, her actions of late don't reflect well. But I'm not her judge."

"No, and neither am I. But if anyone can convince her to change her ways, Artie can." Booth's expression softened and he looked into her eyes. Those blue eyes that Hestia had grown to care for concentrated on her face, making her feel…loved. Shyness overtook her. Why did she think such thoughts? His next question brought her out of her daydream. "So since Selene's here, you'll be helping with her?"

"As long as I'm in town, yes." She was glad he cared enough to ask, but she didn't want to be forward enough to admit it.

"When is the baby supposed to arrive?"

"We think it's supposed to be in the spring. Late March or early April. Then one of Aunt Louisa's distant relatives is supposed to take the baby." Hestia prayed they would treat the baby well.

"Oh. That must be sad for Selene. But at least maybe she'll get to see the baby sometimes."

"Maybe. But they're in Georgia, and I doubt they'll encourage visits."

"Selene's time here will be difficult for her with just your aunt. I know Miss Louisa is strict."

Hestia remembered Selene's having to break her habits of smoking cigarettes and wearing face paint. "Much more strict than the adults she knows in New York. Maybe being with Aunt Louisa for a spell will do her some good. She may be able to slow her down and ground her in solid values."

* * * * *

Meanwhile, Selene tried not to shake as she and Artie went into the kitchen. Why did she feel this way? Surely it wasn't Artie.

Happy to have a distracting task beckon, she piled dirty dishes into the sink and allowed water to loosen the few remaining crumbs. By this time she knew where Aunt Louisa kept the dish towels. She withdrew a white cotton one embroidered with hummingbirds and handed it to Artie. "Sure you don't mind doing women's work?"

"I wash and dry my own dishes at home. Why not here?"

She poured Purex soap flakes into the water. "I can't imagine my father saying that. My, but you are an unusual man." She laughed. It felt good.

His lopsided grin made her feel good, too. "I can't say I love doing the dishes, but I'll bet Hestia and Booth appreciate the time to talk."

"I think they do. I'm amazed that Hestia can breeze into town and find an eligible bachelor right away." She hadn't meant to blurt such a jealous comment.

Artie took a dish from her. "Hestia does have her charms, but so does my present company, if you don't mind my saying so."

"Maybe it's the glow of motherhood." She'd never been so glad to be occupied with dishes, not wanting to look at him as she reminded him of her shame.

"Maybe. But I have a feeling you have always been lovely."

"Tell it to Sweeney."

"Huh?"

"Sorry. I mean, you don't need to flatter me."

"I am not being kind," Artie protested. "I'm being truthful. I have a feeling you could use a friend and a little conversation once in a while. Am I right?"

The conversation she had with Artie hardly qualified as the type of quick-witted banter she was accustomed to with her New York friends, but conversation with a man offered a refreshing perspective she hadn't experienced in recent memory. For the first time, she realized she'd never been friends with a man, any man. The men she knew either paired off with her friends and were so off-limits she barely greeted them, or they were interested in her as a girlfriend.

She remembered one of the many times she and her New York friends had talked about men. Bessie had insisted that men and women could never be just friends. But Artie, with his unaffected magnetism and easy manner, made her wonder if Bessie, for all her sophistication, could have been mistaken.

Artie stopped drying in mid-swipe. "I'm sorry. I shouldn't have suggested you'd want to see me as a friend or anything else. I didn't mean to overstep." His soft tone betrayed hurt, not malice. "I won't stop by again."

"No!" Her answer spewed from her mouth so quickly she embarrassed herself, but the way he relaxed his posture an inch told her he felt relieved by her answer. "I was just thinking about New York and how different it is from here. How different the people are."

"I imagine I don't compare favorably. You think I'm a country bumpkin, I bet."

"No, I don't." Still, she swallowed.

Artie, with his plain but strong looks and straightforward ways, would have fallen under that label for her not so long ago. But away from her crowd, when she could look at people without her city lenses, she could see them differently. She remembered long-ago visits to this very place and how Mother had complained all the way on the train as Father insisted they visit. Mother would pout and grouse, but Selene tried to look forward to the trip as part of a big adventure. She could always relax in Maiden, something impossible to do in the social whirl of New York. Eventually they returned home, too soon for Selene and Father but not a moment prematurely for Mother. The instant Mother returned she'd telephone the beauty salon for one appointment, then the fashion salon for another, and then she'd telephone her friends to schedule lunch at the Algonquin. A gift of jewelry from Father would follow, usually involving diamonds, and Mother was happy again.

She couldn't imagine Artie even considering consoling anyone with jewelry, regardless of whether he could afford to do so. She wasn't sure whether or not he could, but she had a definite feeling he could never buy anything as large as the stones in her mother's jewelry box, the box she had inherited. She would have much rather had her mother in her life.

"Are you sure you don't think I'm a country bumpkin? I'm not certain I'd pass muster with your New York friends."

"You wouldn't fit in there, but you fit in here just fine. And for now, I'm planning to fit in here, too."

Chapter Ten

Hestia couldn't have wished for a better day for the hayride. Brisk air smelled of musty leaves and smoke from burning fireplaces. Late afternoon sun shone for all it was worth, but it was descending into the tree tops. Evening would soon befall them.

Standing on its edge, Hestia surveyed the large pumpkin patch. Booth had brought her to a farm a few miles out of town. An abundance of healthy, round pumpkins awaited her. Each seemed to call to her.

Other church members and their guests joined them, arriving in clusters. Hestia spied Judith. She had arrived looking a bit like a third wheel to her sister and beau. Hestia waved. She was glad to see Judith. The other woman had confided earlier to Hestia that she hoped Peter Drum would look her way. Hestia noticed that Judith had taken special care with her appearance. Like Hestia, she had chosen to keep her hair longer, and her auburn hair framed her face in a lovely manner. She looked casual but collected in a cheerful but modest green dress. Surely she wouldn't escape Peter's notice.

Hestia turned to Booth. "I'm glad you talked me into coming early."

"Maybe I shouldn't point this out, but I didn't have to do too much convincing."

"True." She laughed. "Maybe next time I'll put up more of a fight."

He stepped closer. "You don't have to do that. I'm not a thrill-of-the-hunt kind of man."

His statement gave her pause. She thought of Selene and her terrible situation. Apparently her beau, Ned, had been an adventure seeker. Not that Hestia had fared better. Luther's immediate attraction to a flapper as soon as Hestia left town showed him to be one to seek excitement, as well. Funny how Selene had lost her beau for being too exciting, and part of the reason Hestia had lost hers was because she'd been perceived as not exciting enough. Could a woman really read a man? How could any man be understood?

Hank Beasley waved to Booth. "Got a knife with you? Like a dunce, I forgot mine."

"Sure!" Booth touched Hestia's arm briefly. "Guess he ran into a tough vine. Sorry. I'll be right back."

Judith slid beside Hestia. "Hey, you."

"Hey, yourself. Ready to pick out a pumpkin?"

"Not yet." Judith tugged on her arm. "Look. There's Peter. He must have come with Bob. They've been friends forever."

Hestia spotted a rugged-looking blond. "I think he's looking your way."

He approached, and Judith seemed suddenly shy. "Hello, Judith."

"Hello." She blushed and looked at the ground.

Peter made a stab at pleasantries but got to his point without delay. "Care to introduce me to your friend?"

"Oh. Of course. Wh–where are my manners?" Judith stammered and made the introductions. Seeing her friend's distress, Hestia brought Peter up-to-date on where she was living and why...and the fact she would only be in Maiden a short time.

"That's too bad." Peter's slight downturn of lips showed her he meant what he said. The fact made Hestia nervous. "Maybe we will come to know each other before you leave anyway."

"Maybe." Hestia couldn't bring herself to sound cordial. She didn't want to disappoint Judith. How could he look through Judith and keep his attention focused on herself, when she wasn't the least bit interested? True, she had donned a flattering skirt and blouse, plus taken extra care with her toilette, but those measures were meant to impress Booth, not Peter. Hestia had made a point not to send an encouraging look Peter's way.

"Excuse me, but I just realized I need to ask Booth something." She touched Judith's arm. "You and Peter can sit by us on the hayride, can't you?"

"Oh, that would be fine." Judith's voice brightened.

Hestia made haste toward Booth in the pumpkin patch. He held up his knife. "Good thing I brought this. Some of the vines are right tough. I've had to help with more than one pumpkin today." He returned the knife to the brown leather sheath hanging from a belt loop on his sport trousers and patted it as though it were a trusty hound dog.

"Good. You're always prepared, it seems. So when is the hayride?"

"Soon. Why, are you anxious?"

"Not really. I was just wondering. I hope this evening never ends." She regarded the autumn sky. Twilight would be falling soon.

"Me, either. So are you ready to choose pumpkins for us?"

"Yes." Together, they strode through the immense pumpkin patch, being careful not to trip on vines or twist their ankles in the occasional spot of uneven soil. Hestia's favorite type of pumpkin was small and deep orange, because she thought those to be the most flavorful for pies, soups, and breads.

Booth picked up a pumpkin so large he could barely hold it. "How about this one?"

"Oh my, but that's impressive. Just how many pies do you plan to eat?" she teased.

"As many as I can get. But judging from the expression you're wearing, this one is too large?"

"Yes, and it has yellowed and become encrusted with too much dirt on one side for my taste. Here, let me show you how to select pumpkins for pies and soup."

"And bread, I hope. Pumpkin bread is one of my favorites."

She made a mental note to recall this trivia about Booth. "I'll be sure to make several loaves for you."

"Okay." She expected him to set the pumpkin back, but he didn't. "I'm taking this one for our front porch. Mother likes to decorate for fall."

"Suit yourself. For a decoration, I'm sure that one will be wonderful. It'll show up very well on the porch."

"People should be able to see it from the road." His pleased expression made him seem more like a little boy than a grown man. Hestia found his enthusiasm endearing.

"Is your mother planning to use pumpkins for pies, too? If so, we'd better bring her at least a couple of smaller ones."

He agreed and walked through the patch to inspect more pumpkins. Hestia took time to find several that suited her for her own needs and for Mrs. Barrington.

He watched her reject one pumpkin after another. "You're really picky."

"That's right. I am. It's worth taking the effort to find just the right ones." She noticed Peter and Judith walking through the patch as a pair. Since they were well out of earshot of the couple and other prying ears, she shared her feelings with Booth. "Will you take a look at that? Maybe she got his attention after all."

Booth looked in their direction. "Oh, Judith? Everyone knows she has a crush on Peter. Even Peter."

Suddenly Hestia felt foolish for pushing Judith in Peter's direction. She hoped she hadn't helped her friend make a fool of herself. "Oh. Do you think he's interested?"

Booth shrugged. "Maybe a little more than usual."

"Do you think they'd be a good match?"

He thought a moment. "I guess there could be worse."

"Let's invite them to sit with us for the picnic."

Booth's expression took on a conspiratorial look. "I see. You're playing the matchmaker, aren't you?"

"Maybe just a little. If I can make someone happy before I have to go back, I'd say my trip was a success."

"You've already made a lot of people happy. You just don't know it."

Hestia had a feeling he meant himself, but she wasn't vain enough to give herself credit. She resolved instead to enjoy this evening with Booth as though it would be her last.

During a picnic dinner of fried chicken, potato salad, and rolls, the two couples sat on the large dark brown horse blanket and chatted. Hestia couldn't read Peter's feelings for Judith, but they seemed to get along well. She couldn't help but root for Judith. A nice beau would make her life better.

Sharing time with Booth, even though they weren't a couple, made her realize how much she missed having a beau. At the same time, she realized she didn't miss Luther in particular, just the idea of a man's company in the romantic sense—sharing hopes and dreams and plans for the future. When had Luther decided they had no future? Was it the day she said she wouldn't bob her hair? The day she said she wouldn't don a linear-cut short dress? She felt more confident helping Papa with his patients with her hair pinned back, out of her face and looking neat. Hair flopping forward and swinging backward didn't seem professional to her. And a short dress hardly seemed practical for her needs. Why couldn't Luther understand?

She was just glad Booth didn't seem to mind her appearance. In fact, he seemed to appreciate her. At least, that's what he told her in a friendly way when they met for an outing.

At that moment, Booth leaned near her on the blanket, near enough that she could smell the pleasing scent of the Bay Rum shaving lotion he wore. She had grown comfortable with the scent since he wore it exclusively and always when he escorted her anywhere. She had come to associate it with him and appreciated its familiarity. She would miss the scent—and him—when she returned to Haw River.

She wondered if he knew his effect on her. If he did, he acted oblivious. Men! They were so lucky to be strong.

Soon most of the group gathered for the hayride, leaving only a few sitting by a bonfire to sing camp songs. A mule team was set to pull the wagon. Night had fallen, bringing brisk air filled with falling leaves that rustled as they swirled in the wind, hitting the wagon and landing on the ground.

"Let's go." Booth took her hand and led her to the wagon. Hestia realized he made the motion out of the desire to get a good place rather than romantic inclination. Why, he would have grabbed the hand of any friend he wanted to sit near on the ride, she reasoned. Their haste was rewarded as they scrambled with others to compete for prime spots. Thanks to Booth's quick movements, they grabbed a position where they could rest their backs on the side of the wagon. While not a luxurious overstuffed chair to be sure, the wooden planks offered a degree of comfort. The slower—or perhaps more polite—among them were stuck sitting in the middle of the wagon with plenty of hay but nowhere to lean. The clean hay, damp with night dew, smelled of a pleasant mustiness.

Hestia shivered. "I'm cold." She instantly regretted her admission.

"Here, take my coat." Without delay, he whipped it off and placed it around her shoulders. His warmth still saturated the wool.

"I can't take this. You'll freeze. I'm the one who should suffer since I was foolish and failed to bring my shawl." She made a silent resolution not to be so vain in the future.

She hadn't forgotten the shawl but had skipped the plain wrap so he could see her beautiful embroidered blouse. Out of courtesy to him, she made a motion to take off the jacket.

"I won't hear of that," Booth protested. "I'll just sit closer to you, if that's okay."

She didn't want to seem too eager. "Seems that's the least I can do."

After the driver made sure everyone was seated, he made a clucking sound and pulled on the reins to urge the mules forward. Anticipating a rough start, everyone held on and tried not to lose balance when the wagon took off slowly, but with a jerk.

Booth settled comfortably beside her, close enough that their combined body heat warmed them. He placed his arm around her shoulders, which helped them ward off the chill. Soon Hestia felt comfortable and snuggled closer to Booth. On one hand, she found she welcomed the excuse, but on the other, she felt guilty that he had sacrificed his jacket for her.

The wagon bumped along an uneven country trail. Hitting ruts, they swayed back and forth. There was little chatter as everyone admired the harvest moon, which lit the night enough that, once their eyes adjusted, allowed everyone to appreciate their bucolic surroundings. Hestia breathed in the night air. The heavy scent of burning leaves filled her nostrils at one point. She always enjoyed raking leaves and then burning them, filling the air with an aroma that told the world fall had arrived and was ready to settle in for a time. The sound of wagon wheels churning and the mules' hooves plodding on the ground offered a comforting rhythm. All was right with the world.

A vigorous bump threw Booth closer to her. "You okay?"

"Fine." She looked into his eyes. Though their blueness wasn't evident in the night, she could see them sparkling. The way he looked at her said he wanted to be even closer. Did he want to kiss her? She wished she were bold enough to bring her lips to his. But she couldn't make such a promise. A kiss would be a commitment that she would stay in Maiden forever.

* * * * *

The next day, Selene and Hestia shared time by sewing in the back den. The room held even more mementos than other rooms in the house. Aunt Louisa's skill at embroidery evidenced itself in a bell pull stitched in a crewel floral pattern, along with two complementary pictures and several pillows tossed on the sofa and two chairs. Heavy blue draperies had been installed by Tillie for winter, to keep out the draft. A worn blue Oriental rug covered the floor, offering additional warmth against the anticipated chill.

Hestia had just taught Selene how to darn stockings. Selene's enthusiasm for the project left much to be desired, but at least it gave her something to do. Hestia could have mended much faster, but in her view, Selene needed to learn a few domestic skills. The task wasn't urgent, so the time learning proved to be well-spent.

Having saved the more challenging tasks for herself, Hestia had almost finished mending a few odds and ends. Next, they would shell the pecans Artie had brought, which had been harvested from two trees in his yard. Selene had already claimed some of the nuts so she could cook a pie for Artie. Hestia's heart warmed at how her cousin had taken to baking.

Selene let out a breath strong enough to blow the wisps of hair framing her face. Dark roots had grown uncomfortably visible, but at least Selene had given up complaining about her lack of fresh hair dye. "I wish I could find something to do other than mindless chores. Even that silly hayride you went on last night sounds good in comparison to dying a slow death here."

Hestia's mind focused on the time she and Booth had spent side by side. All morning she'd been giving thanks for the previous evening.

The needle moved faster as her good mood increased. "Everybody has to do a few mindless chores. That's part of life, whether you realize it or not. The sooner you become skilled at small tasks, the more quickly they shall pass. After we shell the pecans, you can read for entertainment."

"Read?" Selene groaned.

"What's the matter?" Hestia couldn't understand her cousin's unhappiness. "Don't you like the periodicals I bought you?"

"Sure, but I can only read them so many times. And I can only rest and sleep so much. I really miss New York."

Hestia stopped sewing and set the blouse in her lap. "I know you had parties at night. What did you do all day?"

A dreamy look lit Selene's eyes. She stared, unseeing, into the corner of the ceiling. "Oh, I slept in most mornings."

"Just as you do now. See, not everything's changed."

Selene stuck her tongue out at Hestia in a playful manner. "I would have a light lunch and then go in for a beauty treatment and maybe a little exercise. Most days I'd shop. Sometimes my girlfriends and I would play cards and eat at restaurants. Then we had parties. Lots of parties."

Hestia considered Selene's currently lean schedule. "I'm sure living here is quite an adjustment for you."

"Sure is. Why, you can't hear anything here. It's so quiet, except for the trains passing through. Like living on the moon or something." She sighed.

"Well, this is a different kind of life. You'll have to learn to take your pleasures in simple things and little joys." Hestia resumed her mending.

Diamond entered the room, fresh from her nap on the kitchen rug. She made her way to Selene and rubbed herself against Selene's legs. "Good girl, Diamond."

The cat ventured to Hestia and repeated her rubbing. Hestia bent over and stroked the animal on her head.

"Is this what you meant by simple pleasures and joys? I have my own cat in New York." Selene sewed a stitch and then studied her handiwork. "How does that look?" She held it up for Hestia's inspection.

"Good." Hestia nodded.

"You know, it might be easier if Aunt Louisa would let me out of the house, but I'm trapped in here all the time. It's not like the whole town doesn't know that she's got two nieces on her hands. One is wayward Selene and the other is saintly Hestia."

"I doubt people are talking like that. At least, I hope not." Hestia completed her work on the blouse and finished it off. "What about Artie?"

"What about him?" Hestia detected yearning in Selene's voice.

"He seems to like you despite your condition. Not every man would be so fearless, you know."

"I know. And I do like him. But I'm going back to New York after all this is over."

"Are you certain you want to go back? Sure, life here isn't as fancy as the way you live in New York, and it never will be. But I've seen how you look at Artie. You've got a crush."

"No…" Selene made a point of avoiding Hestia's gaze.

"Have you ever wanted to bake pies—or anything else—for any other man?" Hestia folded the blouse.

"No, but I still haven't given up on going back."

"You'll have to give up the baby, and nothing will be the same."

"Sure it will. I can go right back to my life as I knew it." She set the mended stocking aside and pulled a piece of stationery out of her pocket. "They haven't forgotten me. Look. I just got a letter today."

"Oh, that's good to hear. Who wrote it?"

"My best friend in New York—in the world, really. Flora Wallace." Selene sighed. "Oh, you should see Flora. She and I are the perfect team. She has hair blacker than coal, and her complexion is a bit darker than mine. She's really tall. We're opposites in appearance, but we dress alike, with our shimmery dresses cut right to the figure. And of course, we both adore face paint from Paris. Everywhere we go, we get stares and whistles. When we arrive, the party starts."

Despite Selene's excitement in describing her friend, Hestia couldn't understand the appeal. "I see."

"Look at this letter." Selene handed it to Hestia.

The paper was of heavy stock, and the penmanship looked girlish but not childish. Hestia read:

Selene, darling:
    What is taking you so long to come back to New York?

Hestia stopped reading. "Selene, you didn't tell her about what happened with Ned?"

"No. I don't want anybody at home to know."

"Not even the person you say is your best friend in the world?" Hestia understood, but how could such a thing be kept a secret from someone so close?

"If I'd wanted everyone to know, do you think I'd come all this way to wait out my pregnancy? Keep reading."

    We miss you awfully. Things here are dreadful without you. Ned is all balled up. He says you two aren't an item anymore, and now he's making time with—you won't believe it—Lucy Van Buren! She is such a wet blanket. Ned hardly comes to any parties anymore.

"I wonder what he's doing instead." Selene's voice was laced with sarcasm. "If Lucy doesn't watch her step, she'll be in the same fix I'm in. Maybe worse."

Hestia couldn't imagine much worse, but she kept reading.

> *Serves him right. If I had to take that dumb Dora everywhere,*
> *I'd stay home, too! You know, you have much better gams.*
> *Everyone says so.*

"That's so true." Selene giggled.
Hestia decided not to comment but kept reading:

> *She had no right to move in on Ned in such a bold way. I'd*
> *like to punch her in the kisser for you. The girls and I are high-*
> *hatting her for you, though.*

"High-hatting her?" Hestia asked.
"Being snobby. Not speaking to her except when they have to."
"Oh."

> *She's too dim to realize it—you know, nobody's home—but she*
> *doesn't have any friends in our crowd anymore. Oh, and speaking*
> *of friends, Bessie, Nina, and Lula all want to know what's taking*
> *that aunt of yours so long to recover. They want you back.*

"So you told them you're taking care of Aunt Louisa?" Hestia asked.
Selene shrugged. "I didn't have a chance to say good-bye. Father put
me on the train and told me not to get into any more trouble. He must
have told them that. It doesn't matter. Keep reading."

> *Oh, and Willie and Rudy were asking after you—and that*
> *was before they got spifflicated, so you know they meant it.*

"What's spifflicated?" Hestia asked.

Selene sighed as though she were an impatient teacher instructing a particularly dull student. "You know. Zozzled. Fried to the hat. Plastered."

"You mean, intoxicated?"

"Yeah, I suppose that's a word you could use, too." Selene rolled her eyes. "Man, don't you ever have any fun?"

"I already told you. Not that kind of fun." Hestia kept reading:

> *Maybe all four of us can go on a double date after you get back. I always did think Rudy was swell. You don't mind Willie so much, do you?*

"Not at all!" Selene spoke as though Hestia knew Willie. "Oh, doesn't that sound like loads of fun?"

"I don't know. Do you really want to keep company with a drunk?"

"A drunk?"

"Yes. Your friend admitted as much in this letter."

"Oh. But they don't get fried to the hat all that much. Just sometimes. You know, to loosen up. I'll bet if you tried a little sip now and then, you could loosen up, too."

Hestia had no desire to keep the conversation on herself. "Ned imbibed in spirits, right?"

"Yes."

"Then I don't think that's a good idea, Selene. You might find yourself right back here if you take up with another man like Ned. I'd think you could see that, all things considered."

Selene patted her belly. "Oh, this won't happen again. I can promise you that. You're such a killjoy."

"I'm sorry. I know I seem that way, but you have to see reality."

"I don't want to see reality. I want to go back home, where my friends are. I want my life back!" Selene snatched the letter from Hestia's hand. "I can't share anything with you. You just don't understand. I don't have any friends here. Not a friend in the world." Selene rose from her chair, abandoning her chore. Instead, she rushed to the bedroom. Hestia could hear Selene slam the door.

Aunt Louisa soon emerged from washing the breakfast dishes, her gait slow but her color looking better than when she was still confined to bed. "What was that all about? I don't take kindly to slamming doors in my house. It's unladylike, not to mention being hard on the house."

"I know. I'm sorry. It's just that Selene and I don't see eye to eye on how she should behave once she goes back to New York. She received a letter today from one of her friends back home that got her all excited and homesick. I don't think she realizes the folly of going right back into the same type of life she left."

Aunt Louisa sat in the chair that Selene had just vacated. "She's emotional. She'll get over it. Don't worry. I'm sure you told her the right thing. But this is one decision she'll have to make on her own."

"I think I need to go in and see her." Hestia rose. "Will you excuse me?"

Aunt Louisa nodded but examined the stockings Selene had left. "I hope she plans to finish up this mending. Crying and pouting won't get any work done."

"I know. I'm sure she'll resume once she's feeling better." Hestia took her leave of her aunt then quietly entered the room she and Selene shared. Since she'd had this type of confrontation with the volatile Selene in the past, her cousin didn't bother to try to get rid of her with a twenty-three-skidoo. Instead, Selene sat on the bed, hugging a goose feather pillow and rocking back and forth. Tears streamed down her face. Hestia watched one drip from her left cheek onto the pillow.

Fighting the urge to sit on the bed and comfort her cousin with an embrace, Hestia made herself content to sit on her own twin bed. The beds were close enough to allow for a quiet conversation but not so close as to make Selene feel that Hestia intruded.

"I know it's hard."

"No, you don't. You don't have any idea." Fresh tears fell.

Hestia bit her tongue to keep from reminding Selene that she had made the decision to live the fast life, so now she reaped the consequences. Instead, she offered consolation. "You said you don't have any friends here. Do you really believe that?"

Selene hesitated. Hestia thought she might admit she had several friends, but, instead, a stubborn knitting of the brows was followed by a frown. "Yes."

"Don't be a silly goose. You have lots of friends, especially for someone who doesn't get out much. Think about Booth. He's friendly with you. And you know you can count on me."

"Can I?"

"Of course. Why would you think anything else?"

"Because you're leaving me all alone with Aunt Louisa, that's why. How will I ever stand being by myself with her until April? The thought makes me want to die."

"Did it ever occur to you that she's making a sacrifice for you? She's old and feeble, and being responsible for a vibrant young woman such as yourself has to be trying on her. Why, even your father couldn't handle you."

Selene started and an angry look entered her eyes. Hestia thought she might deliver a retort, but then Selene relaxed. Apparently she saw the truth of Hestia's statement even if she didn't agree.

"I'm sorry. I don't mean to be harsh. But you have to admit it's the truth."

"I guess I am a handful. I can try to make things easier for Aunt Louisa. Really I can. But you're right—she's old and feeble, and we don't get along so well even with you here. Whatever will I do without you? You might be a Mrs. Grundy, but you're a young Mrs. Grundy, and you have an idea about what it's like to want to have a little fun once in a while."

"Aunt Louisa was young once, too."

"When? During the Civil War?"

Hestia couldn't help but shake her head in amusement at Selene's exaggeration. She twisted her heel into the multicolored braided rug. "I'll agree she grew up in a different world, a different time. But people never change. Not really. That's one of the many reasons the Bible is timeless. Scripture talks about human nature, both good and bad. That will always be with us, whether we're ancient Romans or flappers."

Hestia halfway expected Selene to rebuke her for mentioning the Bible. "I have something to tell you." Selene sniffled.

Hestia tried to hold back her surprise. "Yes?"

"Artie mentioned the Bible the other night when he was here. He says he's read it all the way through. Twice."

Hestia arched her eyebrows. "That is admirable. I've read it all the way through once, but I confess, after that I have tended to linger on my favorite books and passages, the ones that speak to me. He shames me. I really should revisit the whole book again. But you know who shames just about everyone?"

"Who?"

"Aunt Louisa. Did you know she's read the entire Bible straight through almost twenty-eight times?"

Selene let out a breath. "I know there's not much in the way of entertainment here, but that's ridiculous."

"Maybe it sounds that way to you, and maybe it sounds that way to a lot of other people, too, but it doesn't to me. I think being so persistent takes a lot of discipline. I admire her."

"I guess I do, too." Selene shrugged.

"Would you believe she tells me it's like reading a different book every time? I suppose that's because you focus on verses that mean the most to you according to where you are at that point in life."

Selene became engrossed in thought. "She must be taking comfort in verses about the sick, then."

"Maybe. Or verses about hope and patience. I know that's where I'd be looking if I had to stay in bed several weeks." Hestia eyed her cousin and crossed her arms. "You know, you might be well-served to memorize some verses on patience while you're waiting for the baby to come. Who knows? They might help you be more patient with Aunt Louisa, too."

"Like what verses?"

Hestia searched her memory for recent Bible lessons. "How about Ecclesiastes 7:8? 'Better is the end of a thing than the beginning thereof: and the patient in spirit is better than the proud in spirit.' "

"So you think I'm proud, do you?"

"Maybe a little bit. But considering your upbringing, it's not surprising. Not everyone attended private schools only to end up living in a Manhattan penthouse and having all day to spend at the beauty salon, you know."

"I do miss being pampered." Selene lifted a strand of hair and looked at it almost cross-eyed since it was so short. "I'm liable to look like a zebra before all my hair dye grows out."

"Maybe that's one way of getting rid of pride." Almost feeling sorry for Selene, Hestia didn't allow admonition to enter her voice.

"I can dye it again as soon as I get home."

"True. There will be no one to stop you." Hestia could understand her cousin's frustration at sporting two-toned hair.

"Got any more of those verses? I don't really like the one you gave me."

Hestia decided not to pick a fight by commenting. Surely the verse she had remembered hit too close to home for her cousin. Besides, since the Lord had led Hestia to mention His Word and her cousin was actually asking to hear more, that in itself was a miracle—or at least a blessing beyond measure. She racked her brain but couldn't recall the right verses from memory. "Hold on. Let me get my Bible. I have some verses marked."

"Isn't that something? For one, I can't believe you don't have most of the Bible memorized, and two, I can't believe you have to mark verses on patience."

Hestia picked up her Bible, bound in white leather, from where she had left it on the oak nightstand. "Maybe you don't believe it because I do read the Bible and think about what it says. It does give me courage and strength." Hestia thumbed through the pages. "Here's one in the first letter to the Thessalonians: 'Now we exhort you, brethren, warn them that are unruly, comfort the feebleminded, support the weak, be patient toward all men.' "

"That describes you. You're warning the unruly and being patient with me."

"That took courage to admit, Selene." Hestia gave her an approving smile. "I wish I were as good as you say I am, but thank you." Hestia noticed that no more tears watered Selene's cheeks. At least she had distracted her enough to give her a goal and take her mind off her problems. She flipped through more pages but, upon reading the marked passages on patience, decided that Selene might be better off with Psalms. "I have a suggestion. Why don't you commit a psalm of praise to memory? Here's a short one, Psalm 150: 'Praise ye the LORD. Praise God in his sanctuary: praise him in the firmament of his power. Praise him for his mighty acts: praise him according to his excellent greatness. Praise him with the sound of the trumpet: praise him with the psaltery and harp. Praise him with the timbrel and dance: praise him with stringed instruments and organs. Praise him upon the loud cymbals: praise him upon the high sounding cymbals. Let every thing that hath breath praise the LORD. Praise ye the LORD.' "

Selene took the Bible from Hestia. "That is a lot to memorize."

"You have time."

She studied the passage. "You know, I took piano lessons a long time ago. Do you know how to play?"

"Passably. I know a lot of hymns and a few popular songs."

"Name some."

"Oh, 'Good Morning, Mr. Zip-Zip-Zip' and, let me see…'Rock-a-Bye Your Baby with a Dixie Melody' for starters."

Selene hummed the melodies. "Not too shabby. Would you help me refresh my memory? Let's see, Every Good Bird Does Fly, right?" She recalled a pointer on how to read musical notes. "That big old piano in the parlor looks lonely."

"I—I doubt I'll have time."

"Sure you do. If you promise to stay until the baby comes."

"Until…April?" Such a possibility had entered her mind, but only as a tease. To stay for several months?

"Time will fly. I promise."

"But I have a life in Haw River. I have to help Papa."

"Really? I thought your mother was helping him just fine."

Hestia swallowed. No doubt Mama was doing an exemplary job for Papa. What would they say, or think, if she lingered in Maiden? "I–I'll write them and see what they say. In fact, I'll do that right away." To demonstrate, she made a move toward the place she had stored her writing paper.

Selene gasped. "You mean you'll do it? You'll stay here with me until the baby comes?"

"If my parents raise no objections, yes. And of course, I'll be sure it's okay with Aunt Louisa. But I doubt she'll object." Part of her hoped they would, but another part of her hoped they'd be happy to let her stay. An unbidden image of Booth entered her mind.

Chapter Eleven

. . . .

A few days later, Hestia was on her hands and knees waxing the dining room floor when she heard a knock on the front door. They weren't expecting visitors and the mail had already been delivered, so she wondered who it could be. Hopefully the person waiting on the veranda was a door-to-door salesman and Aunt Louisa could dismiss him. Looking frazzled and not at her best since she was in the middle of a big chore, Hestia had no desire to see anyone herself. She listened for footsteps but heard no one stir.

"Aunt Louisa? Selene? Could one of you get the door?" she called.

"Selene's napping. I'll answer it!" Aunt Louisa shouted from the kitchen. "Just let me get this teakettle situated."

"Thanks." Hestia dipped into the wax, applying a clump of soft tan paste to the cotton rag that had once been white. Though the task was hard on her knees, she enjoyed rubbing the smooth, fragrant paste into the wood, giving it a well-deserved drink. Applying wax wasn't the bad part; the real effort happened after it dried and she had to take a clean rag to it, buffing the wax into the floor until the pine planks shone. The pungent, clean smell would likely linger at least a week, reminding her of such accomplishment in keeping a sparkling home. The floor would be slick for some time after waxing no matter how much Hestia buffed. They'd have to remember not to slip and fall.

Her aunt's footsteps signaled her approach. "Hestia, it's for you."

She stopped in midstroke. "For me?"

"Yes. It's Judith Unsworth from church."

"Oh." She rose to her feet and wondered what had prompted a visit from her friend. There was no time to make herself presentable other than to give her hands a quick rinse. At least Judith would understand her sorry state of appearance and wouldn't mind seeing her in her worst housedress and a white cotton scarf holding her hair out of her face.

"Hey, you," she greeted her friend in the parlor. She didn't want to sit down on the good furniture lest she get wax on it. "I'm so glad to see you. Sorry I look a fright."

"Hey, yourself. I'm the one who should apologize for coming here unannounced, but I wanted to stop by and ask if you and your family would like to share Thanksgiving dinner with us this year."

Hestia had been so concerned about Selene that Thanksgiving had slipped up on her. She hadn't even thought about preparing a meal. Perhaps she'd procrastinated about planning. The prospect of cooking an entire turkey for three people was too depressing to contemplate. "Do you mean Aunt Louisa and me?"

"No, I mean you, Miss Louisa, and your cousin."

"Selene?"

Judith grinned. "Yes, unless you have another cousin staying here that you haven't mentioned."

Hestia recalled a stern-looking Mr. and Mrs. Unsworth. "Your parents won't mind?"

"They understand and say they are glad to include Selene."

Hestia didn't know what to say. On one hand, she was sorry yet another family in town knew about Selene; on the other, the fact that Judith and her family would reach out to them in such a gracious way touched her. "That is very generous of you, and I'd love to accept. But I must consult with Aunt Louisa first. May I give you our answer at church this Sunday?"

"Of course. That's plenty of time. Mother is preparing a feast for twenty-two, so another three won't matter."

"Twenty-two! My, but that's a houseful."

"Yes, she invites many friends and family every year. It's quite a party—one of the highlights of our year. So I do hope you'll be among us."

"Thank you. And if Aunt Louisa does agree, please allow me to contribute to the meal. I can bring an apple or pumpkin pie and perhaps a macaroni-and-cheese casserole."

"Sounds wonderful."

After Judith left, Aunt Louisa sought out Hestia in the dining room. Hestia was prying open the tin of wax so she could resume her work. "What did Judith want?" Aunt Louisa asked.

Hestia stopped her task. "She wanted to invite us to share Thanksgiving dinner with her and her family."

"Thanksgiving." Aunt Louisa nodded. "I hadn't thought much about it, but that's right around the corner. On the thirtieth, right?"

Hestia sat back enough to give her knees a rest. "I believe so. Do we have plans?"

"I hadn't made any formal plans. With just the three of us, I wasn't thinking I'd put on a huge meal. We'd just have too much left over."

"I'll say. I don't relish the prospect of turkey wings flambé three weeks after the fact, either." She giggled at her own joke.

"We'd be fighting over them anyway since a turkey only has two wings and there are three of us." Her aunt grinned at her own wry humor before turning serious. "I do believe the Unsworths put on quite an event every year. Motorcars line the street every Thanksgiving so there's not an inch left for anybody else to park."

"She did mention that twenty-two people were attending, so we'd make twenty-five."

"Twenty-five! I don't think I want to go anywhere with that big a crowd. So she invited Selene, too?"

"Yes." Hestia noted her aunt's surprise and disapproving scowl. "I think that's terribly nice of them."

"Are you sure they invited her, too, or did you just assume?"

"No, ma'am. She very specifically included Selene."

Aunt Louisa showed her state of being taken aback by jumping a bit. "Well, isn't that something? I'm surprised Edith Unsworth would allow Selene in her house."

Hestia flinched. "Mrs. Unsworth does seem a bit strict, but apparently her heart is larger than we thought. So will you let us go?"

"I don't know...."

Hestia rose to her feet and looked her aunt in the eye. "Oh, Aunt Louisa, this is just what Selene needs. She's going crazy here in the house all the time, barely being able to see the light of day or step foot outside."

"I know you feel sorry for her, Hestia. Compassion is a good quality. But Selene brought her situation on herself. She has to face the consequences. And some of the consequences are that people aren't going to think as highly of her as they would respectable folk."

"Maybe not, but should she be deprived of a few slices of turkey on Thanksgiving because of it?"

"I don't know. I'll think about it. Like I said, I don't like crowds."

Hestia would have preferred a definite yes, but her aunt's promise to consider the possibility would have to do for the present. With two strikes against eating with the Unsworths, she didn't hold much hope.

* * * * *

In spite of their congenial conversation earlier, Selene hadn't expected to see Artie anymore once he got his Model T repaired. She assumed he was just being nice, pretending not to be bothered by her situation. Though she had made fun of the modest cars she'd seen in Maiden, riding in such a conveyance now seemed the ultimate in luxury.

Winter night had fallen, yet someone knocked on the door. "Who could that be at this hour?" With Selene's condition evident by the fact that her belly looked as though she carried a ball, Aunt Louisa had told her she wasn't supposed to open the door to strangers even in daylight, but neither Aunt Louisa nor Hestia seemed to be available.

When the knock became persistent, she decided it was better to answer than not. She indulged in a quick peek in the mirror before venturing to the front parlor. She still hated her hair. It was naturally a deep blond, but new growth against dyed platinum blond made her roots seem to be the color of strong coffee. She felt pale without any face paint even though Hestia and Aunt Louisa insisted her lips were pink enough and her eyes blue enough to add color to her face without enhancement. Still, she didn't feel so confident.

Another knock beckoned.

Confident or not, she had to respond to the visitor. Maybe it was an emergency, someone stranded on the side of the road looking for help. She rushed to the door, being careful not to step on the bare dining-room floor that Hestia had recently waxed. She opened the door. Before her stood a vision who looked more handsome with each passing day. "Artie!"

"Hello. I'd just about given up getting an answer. Had y'all gone to bed?"

"Not yet. I don't know where Hestia and Aunt Louisa are. One of them usually answers the door." She glanced back at the bedrooms, hoping that one of her guardians wouldn't emerge and scold her in front of Artie. "Sorry it took me so long."

"I don't mind. I hope this isn't too late for me to stop by."

"No, but I'm really not supposed to answer the door, so I hope Aunt Louisa doesn't get too cross with me. It's always nice to see you."

"I'll take the blame." He handed her a bouquet of yellow blooms tinged with robust rust-colored edges. "I noticed these asters in my garden this afternoon, and I picked them for you before it got too dark. I do believe these will be the last of the season. I wanted you to have them."

"Flowers? For me?"

He looked around. "I don't see anyone else standing here."

She giggled and realized she hadn't laughed much since she left New York. At least not unless Artie was around.

"I hope you like them."

She took them from him and buried her nose in the biggest of the blooms, sniffing its light aroma. "I love them. I do believe they're the prettiest flowers I've ever seen. Yellow is my favorite color."

"I'm not surprised. You remind me of sunshine."

She smiled. "With a compliment like that, I can't let you stand out there in the cold. Come on in. We didn't prepare a dessert tonight so I can't offer you any sweets, but I'll be glad to fix you a cup of cocoa or coffee."

"No thanks. I just ate."

"Let me put these flowers in a vase, and then we can talk."

She made her way to the kitchen. Artie followed her. "Watch out in this dining room. Hestia just waxed."

"All right. I'll be careful. Better yet, you be careful."

"I will."

Once they were in the kitchen, Artie took off his jacket and sat right in the head chair as though he belonged. And she supposed in a way he did; he'd been to the house quite often before his motorcar was fixed. "Sure you won't take a cup of coffee since we're already in the kitchen?"

"No. I just wanted to see you."

"Me?" She blurted even though she shouldn't have been surprised. With an involuntary motion, she looked at her stomach and back. "I don't know if Aunt Louisa would approve."

"Why not? I've been coming here all along. I didn't do anything to offend her, did I?" He spoke with the confidence that he knew he couldn't have insulted her.

Being careful not to trip over Diamond, she found a vase in one of the cabinets and set it on the counter. The clear glass vessel wasn't the right size for the bouquet, but she managed to squeeze the flowers into it anyway. "No. I'm sure you didn't. But good old Aunt Lou looks at me as a tainted woman. And I suppose I am. I—I can't believe someone like you, someone from a respected family, would visit me. And I know you're not chasing my father's money, either, because I understand you have plenty of your own."

"Seems gossip works both ways." Somehow his voice held no rancor.

She chuckled, arranging the flowers. "I wouldn't call it gossip, but you are very well known here. One thing I've learned about small towns since I've been here is that everyone knows pretty much everything about everybody else. That can be good or bad. Aunt Louisa thinks that in my case, it's bad."

"I won't lie to you. Maybe I should, to spare your feelings, but I won't."

Taking a seat in the chair across from him, Selene had a feeling she knew what he planned to tell her. "It's fine to be brutally honest. Maybe if my friends had been more honest with me in the past, I wouldn't be here now."

"Okay then." He took in a breath. "People have been talking about you. Some think you're bad because of what happened to you. But the good news is, you can overcome it. Our God gives us many second chances."

"Now you sound exactly like Hestia. Are you sure she didn't send you here to butter me up with flowers before your sermon? She's got me memorizing a psalm from the Bible as it is. A praise psalm."

"Does it make you feel better to read and think about it?"

She didn't want to admit how enthusiastic she felt. "I suppose."

"Good, because it would do you good to get to know Him better, just as I had to after I fell away for a time. God has given me second chances many times."

Selene nodded.

"So you know."

"People have hinted to me about your past. But I don't care about that."

"Did they tell you I was a gambler and a drinker?"

"I could guess. And I understand."

"I'm glad you do. That kind of life was no good. Through the love of my grandmother—that's her house I live in now—and a preacher who took an interest in me, I realized I didn't need those crutches to live. What I needed was Jesus Christ."

"Oh, dear. Where's the collection plate?" She chuckled, but Artie didn't smile. She straightened her lips to show her regret. "I'm sorry. It's just that my father sends our church lots of money but we only go to church on Christmas and Easter. He doesn't have much use for Christianity. He thinks money is what runs religion."

"A lot of people, especially people like your father who have comfortable lives, think that way." She admired how he didn't sound critical. "They look more to what the church does for them and end up missing the joys of fellowship with Christ. But you have to make an effort toward Christ, just as you might make an effort to make good in business. Worshipping with other Christians can help you grow in Christ. No disrespect meant toward your father, because I'm sure he's a fine man, but if he put a tenth of the effort into his relationship with Christ as I imagine he puts into his business, his life would be better."

Selene thought for a moment. True, Father didn't put much effort at all into Christ. He went to church twice a year and gave some money, but that was it. She could see that Artie went well beyond that. "So Jesus cured you of drinking and gambling? I doubt you drank or gambled all that much."

"You don't give Him enough credit. My parents died when my sister and I were in high school. Grandmother wanted to take in my sister, but she wanted to stay with me. So I tried to raise her myself. She died unexpectedly—in an accident—and I felt like it was my fault. I felt as though our family had a big, black cloud over us. I tried to lose myself to the world because I didn't want to face my loss."

Selene couldn't believe such heartbreak. Her problems almost seemed minor in comparison. "I'm sorry."

"Thank you. I'll tell you, losing yourself doesn't work. Oh, you'll lose, that's certain. I lost a small fortune gambling, and some nights I drank so much that the next morning I didn't remember what I'd done. But no more."

"Booth said you're shy. Are you afraid of people?"

"No. But I don't seek out events where alcohol is served, and I don't take any bets. I rely on hard, honest work. Thankfully, in a small town like Maiden, it's easy to find people who are interested in God and in having a good time in a way that honors Him. In fact, that describes almost everyone I know here."

"I haven't seen much of Maiden, but I'd have to agree. It's quite different in New York, at least in my crowd. I guess it's obvious I wasn't very ladylike by the standards they set around here."

"I know what strong drink will do, and I understand. Now, don't think that means I feel sorry for you. That's not the same thing. We all make our choices every day, and every day is a new day. I just hope since the Lord put you in my path, you'll see fit to let me help you make the right choices every day. And besides, you're easy on the eyes and smell good, too. I would like to call on you, if that's okay with you." He grinned, and she grinned back.

Aunt Louisa chose that moment to enter the kitchen. "I thought I heard talking out here. Why, a decent woman can't even take a bath anymore without being invaded."

Artie rose from his seat out of respect for Aunt Louisa and came close to blushing. "I'm sorry, ma'am. I know it's after dinner, but I didn't realize you womenfolk would be getting ready for bed so soon."

Sensing Artie's discomfort, Selene wanted to defend him. "I waited for Hestia to go to the door, but when she didn't, I thought it would be rude not to answer."

"Hestia's visiting next door at Booth's. Never mind." Aunt Louisa waved her hand. "I should have told you not to answer."

"I'm glad you didn't, Aunt Louisa. I have enjoyed seeing Artie."

"I suppose it doesn't matter on all fronts since your reputation is in tatters and you can't possibly get into any more trouble than you're in already." Aunt Louisa looked longingly at nothing, as though imagining Selene when she was still an innocent babe.

Selene winced.

Artie looked Aunt Louisa in the eye. "I beg your pardon, ma'am. If I discover that Selene isn't properly chaperoned the next time I stop by, I won't come in to your house."

"That would have been the wisest decision, in any case," Aunt Louisa lectured. "What was so urgent it couldn't wait?"

"Well, the flowers I brought her might have died." His sheepish expression conveyed apology. "They're the last of the season."

"Flowers?" Aunt Louisa looked at the asters. "Oh, they are pretty. You brought those to Selene?" She said it in a tone that made it sound as though the gesture was the most ridiculous idea in the world. Selene tried not to show her hurt feelings.

"Yes, I brought them for Selene. And I had something else to say to her, but we started talking about a different topic. An important topic, but it did keep me from asking the question I actually came to pose."

Aunt Louisa crossed her arms. "And what is that?"

"I'd like to know if Selene, you, and Hestia would like to have Thanksgiving dinner with a couple of friends from my church. You might know them. Steven and Arlene Chester. Steven and I are going deer hunting that morning, so the meal is scheduled for three o'clock or thereabouts."

Happy for an invitation of any description that would mean taking her out of the house—and with Artie—Selene nevertheless refrained from clapping.

Aunt Louisa seemed shocked. "Oh, yes. I know them. And they don't mind if Selene comes to their house to eat?"

"No, ma'am. Arlene's sister and brother-in-law plan to come from Hickory to join us, but that's it. Arlene said all three of you could come along with me if you like."

"Oh, please, can we go?" Selene asked.

"Are you sure as respectable a woman as I know Arlene Chester to be would permit Selene to enter her house, let alone dine with her family?"

"Yes, ma'am."

"Times sure are a-changing." She took in a breath. "That is mighty generous of the Chesters, especially to include all of us. I do need to consult with Hestia before I can give you an answer. I'll be sure you know by Saturday."

"Thank you. I'll be taking my leave of you now. Good night, Miss Louisa."

"Good night."

"I'll walk you to the door," Selene told Artie.

"I don't think our house is that large." Aunt Louisa looked toward the door even though it wasn't visible from the room. "He can find his way."

"But..."

"That's fine, Miss Louisa. Good night, Selene." The way he said her name sent goose pimples up her arm.

"Good night, Artie." She smiled her sweetest smile.

* * * * *

"Look, there's Artie," Hestia pointed out to Booth as he walked her home from his house. Though she could certainly find the way home by herself, he enjoyed walking her anyway. "Wonder what Artie wanted?"

"Hard to say. I'm sure Miss Louisa will let you know."

They exchanged friendly waves, after which Booth walked Hestia to the veranda. At times like this, Hestia wished she never had to leave Maiden. Aunt Louisa had been thrilled by the idea of her staying longer, and Papa had sent a letter permitting her to remain until spring—but she had a feeling spring would arrive all too soon.

Booth was so close. She longed for him to embrace her good night. But he always displayed the manners of a gentleman. Never did he presume to touch her, except for the occasional light pressure on the hand for reassurance or to emphasize a point. Perhaps it was better this way.

"I have a question to ask." Booth swallowed.

"Yes?"

"I would like you and your family to have Thanksgiving dinner with us. And of course, Mother and Daddy would welcome you as well. I already asked."

"They would welcome all of us?"

"Of course. Why would we omit anyone?"

She didn't want to answer.

"I know what you're thinking. And yes, we want Selene to be there. I know she's going crazy staying in the house all the time."

"She'll thank you for inviting her."

"It's our pleasure. So do you think your aunt will consent?"

"I hope so, but I'll have to ask." Then she remembered. "We also have an invitation from Judith Unsworth's family."

"I might have known I couldn't keep you to myself forever." His grin looked somehow melancholy.

"I didn't know you wanted to keep me for yourself." The thought left her happy. Very happy indeed. Again she found herself wishing Booth would kiss her, but she knew she shouldn't think such thoughts. After all, she had to leave as soon as Selene delivered her baby.

Aunt Louisa chose that moment to come to the front door. "What are you children doing out here?"

"Just chatting, Aunt Louisa." She suppressed a giggle.

"Come on in, Hestia. You'll catch your death of pneumonia."

"Yes, ma'am." She was just about to invite Booth in when her aunt chirped, "Good night, Booth."

"Good night, Miss Louisa."

Hestia went into the house.

"Aren't you about to freeze?" Aunt Louisa frowned.

"No, ma'am." When she was with Booth, she never thought about the weather unless she'd failed to wear her shawl. "Oh, we got an invitation to eat Thanksgiving dinner with his family. They invited Selene, too."

Instead of being happy, Aunt Louisa lifted her hands in surrender. "I don't know what to think. In my day, if a wayward girl were waiting for her baby at her aunt's, she never would have been permitted anywhere. Now it seems Selene is more popular here than she ever was in New York. What is the world coming to?"

"Maybe things are getting better, Aunt Louisa."

"I'm not so sure they are. Paul wrote that we are not to keep company with fornicators."

"From what I remember, his list to the Corinthians included some others, too. The covetous, slanderers, and idol worshippers, to name a few. But that only includes people who say they are Christians, Aunt Louisa."

"Selene says she is a Christian."

"I doubt she'd claim to be a very good one. And that's not her fault, really, considering her upbringing. And please remember, she has repented."

"So you say. I caught her making goo-goo eyes at Artie here in the kitchen earlier, unchaperoned to boot. I was very disappointed in them both. I know my brother was too liberal with Selene, but Artie certainly should have known better." She harrumphed.

Aunt Louisa's harsh outlook, a result of her times and strict rearing, made Hestia realize all the more that Selene needed an advocate. While Hestia didn't agree with Selene's behavior, she deserved compassion. "Selene will always be romantic. It's her nature. But I would be very, very surprised if she engaged in immoral behavior again. Not after this experience."

"Oh, I'm sure she's thinking about what she did. But I'm still not positive I should encourage respectable people in this town to dine with her. I think I have the solution. I don't much feel like going anywhere most of the time anyway, so I can stay home with Selene. Maybe your hosts will let you bring us a few leftovers."

Selene entered. "Stay home? When?"

"For Thanksgiving. We have three invitations as of now." Aunt Louisa's disgust evidenced itself in her voice.

"Three invitations?"

"Booth, Artie, and Judith." Hestia counted down on three fingers.

Selene took in a breath. "I hope we're choosing Artie."

Aunt Louisa shook her head. "I don't think we should impose on the Chesters."

Hestia looked for a bright spot. "Maybe my uncle can visit us."

"Piffle." Selene crossed her arms and pouted. "He wrote me that he'll be on a steamship to Europe throughout the holiday. He won't miss me at all."

"Oh, I'm sure he will." Hestia wanted to comfort Selene but wondered if her uncle would miss his daughter. Selene knew him better than she did. What a sad life for Selene.

"Miss me? Tell it to Sweeney. I imagine he'll be dining and dancing with his latest paramour, not giving me a second thought." A sad, faraway look touched Selene's eyes.

Hestia's heart ached for her cousin. At least some of her uncle's love should have been reserved especially for his daughter.

"Now, now." Aunt Louisa chastised, but her unwillingness to look Selene in the eye bespoke her embarrassment over her brother's behavior. "You mustn't speak about your own father in such a way. It's not right."

"Yes, it is right, because it's accurate. Oh, Aunt Louisa, won't you let me have a little turkey at somebody's house for Thanksgiving?" Selene touched her aunt's arm.

"Even if I were so inclined, which invitation would we choose?" Aunt Louisa shrugged.

"I know! Three invitations. Imagine! It almost feels like the old days back in New York." Selene sighed. "I wonder what my friends will be doing."

"Eating turkey like everybody else, I suppose," Aunt Louisa ventured.

"I want to eat with Artie." Selene spoke with more enthusiasm than she'd displayed in quite a while.

"I'm thinking the best thing for us to do is eat here and not impose on anyone's generosity."

"Please don't make us stay here alone." Selene's posture deflated with the prospect. "I'm going stir-crazy sitting in the house all the time."

"I'm sorry, but you should have thought of that before you got into the shape you're in now. And you won't be alone. I'll be here."

Hestia felt she had no choice but to intervene. "I know Selene's situation isn't ideal, but obviously people are willing to let her come to their houses."

"I didn't say you couldn't go." Aunt Louisa pointed at Hestia for emphasis. "Just Selene."

"Oh, this is dreadful!" Selene left the room crying.

Hestia couldn't help but feel sorry for her cousin, but she had to consider her aunt, too. "Let's sit down."

Aunt Louisa nodded and followed Hestia into the den. The women chose their favorite chairs in the room. "I don't mean to be disrespectful, Aunt Louisa, but I think you should reconsider. You can see by how upset she is that going out for the holiday would mean a lot to her."

"I'll see. She's got to understand the reality of her situation. She hasn't done what's right, and she has to think about that."

"Oh, I think she has."

"What shall we tell everyone?" Aunt Louisa rocked back and forth.

"I don't know. Whether Selene stays or goes, you're right in that we have too many invitations to accept. Even on the best day, we can't eat turkey three times." Hestia chuckled.

"Clearly it would mean the most to Selene to eat with Artie."

"Artie used to have a reputation as a rounder, but he's changed. I think he's a good man. If anyone can be a good influence on Selene, it's him. You know, I do believe she has eyes for him."

"Me, too."

"Nothing can come of it, though. She's a tainted woman, and she'll be going back to where she came from soon after the baby arrives."

Hestia didn't answer. She'd be going back, too.

Chapter Twelve

....

The next day Hestia added cheddar cheese to the scrambled eggs for breakfast. Perhaps the special touch would put Aunt Louisa in a mood to allow Selene out of the house for Thanksgiving.

The women talked about everything but the upcoming celebration as they shared the meal. Obviously desperate for a topic, Selene even discussed her father's trip abroad. She'd just received a postcard from Paris and shared the image of the Eiffel Tower with them. "Do you want to visit Paris one day, Aunt Louisa?"

"Child, I'm well past the time to think about exotic travel. Why, I've never even seen the Atlantic Ocean."

At first Hestia found such an admission surprising, but then she recalled her own lack of experience. "I've only seen it once." Hestia remembered a long-ago vacation to Carolina Beach. The trip marked one of the few times her father felt he could leave his practice long enough to enjoy recreation. "I'll never forget it."

"It's not so lovely when it separates you from people." Selene picked at her egg.

"Maybe you won't have to be separated for long." Hestia reached across the table and patted her cousin's hand.

Aunt Louisa touched her lips with her napkin. "I know what you girls have on your minds, and it's not the ocean. You want my decision on all these invitations. I have the perfect solution about what to do for Thanksgiving."

Hestia wasn't sure any solution would be perfect, but she wanted to hear what Aunt Louisa had to say. She set down her fork and noticed that anticipation covered Selene's expression.

Aunt Louisa set her napkin beside her plate. "Rather than us going anywhere, I'd like to host a coffee and dessert gathering here in the evening."

"A coffee and dessert?" Hestia thought this a poor idea but didn't want to say so.

"You think that's the perfect solution?" Selene pouted. "Oh, Aunt Louisa, everyone will be so full of turkey and pie they won't be able to eat another thing."

"Then they can just have coffee." Aunt Louisa's tone bespoke her determination. "I think we have time to bake pies and cakes before Thursday, especially with all three of us working. I'm feeling a mite better now, so I should be able to offer more help than I could recently."

Seeing Selene's distress on her face, Hestia decided to give an opinion. "If it's all the same to you, I'd like to accept the invitation with Booth's family."

"Traitor." Selene stared into her cup of coffee.

Aunt Louisa ignored Selene. "Of course you may go."

"Then where will that leave the two of us for turkey, Aunt Louisa?" Selene asked. "It's bad enough that I'm here all alone with none of my friends, but do I have to starve, too?"

"You're hardly starving." Aunt Louisa surveyed Selene's expanding figure.

Hestia tried to think of a way to console Selene. "I'm sure Mrs. Barrington would let me bring you home some food, but rather than imposing on her, I might order a small turkey from the grocer. I can cook that for you and then go to Booth's. Of course, that means I'll have to turn down Judith. I feel so terrible about that." Hestia considered that she might suggest to Judith that she invite Peter Drum in her place.

Aunt Louisa kept her attention focused on Hestia. "Now don't you fret. You don't have to turn down anyone. I think you can go to both. I'll just fix Selene and me a little chicken, and we'll have our own celebration."

Though Aunt Louisa's tone didn't convey regret, Hestia still felt pity for her. "That's not much of a day for you."

"It's more than enough excitement for me. And don't forget, I still have church and my whist party every week. I get out plenty for an old hen." Compassion touched her eyes as she looked at her youngest charge. "Besides, I said I'd take care of Selene, and I will."

Hestia looked at her cousin. "Thank you, Aunt Louisa. Maybe this will be a happy Thanksgiving after all."

* * * * *

Booth felt more anticipation than usual as he entered Miss Louisa's house, cracking open the back door and announcing his arrival. He hoped Hestia could dine with his family for the holiday. Hestia didn't realize it, but he'd never asked a woman to share their family's Thanksgiving meal with them. His mother's ready acceptance of the idea heartened him. His parents had become acquainted with Hestia on their rides to church, and he could tell she'd be an amenable daughter-in-law for them. He tried to put such thoughts out of his mind. He had no reason to think Hestia would stay in Maiden. He vowed to treasure their moments together as long as they were his.

Hestia greeted him with her usual smile, appearing radiant in her plainest dress. "There you are." She escorted him into the kitchen, where Miss Louisa, Selene, and Hestia were shelling pecans. "Wasn't Artie generous to bring us so many pecans?" Hestia took a chair. "Have a seat."

"That's okay. I've been sitting all day and I'm ready to stand awhile. I can't stay long, anyway. I've got chores to do once I go home." He watched the busy women. "Speaking of chores, it looks as though you have your hands full right here."

Hestia nodded. "It's taken us awhile."

"Need some help?"

"We only have three of these." Miss Louisa raised her hand slightly, holding a nutcracker. "If I had more, I'd welcome your help."

"I can get one from my house." He felt he had to make the offer even though his heart wasn't in the task.

"This one is your mother's." Hestia grinned. "We just borrowed it from her."

They were interrupted by a "Yoo-hoo!" He recognized the voice as belonging to Miss Olive.

"In here, Olive," Miss Louisa called.

Booth wondered what had prompted their neighbor to visit. Normally she didn't appear without reason. She didn't have any sugar or eggs in hand. Perhaps she wanted to borrow something. He watched Miss Olive survey the activity. "My, but you're busy bees. Where'd you get all those pecans?"

"Artie Rowland." Selene's voice sounded prideful and shy at once.

Miss Olive's eyebrows rose. "I see. Well, I suppose he's invited you to dine with him for Thanksgiving."

"In a way, yes." Selene smiled and ate one of the nuts.

"I'd invite you over myself, only I won't be here this year. I'll be with my family in Gastonia."

"That's fine, Olive." Miss Louisa squeezed a pecan with the nutcracker. The shell gave way with a sharp snap. "Shall we look after the house while you're away?"

"You sure can. I already asked the postman to drop all my mail here. Otherwise, just make sure all's well. I'll be back on Tuesday." She studied Selene. "So you'll be with Artie?"

"Booth invited us to dine with his family." Hestia's interruption made him wonder if she was trying to distract their nosy neighbor. "Is it still okay for me to have dinner with you that day, Booth?"

"Of course." He tried not to look too happy. Miss Olive had enough to gossip about as it was. "So I can tell Mother to set three more places at the table."

"Just one." Miss Louisa held one finger in the air. "Hestia's the only one who'll be with you."

"You mean Selene and you aren't coming to the Thanksgiving feast?"

"We'll stay home. But I know Hestia will have a grand time with you and your family. Oh, and you all are more than welcome to stop by for pie later in the day. Sometime after five."

He couldn't imagine eating more dessert after indulging in a big slice of his mother's pumpkin pie—a treat she baked only once a year. "That's generous of you. I'll mention that to Mother. But really, Miss Louisa, I wish you would reconsider. Truth be told, Mother has planned for the three of you to be there, and she'll be disappointed."

"She won't be the only one." Selene split open a pecan with so much force that pieces of shell flew in the air and scattered all over the table.

"Pay no attention to Selene." Miss Louisa shot Selene a chastening glare.

"Mercy!" Miss Olive's look mimicked Miss Louisa's. "Don't you know you shouldn't be socializing in your condition? Why, in my day, no girl would have considered leaving her room in a state such as the one in which you find yourself, much less contemplate going out to eat with respectable families."

"Now, Olive, you let me do the lecturing."

Noting the two older women exchanging stern looks mixed with indignation, Booth turned to Hestia. "I'm glad you'll be there."

"Me, too." Her quick nod indicated her relief at the change in conversational tone.

"I'll be on my way, Louisa." Miss Olive sniffed. "Clearly you have everything under control here. I hope you manage to enjoy your Thanksgiving somehow."

"We will, somehow." Miss Louisa's demeanor stayed serious, as though enjoying the day would indeed be a struggle.

"I should be on my way, too. See you tomorrow. I'll be checking in on you as usual." Booth addressed all the ladies, but his gaze rested on Hestia.

"Yes, we can set our clock by you." Aunt Louisa smiled.

Diamond rubbed against Booth's legs. He reached down to pat her head. The cat closed her eyes and purred.

Booth noticed Hestia watching him and the cat. "She must remember that you're the one who brought her to us. I'm glad you did. I haven't seen a mouse since she arrived."

"Not a live one, anyway." By placing her hands in her lap, Miss Louisa stopped her task long enough to observe the cat. "I must say, I've grown fond of the little thing."

"I guess I won't be able to take her back with me to Haw River." Hestia's voice sounded with regret. She glanced at Booth long enough to capture his gaze in hers with sparkling eyes. All too soon, she looked back at the animal. Booth felt his heart beating faster. On the surface, she spoke of the cat, but he sensed that her sorrow ran much deeper.

"I don't think I want Diamond to leave." Miss Louisa bent over and stroked the cat's back. "She'll be a companion for me once you girls go back home."

Booth swallowed. He didn't want to consider the day.

"I know what you mean, Aunt Louisa. I almost wish I could take her with me to New York." Selene looked longingly at Diamond. "Some days she's the only company I have."

"What does that make us?" Hestia asked with a smile.

"Maybe I'll let Diamond answer that."

Booth didn't want to leave, but he soon bid them farewell. As he turned to go, he stole one last look at beautiful Hestia. He walked the short distance to his home, the brick bungalow where he had spent his life. Thoughts of leaving the home his parents had made with each other and their children left him feeling wistful, but not sad. The time to leave had come, and he wanted Hestia to be with him. How he would convince her, he wasn't sure. Deep in thought, he breezed through the back door as he had hundreds of times before.

As he entered the Barrington kitchen, the scent of pork roasting in the oven greeted him. He wondered how Hestia cooked pork roast. Did she add onions to her gravy, the way he liked? Could she make lump-free gravy?

Mother bent into the oven, taking out the meat. She paused. "Oh, there you are."

"May I help you with that?"

"I've got it." She set the meat on the top of the stove, beside a pot where potatoes had already been mashed. Booth watched her check the firebox. The meal was nearly ready to serve.

Booth noticed how she seemed young even though she had married his father decades before. Each day, without fail, she provided a delicious meal, served in a house that smelled of lemon oil, her lavender talcum powder, and soap—all aromas that spelled cleanliness to Booth. Even more important, a sense of well-being and love evidenced themselves in their home. He wanted a wife who would make the same kind of home for him, but he wanted to share his thoughts and dreams with her, too. He wanted to talk with her about things important and unimportant, to share the joys of family.

"Were you able to confirm that we'll be having three extra guests on Thanksgiving?"

Booth snapped himself out of his thoughts. "Just Hestia."

"Just Hestia?" Mother set her pot holders on the counter. "What about Louisa and Selene?"

"Miss Louisa wants Selene to stay home."

Mother let out a breath. "I know the only one you really care about is Hestia—"

Embarrassed, he felt he had to object. "I—I care about the others...."

"Now, listen here. I'm your mother and I can tell by the way you've been mooning around the house that you're interested in her. Can't say I'm sorry about that, but don't get too attached. She's going back to Haw River. But we'd be mighty poor neighbors if we didn't extend Christian charity to them. The Bible says so."

"Yes, ma'am. I'm afraid Miss Louisa was insistent."

"Well, we'll see about that. Fetch my coat out of the closet, will you? I'm going over there right now." She moved the pots to the side of the stove so the food would stay warm.

Booth wished he didn't have to obey. All he needed was for his mother to argue with Miss Louisa and ruin everything.

* * * * *

Hestia had just finished cleaning up shells and putting nuts into a covered dish for later use when she heard a knock on the door. Selene was washing up, and Aunt Louisa had started preparing dinner. "Booth must have forgotten something. I'll get the door."

"That's fine. Don't dawdle."

Hestia whisked off her apron. "It's funny that he'd knock on the front door instead of coming in through the back. Maybe it's not Booth."

"You won't find out who it is if you don't answer it." Aunt Louisa dished a spoonful of lard into the frying pan. "Run on now, or whoever it is will leave and we'll never know."

Hestia rushed to answer. Mrs. Barrington stood on the veranda. Hestia could never look at her without being reminded of Booth.

"I hope I'm not disturbing you."

"No, of course not. Please come in." Hestia opened the door wider and stepped aside for her to enter.

"Is it Booth?" Aunt Louisa asked as she made her way into the parlor. "Oh, Betty, it's you. What brings you by? It's suppertime. Your dinner isn't getting cold, is it?"

Mrs. Barrington crossed the threshold and Hestia closed the door. "That doesn't matter today. I wanted to come over myself, to let you know that I really want to include your family in our Thanksgiving celebration. And that invitation is extended to Selene."

"That's mighty generous of you, Betty, but Selene really shouldn't be out and about in her condition."

"Did the doctor say she had to have bed rest?"

"No, but you know her situation." Aunt Louisa stood to her full height.

"I do, and I realize many people think it's scandalous."

Aunt Louisa blanched. "There's been talk about us, I take it?"

Selene entered, but Mrs. Barrington didn't miss a beat. "I don't have to remind you that this is a small town, and people have been asking me what I know. I tell them I know very little and then I change the topic. Of course Selene's situation isn't ideal. But our God is a God of second chances, and I think He'd want us to share our meal with Selene."

Selene spoke, to Hestia's surprise. "That's the second time I've heard someone say that about God in the last few days."

"Is that so?" Mrs. Barrington looked at Selene. "Then He must be trying to tell you something."

"Maybe He's telling me not to cause trouble." Selene looked at the floor and back. "I would like to get out of the house, but I don't want to cause problems for anybody. I'm enough of a problem as it is."

Mrs. Barrington's voice displayed compassion. "Don't speak that way about yourself. Mr. Barrington and I have always thought highly of your aunt, and I remember you as a sweet little girl who used to visit here over the summer. Inside, I think you're still that sweet little girl. You just fell in with the wrong crowd, that's all. I hope you'll reconsider and spend Thanksgiving with us. It's a special occasion, after all." Mrs. Barrington turned to Aunt Louisa. "And if you're worried, Louisa, please know that it's just going to be Harry and me this year, along with Booth. We'd welcome doubling the size of our party. I do hate cooking such a feast for three."

"But what about Effie and her family?" Hestia knew that Aunt Louisa referred to Booth's sister.

"It's their turn to be with her husband's family this year. So you see, Selene's condition won't be out to any more people than already know about her."

"That's not the case with Artie's party, or Judith's, either." Hestia hoped such arguments would work with her reluctant aunt.

"Artie and Judith?" Mrs. Barrington asked.

"We got three invitations this year." Aunt Louisa crossed her arms. "Seems Selene is quite popular."

"I can't believe it, either," Selene admitted. "It's almost as good as being home."

Mrs. Barrington chuckled. "I'm glad we can make you feel welcome. So is it settled, then?"

Aunt Louisa hesitated. "Well…"

"Oh, please, Auntie?" Selene clasped her hands.

"I'd like to go, too," Hestia added, thinking of Booth. "I'll be glad to bake a pie to bring, and a macaroni-and-cheese casserole. Or rolls."

"You don't need to bring anything. Just bring yourselves."

"Oh, but I insist."

"In that case, macaroni and cheese would be a wonderful addition, as that's one dish I hadn't planned to bake."

Aunt Louisa opened her mouth to protest, but Mrs. Barrington interrupted. "And you know, Louisa, I never would have come over here myself to invite you if I didn't mean it."

Her aunt let out a labored sigh. "Oh, all right. I can see I'll have no peace until I relent. Betty, the girls and I will come."

Selene and Hestia rushed to their aunt and hugged her. Mrs. Barrington smiled with more feeling than Hestia had ever seen.

"That's enough, girls." Aunt Louisa, never being demonstrative, pushed them away with a gentle motion. "If I don't get back in the kitchen, we won't be eating until breakfast tomorrow."

They bid Mrs. Barrington farewell, with thanks. After the door shut behind their guest, Hestia moved to help Aunt Louisa, but Selene held her back in the parlor. "Seems getting me out of the house is quite a production."

"Aunt Louisa's trying to protect you, that's all."

"She'll always be a Mrs. Grundy." Selene pouted. "If this is what it's like to be expecting, what must it be like to be a mother?"

"You'd have even more responsibility, I can assure you." Hestia recalled anxious parents bringing their children to her father's office. "But don't let this scare you. When the time is right and you have a husband who loves you, you'll find a baby a blessing." Hestia couldn't help but indulge in a daydream. She imagined herself as a mother, with little blond tykes running afoot and a talcum-scented baby in her arms. Her husband would walk through the door, wanting dinner after a hard day's work. The husband she pictured materialized as Booth. Embarrassed by how easily she allowed him to fit into the scenario, she forced the thought out of her mind.

"I hope my cousin will take good care of the baby." Selene rubbed her midsection.

"She will." Hestia recalled a time she had helped her father bring down a little girl's fever. She prayed at the girl's bedside, watching the poor motherless thing writhe and moan while the father, strapped for pennies, went to his work. When the fever broke, the little girl came alive, cheerful as spring sunshine. That moment led her to want a career in medicine. She had no idea her family would object or that her own doubts, along with love for a man, might get in the way.

Chapter Thirteen
....

On Thanksgiving Day, Selene picked at her turkey. She had gotten over
being queasy each morning, but her dresses, even relatively loose ones
she had brought from New York, felt tight. She would have to send for
at least a couple of maternity dresses soon. She dreaded the thought. So
proud of her slim figure, she no longer looked good in the linear fashions
she adored. At least her condition wasn't permanent.

She wondered how her friends fared back home. No doubt
they planned a big bash at the Algonquin to celebrate on Saturday,
according to their custom. Today they'd be dining with their families,
and she would have been invited to several of those celebrations.
As in Maiden, in New York her friends' families also seemed to feel
sorry for her, always including her in their plans since Father was
never home over Thanksgiving. Of course, he'd try to make up for
it on Christmas by never letting his latest mistress anywhere near
their penthouse. He would devote the day to her, giving her eggnog
laced with forbidden bourbon and presenting her with a bauble from
Tiffany's. She wondered if he would send her a piece of jewelry for
Christmas this year by post. She didn't care. His attention would
have been better. If only he would visit for Christmas—but she knew
without asking that he wouldn't. His own life and New York friends
were too important to him.

She considered her hosts as they dined. The Barringtons had aged
well, looking hale and hearty though they were past their prime. They
seemed to get along well. Some couples would put on a front of civility
for guests though one could feel seething rage below the surface.

Sometimes her own parents had acted that way before Mother died. But the Barringtons seemed to care for each other, as though they were close friends near and dear to each others' hearts. Their marriage seemed enviable. Could she ever aspire to such a match? With her past, she doubted such happiness awaited her in the future.

Booth, meanwhile, couldn't take his attention away from Hestia. Didn't he know she'd be going back home in the spring?

Even Aunt Louisa seemed to be having a good time. For once, the lines on her face looked softer, and she laughed. Some moments hinted at what she must have been like as a young woman. Clearly not as strict, or as provincial. She wondered why Aunt Louisa never had children of her own and if she regretted her decision. Or had poor health sealed her fate? She wanted to ask, but the older generation made such topics off-limits, acting insulted if anyone even dared to broach what could be an honest conversation.

As she swirled her fork in a mound of sausage stuffing covered with gravy, Selene's thoughts turned to Artie. She wished she could have finagled him an invitation to the Barringtons', but of course to suggest the presence of an extra guest would have been the height of rudeness. She hated breaking the news that she couldn't accept his invitation. When she did, his disappointment seemed genuine. A fantasy that he might invite her to another event entered her mind, but how could he? The fact that she expected a baby in a few months made such an idea nothing more than a dream.

* * * * *

"I don't remember when I've had a nicer Thanksgiving," Booth confessed to Hestia after the feast. He had taken her outside to the back porch of the Barringtons'.

"Neither can I." Hestia looked at the moon. Crossing her arms, she stared at the backyard. "I'll have to say, your mother puts on quite a meal. I haven't been so stuffed in a long time."

"Neither have I."

"I'm glad Aunt Louisa called off the dessert and coffee at our house. I couldn't eat another bite."

Booth groaned. "Maybe tomorrow." Following Hestia's lead, he gazed at the yard he had played in many times as a boy. Since it was autumn, he especially recalled how he had jumped into the piles of leaves his father raked. Now Booth did most of the raking, and no one jumped in the leaves. The thought of raking leaves into piles so his children could jump into them popped into his mind. Would they giggle and wave their arms, feeling crisp brown leaves against their hands, hearing the light crackle of them rubbing against each other?

"A penny for your thoughts."

Considering she'd be leaving Maiden soon, he feared scaring her with such definite thoughts of the future. "I think I'd better let you keep your penny."

"Oh, I'm sure you underestimate the value of your thoughts." Sending him an indulgent smile, she changed the topic. "I appreciate how kind you and your parents are being to Selene. Not everyone would be, you know."

"There are judgmental people anywhere you go. I'm glad Selene hasn't met any of the ones we have here."

"Miss Olive is probably the closest I've encountered, and though she likes to talk, she doesn't have a malicious bone in her body." She sighed. "You have such good people here."

He couldn't argue that. "Don't tell me we're that much different than Haw River."

She shrugged. "Of course we have the same ideas about how to live. Most of us love the Lord. But Maiden is a special place."

With her face shadowed by the moon so that the curve of her cheek evidenced itself, beams of soft light captured the black irises of her eyes. Hestia seemed mystical. He couldn't resist expressing his feelings. "It's more special now that you're here. And it will be lonely once you're gone."

"You, lonely? I don't believe it."

"I won't say I don't have friends. God has been good to me and put many friends in my path. But you do add a spark everywhere you go. I know your friends will be happy to see you return." At that moment, he wished he could kiss her. But to do so, knowing she would soon be departing, seemed to be taking advantage of her. "Will we have another chance to go to church, at least? Everyone will want a chance to tell you good-bye."

"Of course I'll go to church with you again. And they don't have to tell me good-bye. At least not this Sunday."

"I heard Miss Louisa mention that she still gets mighty weak."

"She does get weak. But that's not the only reason I'll be here a little longer. I've agreed to stay until Selene's baby arrives this spring."

He tried not to look like a little boy at Christmas, though he felt as though he'd just gotten an early gift. "Really? That's swell…if you don't mind me saying so."

She laughed. "I don't mind."

The idea of kissing her entered his thoughts once more. She had just taken the barrier of an early departure from him, yet he still felt the time wasn't right. Maybe it never would be. Maybe the whole idea of her ever being interested in him as more than a friendly neighbor and childhood playmate was only a fantasy.

* * * * *

A few days later, the mail brought Hestia a letter from one of her friends in Haw River named Gertie. Wanting privacy, Hestia went to the bedroom and sat on her bed. She opened the letter and skimmed items about friends and acquaintances before reading surprising news:

Oh, and I have such exciting news. Mama and Papa let me bob my hair! Now please don't be cross with me, my dear friend, because I know we sort of made a promise to each other that we would never let scissors touch our hair. But a few of the girls here have started taking the plunge, and we were so tired of feeling as though we looked like our mothers, we—yes, I said "we"— decided to take the plunge, too. Last Saturday, the week before Thanksgiving, June and I cut each other's hair! I was so nervous! She was, too, but everything turned out just peachy. Do you know I actually lost three pounds when I had my hair cut? Isn't that unbelievable? I feel so different, and everyone says it's a good look for me. June likes hers, too. When you come home, we want to cut your hair, too. Now that we have, I think your parents will allow you to cut yours. Of course, Mama cried her eyes out when she saw I didn't have any hair. She made me keep a long lock of hair. We braided it, and she's going to frame it like a picture. She's such a silly thing, but aren't all mothers sentimental like that? June's mother is framing hers, too. I won't tell a falsehood—it felt very strange to look at myself in the mirror for a while. I had to get accustomed to the new me. But it didn't take too long. And when I went to June's annual Thanksgiving party, I got so many compliments! That surprised me the most. Let me correct that. What surprised me most is that now Mama is thinking of bobbing her hair! I wonder if you'll recognize any of us when you come home.

Her stomach lurched. Now that her friends—and perhaps even their mothers—were bobbing their hair, she would look ridiculous among them, with her waist-long locks. Clearly, fashion was catching up to them all. She wondered about the rest of their new look. Would it be complete without dresses? Gertie didn't say anything about sewing herself new dresses. Those linear styles tended toward the short side, not as modest as they all wore now. Shorn hair was bound to lead to short dresses. Surely her friends' dresses would be more modest than the flappers', perhaps longer. As for rouge, she doubted even the most daring girls in her set at home would paint their faces.

Hestia ran her palm over the top of her hair. Maybe she could get used to the idea of shorn locks. If she didn't dye hers platinum like Selene's, then perhaps people wouldn't look askance at her. On the one hand, she wanted to look modest. Yet if she went too far to the extreme, she would look odd and out of place. Such a stance would be acceptable if she lived in a community known for separation, such as the Shakers or the Amish, but she lived as a doctor's daughter in Haw River. If she drew stares for being too old-fashioned for her age, would that be honoring the Lord?

"Lord, I know You care about everything concerning me, even something as trivial as my hairstyle. Guide me so I represent You in word, deed, and appearance."

She didn't want to think about hair anymore. Looking back at the letter, she took in a breath when she saw Luther's name.

My dear, I hate to be the bearer of bad news. I know you are aware that that skunk Luther has already begun courting a new girl here, one who couldn't hold a candle to you. Well, you'll never guess what. He is now engaged to her! It makes all of us sick to see him. We are doing our best to avoid the both of them, but it's hard

*since they're on everyone's guest list. I'm only glad you're not here
to witness such a sickening development.*

Hestia read the passage again to be sure she'd read it right. She had.

"I will not cry. I will not cry. I will not cry," Hestia muttered to herself.

Regrettably, mind did not conquer matter and tears flowed. She
had long ago reconciled herself to the fact that she and Luther were
through. She didn't want to see him, and he hadn't contacted her. In a
way, she wished he'd write and beg her to come back to him. Yet that
wish was only pride talking. Reading that he was courting someone
was bad enough. Of course he'd start courting someone. Why wouldn't
he? She had no claim on him now. Besides, it had all started when he
decided being engaged wasn't enough to stop him from flirting with
other women. Surely she would have lived a life filled with insecurity and
mistrust had she gone through with her marriage to Luther. Yet reading
that he had taken his courtship to the next level—engagement—well,
that hurt. Hurt much more than she ever thought possible. She hated the
tears she cried and hated herself for caring.

Rising from the bed, she felt the need to release some energy. She
peered out the window beyond the lace curtains. Thankfully, many leaves
awaited in Aunt Louisa's yard. The leaves on the maple trees, recently in full
red glory, had fallen almost as quickly as they turned. She suspected the
oak's brown leaves would linger into winter, but in the meantime she'd been
trying to keep the yard as clean as she could during the past two weeks.

She hid the offending missive in the top drawer of her side of the
vanity and headed for the coat closet in the front parlor. With more energy
than necessary, she threw on the gray wool coat she wore for work.

"I'm raking," she called to Selene and Aunt Louisa.

"You've been working like a madwoman on those leaves. Don't
overtax yourself," Aunt Louisa called back.

"I won't."

On most days, she enjoyed the musty smell of autumn air, but not today. Today she was on a mission. She headed for the woodshed in the backyard, passing a small load of laundry hanging on the line. She touched the hem of a petticoat, drying as it whipped in the wind. It still felt too damp to bring in, although the chilly weather made it hard to discern exactly when fresh laundry had dried. She decided to let it hang outside a bit longer. She wouldn't set fire to the leaves until late in the day, when the women had taken in their laundry, so the smell of smoke wouldn't affect anyone's clean clothes.

The wind was a bit more energetic than she preferred for her task, but nothing would stop her. Rake in hand, she headed to the front lawn. With vigor she raked and raked, bringing fallen leaves to the small ditch at the edge of the front yard. A neighborhood mutt she recognized trotted through the leaves, and she waved her rake in his direction to shoo him away with more anger than she meant. The poor little thing took off yelping.

At times she raked so hard she almost stripped the grass from the topsoil. She muttered to herself, "Why? Why am I still so hurt?"

"You're hurt?"

She jumped, almost dropping the rake. "Booth! What are you doing, sneaking up on me like that?"

"I'm sorry. It's just that you were muttering to yourself and I wondered what you were saying. Who hurt you?"

She wasn't sure what to say. Embarrassed though she was, the only thing she could do was tell the truth. "Luther. He hurt me."

"Oh. Your fiancé."

"Former fiancé." Frowning, she resumed raking as though a strict employer had issued an urgent deadline for the job to be complete within the hour.

He placed his hand on her shoulder in an unspoken request for her to stop working. "You know, we've talked a lot, but you never told me what happened."

She couldn't look in his eyes. "I don't want to talk about it."

"Oh, but I think you do. Or, at least, you need to. It upsets me to see you let him affect you this way. You still love him, don't you?" He sounded almost hurt himself.

"No. No, I don't."

"Do you mean that?"

"I—I do. He's been seeing someone else for quite a while now, but I didn't think he'd get engaged almost the moment I left Haw River."

Booth's eyes widened, reminding her of their blueness. "Already?"

"I must be forgettable."

"No. Never."

"Thanks for being a friend, Booth. I wasn't fishing for a compliment." He opened his mouth to say something else, but she stopped him. "My pride is hurt more than anything else. Okay, you got me to admit I'm prideful. And upset. Are you happy now?"

"No, I'm not. I'm never happy when I see you upset."

She kept raking.

"Please stop working long enough to tell me what really happened."

"No."

"If you don't, your aunt won't have any grass left and I'll have to come over next spring and plant grass seed. You don't wish all that work on me, do you?"

"No, I guess not." She stopped raking.

"So, please, tell me."

"Why do you want to know?"

"Why do you think? Because I care about you, that's why."

"You want to know why he broke it off with me?" She didn't want to admit her humiliation to anyone, but maybe the time had come to share it with Booth.

"I thought you broke it off with him."

She swallowed. "I did, formally. It's just that he had left me long before I drew up the courage to confront him." She stared at the steps leading to the veranda—anything to keep from looking into his handsome face. She couldn't stand the thought of witnessing his pity. "You see, he found other women more attractive than me, his future wife."

"Then he's a fool."

Hestia would have protested, but Booth's vehemence told her he spoke the truth as he saw it. "Thank you for saying so. I wonder if it wasn't partly my fault. He thought I wasn't modern enough, with my style of dress, and the fact that I don't sport a bob." She touched her long hair. "I can't help but wonder if things would have been different if I'd been more fashionable."

"You mean, if you had betrayed yourself? No, that's never a good idea. An unfaithful man will find any excuse. That just happened to be his. Better that you found out sooner than later what he was really like. And as for fashion, I think you look swell. Only a very few girls dress and cut their hair like Selene does. I imagine bobbed hair and short dresses will be out of style by this time next year."

Glad for a more cheerful topic, Hestia answered with dash. "I don't know. I just got a letter from one of my friends back home. Not only has she bobbed her hair, but her mother is thinking of doing the same thing."

"That's hard to believe."

"Maybe it's not so bad. Gertie—that's the friend who wrote to me—seems to think she looks very good in the new style. I know you think Selene is pretty. And I do, too. Would you like me to sport such a new look?"

"I'll borrow a phrase from Selene. You'd look copacetic no matter what."

She laughed. "So you wouldn't mind if I bobbed my hair? Or if I wore my dresses a little shorter?"

"Not if it made you feel more comfortable. I look at the heart. And I believe yours is pure. I don't think dressing in the new fashions and changing your hair makes a person bad. But I do think that if you wore face paint it would cause quite a stir, so I hope you would stay away from that."

Maybe she could live with that. She looked at the leaves in the ditch and set down her rake. "See that pile of leaves?"

"You've been working hard."

She eyed them and grinned. "Want to jump in those leaves?"

"Jump? In those? Why, sure!" He took her by the hand, and they ran together and leaped feetfirst into the pile. Leaves flew and rustled when they made impact. Booth took handfuls and threw them at her. She threw handfuls in return. Each of them flailed their arms in the air, swishing leaves up and around. Before they knew it, they were laughing together as though they were kids instead of responsible adults. They laughed until they were winded, and Hestia realized she'd needed the emotional release.

Their energy spent, Hestia and Booth dropped into the leaves and laid beside each other. Hestia didn't want to rise, and Booth made no motion to stand. She looked at the fall sky. From the corner of her eye, she noticed he looked upward, too.

"See that cloud?" He pointed to a fluffy confection. "What does it look like to you?"

"An elephant."

"An elephant. Yes, I'd say you're right. I can see the trunk and ears. How about the one beside it?"

She didn't know what she saw. "Your turn to go first."

"A heart."

"A heart?" She noticed that, indeed, it did look like a fat heart. "Yes, I see what you mean."

She sensed that he had turned his head to look at her. She turned to look at him, too. Those blue eyes. She could look into them forever. His eyes reminded her of the sky, but she didn't dare tell him so. She longed for the freedom to share such thoughts, but she couldn't. She had to settle for something anemic. "I'm glad you came over when you did. You always seem to know just when I need you."

"Do I?"

"Yes," she whispered.

He drew his face closer. She felt her eyes closing ever so slightly. She wanted him to kiss her. Very much.

"Mercy!"

Hestia jumped and sat up, and Booth followed suit. Hestia hadn't heard Miss Olive approach, and judging from the way he mimicked Hestia's shock, Booth had also been oblivious. They greeted the older woman with shy voices and rose to their feet. Ever the gentleman, Booth extended his hand to help Hestia rise even though she didn't need assistance.

"You had better be standing upright. This is an absolute disgrace! The two of you lying down like that. What do you think you're doing?"

"We were just playing, Miss Olive." Booth brushed leaves from his jacket.

"Playing? I'll say you were playing. Just wait until I tell your aunt, Hestia. She will be very disappointed. Don't you think your family has enough disgrace with Selene being in the shape she's in, without you acting in such a way?"

"I'm sorry, Miss Olive." Hestia felt confident that she blushed enough to show her chagrin. "We really were just having a little innocent fun. Please forgive me. And if you don't mind, I wish you wouldn't burden

Aunt Louisa. You're right—she does have enough on her without worrying about me, too."

"What about you, Booth? I expected much better of you."

"Yes, ma'am. I'm sorry I caused Miss Hestia to appear anything but the most virtuous woman that I know her to be. Please forgive me. And I beg your forgiveness, Hestia."

She nodded.

Holding a basket of pecans, Miss Olive stood before them like a grumpy schoolmarm. "I came to bring these pecans I had left over from harvesting my trees. I know you have some from Artie Rowland, but mine are the kind that are easy to shell." Having outdone Artie, she peered down her nose at them. "It seems you two have other things to do than worrying about pecans."

"No, ma'am. I don't have anything else to do. I can shell pecans this afternoon," Hestia hurried to assure her. "Thank you for bringing them."

"I can help you, Hestia." Booth sounded as though he were a dull student trying to gain the teacher's favor.

"In the presence of her aunt, I hope." Miss Olive squinted her eyes at them.

"Yes, ma'am." Now Hestia sounded like the dull student.

"Mercy! The two of you are acting as though you're children." Miss Olive surveyed the misplaced leaves. "Now just look at all the extra work you two created for yourselves."

"Yes, ma'am." Booth surveyed the leaves as though he'd never seen them before. "I'll help Hestia rake them back."

"I would certainly hope so." The topic exhausted, Miss Olive ventured elsewhere. "Is your aunt home?"

Hestia nodded. "Yes, ma'am. I know she'd love to see you."

As Miss Olive took her leave of them, shaking her head all the while, the two recalcitrant young adults watched her.

"I'll rake." Booth grabbed the rake from where Hestia had left it propped on a nearby tree.

"I can do it," Hestia protested, although her enthusiasm for the project had waned.

"You can take a turn." Hestia doubted he planned for her to work, but she admired him for saying she could. "If I were a little younger, I'd be tempted to stick out my tongue at her."

"Now, Booth!" Hestia mocked. "I can't believe you'd consider such a thing."

He gave her a sheepish grin.

"Truth be told, I was tempted to do the same thing." Hestia giggled, and Booth laughed. Hestia looked back toward the house and saw the front parlor curtain open a couple of inches and shut back. "She must be tattling on us now."

"Your aunt knows Miss Olive pretty well. I imagine since we're now hard at work raking, she'll excuse us. Let's just pray she doesn't make this out as more than it was."

"True." She wondered what would have happened in that moment, had they not been interrupted. Would there ever be another moment like it again?

Chapter Fourteen

Hestia's energy spurred Booth to take action on his own yard. He was glad Hestia had gone into her house. What had he been thinking? He had come so close to kissing her. He never should have gotten close enough to be tempted. With wistfulness, he recalled the moment. She'd been willing. So had he.

The Browns' black-and-white mutt wandered into the yard and sniffed a pile of leaves, digging into them. Booth looked at Rover for help, but the elderly dog had no intention of leaving his position on the front porch. Booth shooed the mutt with a voice louder than he intended. The little dog ran away with a little howl.

His thoughts returned and swirled like falling leaves. What was he to do? He stopped and realized the truth. They were in love.

* * * * *

Hestia felt justified in taking a break after so much raking, but she couldn't concentrate on anything in the newspaper. She sat in a chair in the parlor since Selene was occupied in their room, but she couldn't situate herself comfortably. Looking up from the paper, she stared at the philodendron plant in the corner without seeing it.

What had just happened? Or almost happened? Booth had seemed to want to kiss her, and she had yearned to kiss him. But Miss Olive had interrupted. Maybe it was for the best. If she didn't go back to Haw River, she could forget any career in medicine. Not that her family supported such an idea. She wondered if Papa had insisted she help her aunt just to discourage her. During her stay she'd learned almost nothing about medicine but much about housework.

Sighing, she decided to do a little dusting and headed to the kitchen to retrieve a dust rag from a drawer. Once in the kitchen, Hestia heard the whir of the Singer sewing machine coming from the little room off the kitchen. She ventured into the room and found Aunt Louisa engaged in a project. The fabric she was sewing looked to be of quality. The pretty green color reminded Hestia of spring.

Aunt Louisa stopped pumping the machine with her feet and looked up. "Oh! It's you. What a relief."

"I'm glad. I think." She laughed. "My, but you've gotten ambitious."

"Did I tell you the quilt brought thirty-five dollars for the church?"

Hestia whistled. "That's wonderful."

"The news encouraged me to get back into sewing. I always did love to sew. Come here." Aunt Louisa crooked her finger. "Look." Standing, she held up a garment for Hestia to see. It was a dress in the linear style Selene preferred, only with plenty of room in the waist. "It's for Selene. What do you think?"

"It's a maternity dress?"

Aunt Louisa nodded.

"That's a grand idea. She certainly needs some clothing that fits loosely."

"I can take it in at the sides for her once she has the baby."

"Oh, that is so thoughtful of you. I haven't thought about Christmas yet. Maybe Booth wouldn't mind taking me into Lincolnton to shop."

"Good idea." She smiled. "I have a feeling he won't mind. And I suspect you wouldn't mind, either."

"I'm that obvious?" She felt herself blush.

"Young love is always obvious, especially to us old folks." Aunt Louisa sighed as though the years had melted from time. "I remember young love very well. I was happily married for many years."

"Yes, you were a fine example."

"Enough of this sentiment." Aunt Louisa flitted her hand at Hestia. "Now don't you mention that you caught me in here sewing. This is a surprise for her for Christmas."

"So when did you get the fabric? It's lovely."

"Oh, I have my ways."

Hestia wondered if she happened to have the material on hand or what. Why was she being secretive?

* * * * *

As Judith and her mother dropped off Hestia at Aunt Louisa's after the quilting bee, she bid them farewell and watched the motorcar depart. Seeing that Hestia could use a weekly break, Judith had invited Hestia to take part in her quilting bees. The meetings had become events that Hestia anticipated, a time to be with women of all ages as they sewed to raise money for missions.

Hestia breezed through the front door, refreshed by the fellowship.

"Is that you, Hestia?" Aunt Louisa called.

"Yes, ma'am."

"Look on the table. There's a letter for you."

Following her aunt's instructions, Hestia saw a letter from her old friend Gertie. In the recent past, she would have been eager for news. Not anymore. She almost couldn't remember Haw River. Sighing, she took a moment to sit on the sofa and read the correspondence. It opened innocently enough, with news about all their friends and acquaintances. Learning about their comings and goings made her feel wistful. She had gone from feeling a sense of immediacy about their concerns to discerning that she had become an outsider, someone they'd ask about on occasion but not thought of with the urgency of the past.

"What's taking you so long?" Aunt Louisa called.

Obviously her aunt wanted to learn all about the meeting. Shaking her head and smiling to herself, Hestia put the letter back in its envelope and went to see her aunt.

Aunt Louisa's expression reminded Hestia of a little girl waiting for a new doll. "Did you have a good time at the quilting bee?"

"Yes, we're making progress. Next time I'll take a batch of sugar cookies. I have a new recipe I want to try for Christmas festivities."

"So you don't mind spending Christmas with us?"

Hestia didn't answer right away. "No, I don't mind. I won't say I don't miss anyone back home, but I do enjoy being here." She thought of Booth.

"Good. I imagine your letter is from one of your friends."

"Yes. Are you afraid I'll be homesick?"

"A mite."

"You really do want me to stay for Christmas, don't you?"

"I'll admit I've grown fond of having you here."

Hestia smiled. The admission of fondness was as close as her aunt would ever admit to love. "Thanks for the letter. Is Selene in the bedroom?"

"No. She's decided to try to make us dinner tonight. Candied yams and pork chops, I do believe."

"She's become quite domestic of late."

"I do believe she has a hankering to impress Artie. For a time the postman flirted with her mightily, but she didn't seem interested. He's a handsome fellow, too. She could have done worse. But her eyes light up when she's around Artie."

Hestia couldn't argue. "Funny, I never would have judged her to become interested in someone as conservative—or as devout—as Artie."

"Me, neither, but you won't see me complaining. He's been encouraging her to read the Bible, and they've been discussing the hard verses and teachings, such as Paul's admonitions about women's roles in the church. Seems our New York flapper doesn't take too kindly to such restrictions." Aunt Louisa chuckled.

"If anyone can help her understand the Bible, I have a feeling Artie can. She'll listen to him sooner than she'll pay attention to us. They seem to have respect and regard for one another."

"Yes. That's got to be the Lord's doing, His way of using this scandal to bring her to Him. Sometimes it takes a tragedy in one's life to get one to come to the Lord."

"True. I hadn't thought of it that way before." Hestia stared at the curtains but didn't truly see them.

"Too bad nothing more can come of it. Once she goes home, Artie will be back where he was, with no one. Such a shame, too. He's a nice fellow. We must pray for him not to be lonely after Selene leaves, and we must pray that once Selene gets back to her home, she won't fall back into her old habits."

Hestia thought about Selene. Her manner had become humble, and she no longer reminisced about her old life. "I have a feeling she's learned her lesson. And I know she won't be seeing Ned anymore. He's courting some other flapper."

Aunt Louisa harrumphed. "I hope someone warns the new girl what a rounder he is."

"I have a feeling word gets around about things, even in New York." Hestia held up the letter. "Speaking of word, let me see what Gertie has to say."

"Hope it's good news."

"Me, too," she said.

"Oh, and a letter also came for Selene. Can you take it in to her?"

"Of course. Seems we're popular today." In no hurry to read Gertie's letter, Hestia stopped by the kitchen to check on Selene and let her know she received mail.

"How's the new dish coming along?"

"Why don't you tell me?" She took a clean spoon from the silverware drawer and dipped out some of the dish for Hestia. "Taste."

Hestia obeyed. The flavors blended very well. She nodded. "As you would say, it's copacetic."

Selene giggled. "It doesn't need more salt?"

"No. Besides, people can always add salt to taste, but once it's in, you can't take it out."

"True."

"I think Artie will be impressed. That is what this is all about, isn't it?"

Selene shrugged. "Ask me no questions and I'll tell you no lies."

"So it is about Artie."

"Yes. And no. Sure, it's the bee's knees to have a fellow to impress, but I figure I'll be home soon enough. Might as well make the most of my misery here by picking up a new skill. Maybe one of the fellows back home will like a woman who can make a meal on the cook's night off."

"You have a point. Aunt Louisa was just saying Artie will miss you when you're gone."

"Yeah. Sure."

Hestia thought she caught just the slightest touch of wistfulness in Selene's voice, but she decided not to ask about it. "Here's a letter for you. It just came in today's mail."

Selene stopped her task long enough to take the letter from Hestia. "Oh, good, it's from Flora. She'll fill me in on all the news."

"I'll leave you to your letter."

"Don't bother. It'll be more fun to share."

"Are you sure?"

"Sure, I'm sure. Flora's already told me that Ned has someone else. It can't get any worse."

Touched by Selene's willingness to share her life, Hestia agreed to stay. "Read away."

Dear Selene:

What's the latest with you? We still miss you. You're missing so many things here. When are you coming home? What's the holdup?

"So she still doesn't know." Hestia found such a fact hard to believe. "No, and she never will."

Everything's jake here. Some new fellows from Chicago attracted Mildred's attention at the Saturday bash, and she asked them if they'd take us out to a swanky joint.

Hestia gasped. "You mean, your friends asked two gentlemen if they'd take them out for an evening?"

Selene looked at Hestia as though she were a dullard. "That's right. What's wrong with that? I think the fellows like it."

Hestia wasn't sure but decided not to argue.

At first I was worried that we'd be in trouble once the check came. What if we didn't have enough money to pay? But they both turned out to be darbs, so we didn't have to wash dishes after all.

"Darbs?" Hestia asked.

"They can be counted on to pick up the check," Selene explained. "The girls were really lucky. I don't think I would have taken a chance like that."

*I wasn't so keen on the one I got. He turned out to be a flat
tire. But Mildred's gotten stuck on her date. I think they'll be an
item soon. By the by, she wants to fix you up on a blind date with
his brother. You'd better hurry back before they're gone for good!*

*Speaking of dates, you might as well take any opportunity you
can. If you think Ned's carrying a torch for you, you can forget it.
He eloped!*

Both women took in a collective breath and said, "Eloped!"
Selene looked at the letter as though it were written in Chinese.
Hestia took the letter from her. "Let me see that."

*And not even with the same woman he had a crush on right
after you left town. This is someone altogether different. I don't
know the girl—she's apparently someone from the Catskills and
they met while he was visiting his uncle in August. Well, I say
good riddance. Who needs him? All the swell guys think you're the
berries, and we can paint the town red once you get back.*

Selene seemed dazed. "I can't believe it."

"It sounds mighty suspicious to me. Do you think it possible that
he—no, I don't even want to suggest it."

"What?"

"Read for yourself."

Selene took the letter. "We don't even know the girl? And he hardly
knows her himself, it seems."

"The timing of when they met in relation to this elopement is
strange to me." Hestia paused, hoping Selene could make the deduction
for herself.

"Why?"

Hestia sighed. "I just hope he didn't let the same thing happen to this girl that happened to you."

Selene let out a cry of frustration and anguish. "No. It can't be. Why would he leave me on my own but give someone else's baby a name? I pray it's not true."

"I do, too, Selene. Maybe I'm wrong. Sometimes I'm too pessimistic for my own good. Don't pay any attention to me."

Selene put her face in her hands and bawled. Hestia wrapped her arm around Selene's shaking shoulders. The news from her friend's letter was bad enough, but why did she have to open her big mouth and suggest that Ned had gotten yet another woman in trouble?

Selene sniffled. "You want me to be miserable, don't you? Nothing makes you happier."

"That's not true. I'm so very, very sorry about the whole mess. I really mean that." She tried to embrace Selene, but her cousin pushed her away.

"I wish I'd never asked you to stay. As far as I'm concerned, you can go back to Haw River and stay there. You can fly to the moon, for all I care!"

"I'm sorry—I didn't mean—"

"Leave me alone!" Selene broke away and rushed out of the kitchen and to the bedroom, slamming the door behind her.

"She must really be upset," she muttered to Diamond, who had witnessed the entire episode.

Diamond, more concerned that she had been awakened from her nap on the kitchen rug than with Selene's romantic entanglements, stretched and blinked.

Aunt Louisa entered. "What's all the commotion? I heard enough noise to wake the dead. You girls have got to get out of this habit of slamming doors. Did you two fight?"

"In a way." Hestia felt on the verge of tears herself. She explained the exchange to her aunt. "I wish I hadn't made matters worse with my tactlessness. That wasn't my intent, but she seems to think so."

"She's overly emotional in her delicate condition. I knew better than to let her tire herself with cooking, but she wanted to cook so badly that I consented. No more."

"I don't think she was tired; I think I introduced a possibility she hadn't considered, and I upset her. She won't accept my apology. Can you help me?"

"I'll try talking to her."

Hestia prayed her aunt would be successful. If not, she would surely be better off returning to Haw River.

* * * * *

The next day, Selene woke up in a foul mood and tried to remember why. That's right. She had argued with her only ally in the house. How dare Hestia suggest that Ned had taken up in such a big way with another girl as soon as she'd left for Maiden.

She looked at Hestia's empty bed. Of course she was up, bright and early. Hestia, always perfect, never lacked for energy. Selene wished she could say the same. But of course, Hestia wasn't expecting a child.

As though the child could detect her thoughts, it kicked. The motion made her stomach move up and down. She placed her hand on her belly and waited for the baby to kick again, but it didn't. At least it had made its presence known. The larger the baby grew, the more conflicted Selene felt about giving it away. Of course she could never go back to New York and resume the carefree life of a flapper with a baby in tow, especially a baby whose father wouldn't give it a name—a father who had already married another woman.

Hestia's idea that Ned had gotten yet another woman in a family way infuriated her, even though she was probably right. Still, why couldn't Hestia keep her awful conclusions to herself? Why did her cousin want her to believe that Ned cast her aside but took responsibility for his child with another woman? Did he hope to find some sort of redemption in a second chance? She didn't get a second chance. She should bear responsibility for her baby, and that fact would always be with her. Forever. She would think about the baby on every holiday, especially its birthday.

She could hear Aunt Louisa's voice whenever she expressed such concerns. "You can't think about things like that. You have to consider the baby's best interests. Its best interests are for you to give it to our relatives. They'll take care of it. If not, your father never would have consented to letting them take it."

She didn't doubt that, but she also knew her distant cousin already had a brood and Father's money was her main motivation for taking Selene's baby. The thought made her ill. Almost as if by her thinking so, she felt a pain in her midsection.

"Please, Lord, let the baby be okay."

She waited, and the pain subsided. Eager for a distraction, she flipped through a mail-order catalog Hestia had left open on the bed. Since she was stuck in Maiden, her needs were few. Still, she usually enjoyed window-shopping. As if to torture her, the book flipped to a page with illustrations of happy babies in nightgowns.

Dainty Things for Baby's Comfort. Hurriedly she turned to another section of the catalog.

Enter the Big Race. Pictures of go-carts and sleds brought to mind a ruddy-cheeked little boy. A ruddy-cheeked little boy she would never know. She tried another time.

So Real They Seem Almost Alive…Dollies to Cuddle.

She shut the book with a bang and threw it on the floor. Never had she cried so much in her life.

Chapter Fifteen

. . . .

The next day, Hestia sat at the desk in the den and reread the latest letter from her mother, which was asking about Christmas. Her parents were the ones she missed most about Haw River. She looked forward to going home, having received assurance from Aunt Louisa that she could spare Hestia for a few days.

Selene entered. "There you are. Aunt Louisa's ready to start on the laundry."

"I'll be right there." Hestia returned the letter to its envelope. "I'll reply to this tomorrow. I need to let my parents know when I'll be home for Christmas. Booth is supposed to take me to the train station later today to buy tickets."

Selene's expression froze in a way that made Hestia think of a fox cornered by a pack of hounds. "You're—you're leaving?"

"Just for a few days. Maybe it's for the best, considering our spat. I'm so sorry about that." Hestia hoped her expression showed her regret.

Selene looked up at her, eyes misty. "Me, too. I shouldn't have acted that way, especially since, considering what Ned's like, you're probably right." She brushed back a tear.

"I wish things were different."

"But they aren't. Hestia, sometimes I've felt as though you're my only friend around here. I wish you wouldn't go. Can't your parents visit us instead?"

"My brother and his family will be with them, so they'll be playing host."

"Oh, please, Hestia. You can't leave me alone here with Aunt Lou. Cousin dear, please stay."

"Selene! You act as though she'll whip you every day."

Selene rolled her eyes. "No, but this Christmas will be miserable enough for me without you being gone, too." She looked both sheepish and fearful. "Besides, I had a bad pain in my stomach yesterday, and I really don't want you to go."

"Pain? Why didn't you tell me?"

"I didn't want to worry you. And yesterday wasn't the first time."

Hestia tried to remember how her father would advise a mother as far along as Selene. "I don't think it's anything to worry about, but you do need to be careful. We don't want anything to happen to the baby.

"All the more reason for you to stay. And not just for me. You'll have every Christmas the rest of your life to be in Haw River, but only one Christmas here in Maiden."

Only one Christmas here in Maiden. She remembered Booth, and judging from Selene's distress, she really needed Hestia. Yet she didn't wish to disappoint her parents and brother. She hated being in the middle of a quandary. "Let me think about it." She rose from her seat. "I'll do the laundry. I want you to rest."

* * * * *

That afternoon, Booth's steps were slow as he walked to meet Hestia. Usually he enjoyed Maiden's mild winters, but not even the invigorating mountain air cheered him. He dreaded taking her to buy the train tickets, even though she wouldn't be gone long. Besides, she deserved time with her family for Christmas.

Hestia answered the door, dressed in her best coat and the wide-brimmed hat that framed her beautiful face. "I'm ready."

"I'm not." He felt his heart pound with the love he felt for her and with regret at having blurted out his feelings to Hestia.

Her mouth dropped. She stepped onto the veranda and shut the door behind her so as not to let cold air in the house. "Oh! Is something the matter? I'm sorry. We can go another time."

"No, nothing's wrong. I apologize. I'm acting like a spoiled little kid. Of course I'll take you to the station."

She didn't try to move. "A spoiled kid? How so?"

He felt suddenly shy. "I wish you could stay here and celebrate Christmas with us in Maiden. This is the only Christmas you'll be with us, but you'll have a lifetime in Haw River. I know it's selfish of me to feel that way, but nothing is accomplished by me lying to you."

"Selene said almost exactly the same thing to me. About how I'll only have this one Christmas in Maiden. I have to admit, the thought makes me sad." A light of unhappiness did touch her lovely eyes. "To tell the truth, I've been conflicted about leaving ever since I spoke with Selene yesterday. I want to be sure she's okay."

Booth had a feeling she wasn't revealing the whole story, but he didn't want to pry.

"So you know what? I'm not ready to go, either." She averted her eyes. "I hate telling my parents I won't be with them. They'll be disappointed."

"Yes, but they'll have other family around them to share in the celebration."

Hestia nodded. "They'll understand."

Booth smiled. Maybe this Christmas would be his best after all.

* * * * *

Hestia peered outside on Christmas Eve. The clear night made her think about the star that guided the three wise men. Surely that night could not have been any clearer than this one. She thought back over the day's celebrations. It was Sunday, so the regular church service had been especially meaningful. The little ones had performed their version of the Christmas story, which both Hestia and Booth found heartwarming.

That afternoon Hestia helped Selene and Aunt Louisa adorn the tree they'd bought from Hugh Drum. Both of the younger women found the selection of a cedar, with its intensely prickly leaves, difficult to decorate, especially since they were accustomed to the more forgiving branches of pines or firs. But the cedar emanated a pleasant aroma and possessed a lovely shape that reminded Hestia of a teardrop. A teardrop of joy on this occasion.

Though secrets were almost impossible to keep in their house, all three women managed to conceal their gifts from one another. The previous week Hestia had walked to the dry goods store for tissue paper, so boxes wrapped in cheerful red and green paper awaited them underneath the tree for a beautiful effect. Hestia felt a sense of peace. She was glad she had stayed in Maiden.

On Christmas, they rose around the same time as any other day, looking forward to a pleasant celebration. Hestia cooked a special breakfast of crepes with strawberry preserves to go along with pork sausage patties.

"Are you ready to play the piano for the sing-along tonight, Selene?" Aunt Louisa asked as she poured cream into her coffee.

"I think she is." Hestia couldn't help but be proud of Selene's progress. She didn't mind practicing and, with Hestia's instruction, had learned easy versions of several Christmas songs.

"I hope I don't play too poorly." Selene looked nervous.

"Don't worry. Everybody who'll be here is your friend," Hestia assured her. "We'll all have fun. Now let's leave the dishes to soak while we open our gifts."

Once they had settled in the parlor, Selene reminded Hestia of a small child as she studied the wrapped treasures. She reached for a big box.

"Not yet." Aunt Louisa tapped the Bible in her lap. "First we'll read the Christmas story aloud."

Hestia expected Selene to howl, but instead she sat patiently and listened. She made a mental note to thank Artie for his influence.

Once the story was read, Selene didn't hesitate to pass out the gifts.

"Do you want to open your gifts first?" Aunt Louisa asked from her perch in the Chippendale chair.

Selene nodded much as a little girl would.

"That little box came for you yesterday." Aunt Louisa pointed to the gift in question.

With no degree of joy, she opened a box from Tiffany's and discovered a small silver brooch flanked with diamonds.

Hestia and Aunt Louisa gasped. "That's gorgeous."

"Yes, typical for Father." Selene chose the two other odd presents under the tree. "These must be from him, too. Want to open them?"

The women nodded. Soon they discovered plain silver brooches. Aunt Louisa's was traditional, while Hestia's was in a geometric art deco form.

"I've never had anything from Tiffany's." Aunt Louisa looked at her brooch in wonder.

Hestia pinned hers to her dress. "I never have either. Uncle Ralph has good taste."

"You mean his secretary has good taste." Selene sighed. "Might we open the other gifts now?"

Aunt Louisa nodded, and Selene tore into the largest box. She revealed a beautifully sewn dress and cried out in happiness and surprise. "This will really help me tolerate the next couple of months. Thank you, Auntie."

"You said green is your favorite color."

"It is. I can't believe you remembered."

"I do listen to you, even if I can't hear well. I'll take it in for you before you go home so you can wear it later."

Selene nodded, her eyes misting.

Hestia had waited long enough. "Open mine."

Selene ripped open the package. "A cookbook. Copacetic!"

"Yes." Hestia nodded. "I asked Mother for all her favorite recipes, and I wrote down a few of my own. Aunt Louisa also contributed. I think you've got enough recipes to put on a meal for just about any occasion."

Selene clutched the book to her chest. "Thank you so much. That means a lot to me."

"You're getting to be such an expert in cooking, you'll easily outdo me in no time." Hestia had noted Selene's determination in the kitchen, so she didn't exaggerate.

"Is your compliment part of my Christmas present?" Selene laughed. "Now open your gifts, Hestia."

"They're both so pretty I don't know which to open first."

"Mine! Mine!" Selene asked.

Hestia was amused by how Selene reminded her of a small child, but she complied. Selene had given her a bottle of perfume. "Jicky."

Selene nodded. "It's by Guerlain, same as mine. Legend says Monsieur Guerlain named the fragrance after the love of his life."

Hestia dabbed a few drops on her wrist and sniffed. "Smells wonderful. Thank you."

"How did you manage to sneak it into the house?" Aunt Louisa wanted to know.

"It wasn't easy. I had to watch for the postman every day and beat you to the door. Thankfully, neither of you were home the day the package arrived. You have something too, Aunt Louisa. Why don't you open it?"

"Why not?" She started unwrapping the gift, taking an inordinate amount of time.

Selene watched with an intense gaze. "Goodness, Aunt Louisa. Are you trying to make Christmas last until tomorrow?"

"If I had my way, it would last all year." Aunt Louisa slid the paper off a turquoise box. "In people's attitudes, anyway. We couldn't afford to give all these gifts every day."

"True. I think I'd get bored with Christmas every day." Hestia tried to imagine nothing but celebrating and couldn't.

"Baloney." Selene flicked her hand at them. "I'd never get bored with Christmas every day."

As she spoke, Aunt Louisa finally uncovered a box of lovely soaps. She sniffed them. "Smells good. I'll bet these cost a fortune."

"They're the same kind we use. I thought you'd enjoy something practical and pretty."

"These are too good to use." Aunt Louisa looked pleased all the same.

Hestia handed her gift to her aunt. With due care, the older woman opened a gift of beautiful stationery and a fountain pen fashioned from ivory.

"I know you write every week to several people, so I thought you might enjoy a new stylus and pretty paper."

"Indeed I shall. And my recipients shall enjoy such tasteful paper as well. Thank you. Now it's your turn to open my gift to you."

Hestia unwrapped the gift. To her shock, she discovered that Aunt Louisa had also sewn her a dress. Hestia's was fashioned for her thin frame, and the blue fabric delighted her. When she noticed the style, she wasn't sure how to react.

Selene clapped. "If you don't want that dress, I'll take it, Hestia."

"No dress can receive higher praise than that." Hestia studied the style. "I've never had anything like this, Aunt Louisa."

"I know."

Selene surveyed the garment. "It's too long. That's the only thing I'd find to criticize about it. But that can easily be fixed."

"Selene!" Hestia chastened her. "You shouldn't criticize my gift. I love it. But Aunt Louisa, what possessed you to sew me such a modern dress?"

"I heard you talking about your friends bobbing their hair. It's only a matter of time before the world catches up with all of us. We can be modest and fashionable at the same time."

"Yes, ma'am."

"But no face paint, you hear me now?" Aunt Louisa wagged her finger.

"Yes, ma'am." That would be an easy promise for Hestia to keep. The idea of making herself look so strange with the use of cosmetics seemed odd to her. Not to mention, Booth didn't like the idea. But she would have to visit the dry goods store for a pair of flesh-toned stockings.

"I almost didn't give you this dress, you know." Aunt Louisa's voice sounded a warning.

"Really?"

"Not after Olive told me she found you and Booth lying in the leaves together the other day."

"The other day" had occurred longer ago than that, though the memory of it visited Hestia almost every hour. She had thought that since Aunt Louisa didn't scold her, the incident had passed without mention from Miss Olive. She should have known better.

"I don't believe it! You were lying in the leaves with Booth? Naughty girl!" Selene's crooked grin told Hestia she was having fun turning the tables on her "perfect" cousin for once.

Hestia groaned. "Did you have to bring that up? We were having such a nice time."

Aunt Louisa gave her a serious look. "We still are. I'm just telling you that I expect you to conduct yourself as a lady if you're going to wear the new fashions, that's all. Keep God close at hand, no matter what the styles or notions of the day may be."

"Yes, ma'am." Hestia cut her gaze to her cousin, who was no longer grinning, wry or otherwise, but had her stare fixed on the wooden floor.

* * * * *

Since everyone had been so good to them at Thanksgiving, the ladies had invited Booth and his family and Artie to Christmas dinner. Only Judith's family declined since they had plans to be with Judith's sister.

Though Aunt Louisa insisted that Selene had to take things easy, she had been allowed to bake pies for the meals. Selene was proud of her accomplishment. Hestia baked her customary red velvet cake. Aunt Louisa said that no Christmas passed without her preparation of gelatin salad, Parker rolls, and country ham. She had ordered fresh oysters at extra expense as a fabulous Christmas treat, and they had arrived just in time so she could make oyster stew to start the dinner right.

"This will be quite a feast." Hestia inhaled delectable cooking aromas.

Selene followed suit. "I do believe we might almost be able to outdo the Algonquin. Or at least come close."

"Maybe." The Algonquin did sound like a wonderful place. "Let me set the table. Since we don't use the dining room much, I'm afraid it still might have some slick spots where I waxed, and I wouldn't want you to fall, Selene."

"I wouldn't want that, either."

"You haven't had any more cramping, have you?" Hestia tried not to let her voice sound worried.

Selene shook her head.

Aunt Louisa hardly ever used her good china and crystal, and the Christmas tablecloth embroidered with images of holly was used only once a year, so the table looked as elegant as any Hestia had seen in recent times.

Later, their guests arrived and greeted them with merriment of the season. When Booth entered, he and Hestia exchanged glances. She noticed he sported a new sweater. He eyed her new dress but didn't say anything about it. She was glad Selene had let her borrow a pair of flesh-toned stockings for the occasion and that her shoes looked stylish enough to fit the dress.

The hostesses' anticipation proved on-target. Their guests enjoyed eating food lovingly prepared among convivial company.

Hestia and Booth sat beside one another. Every once in a while he gave her a shy smile and complimented the meal. She noticed him regarding the new blue dress. His expression wasn't unpleasant, but then again, it never was when she was with him. She wondered what he really thought of her new dress. At least she hadn't bobbed her hair. No doubt two such daring moves at once would have been unduly shocking.

After the meal, the older adults exited to the front room for coffee. Hestia wouldn't allow Selene to help with the dishes, so she made quick work of the task, stacking them on the counter to clear them from the dining room. She would have plenty of time to wash them the next day. The gift she had for Booth awaited. She'd been working on it for a while, and she hoped he would like it.

After she cleared the dishes, she took him to the den in the back of the house where they could have relative privacy but stir no objections. She sat on the sofa and motioned for him to sit beside her.

"Before you say anything, I have something to tell you. Something I've been wanting to say all night."

"What?" She tried not to take in an anticipatory breath.

"Your dress is quite shocking."

Her heart fell into her toes. "Really? I'm sorry. I'll go change into something else." She tried to rise, but he restrained her with a hand on her shoulder.

"No. Please don't."

"But if it offends you—"

"No, it doesn't offend me. Was it a gift from Selene?"

"I thought you might ask me that." She sent him a half-grin. "It does resemble something Selene would choose, doesn't it? Although she did say it's not short enough for her taste."

"I'm not surprised."

"You won't believe it, but Aunt Louisa sewed it for me."

"Miss Louisa?"

"Yes. I was surprised, too. I guess I've got to face the new fashions whether I want to or not. Unless…unless you'd prefer I not."

"I'd never boss you. I meant what I said earlier. Of course I think you look lovely in anything. And you look keen in your new dress. I think you should wear it. A lot."

"I'm glad. I've been wondering all night what you thought."

"As I said, I wanted to tell you all night, but I didn't want to be too bold in front of everyone. I only hope you don't find me too bold now."

"No. No, I don't." Heart beating with anticipation, she hoped he'd take the opportunity to kiss her. She looked him in the eyes, getting lost in their blueness.

Instead of moving toward her, he looked into her eyes and away once again. "Your friends in Haw River will think Maiden is quite progressive once they see your new look."

Haw River. "Oh. Yes. Yes, they will." Realizing there would be no moment as she dreamed, she cleared her throat and switched topics. "Selene and Artie seem to be doing quite well."

"Yes. I never would have put the two of them together, but they get along swimmingly."

"Yes, they do. I'm not sure Selene would have given him a second glance a year ago, but I think she sees the folly of trying to chase after men. This time she's letting him do the chasing."

"That's a tough lesson to learn. Artie is good for her. But can it go anywhere? She'll be leaving about the same time you will. Right?" Did she hear a hint of remorse in his voice?

"Yes. At least we've both been able to enjoy fellowship while we've been here. You've made my stay pleasant. And so, I couldn't forget you today. I have something for you." She handed him a box wrapped in red.

"That's nice of you, but you didn't have to get me anything." Still, he opened it without hesitation, reminding her of an eager little boy. Soon he withdrew a dark blue scarf.

"I crocheted that for you myself. I hope you like it."

"This is swell. Thanks!" He threw the scarf around his neck with aplomb, looking quite dapper in the process.

"You certainly look dashing."

"Your scarf does add to my cachet, I will agree." His voice took on affectation and he showed her his profile as though he were an important figure posing for a formal portrait.

She chuckled. "I'm glad you like it."

"Now this debonair gentleman has something for you." He took a small box out of his pocket. Hestia knew better than to think that the box contained an engagement ring, but her heart was getting its exercise all the same.

She tried not to seem too excited as she removed the white ribbon from the gift wrapped in green tissue paper. Inside was a black velvet box. She opened it and discovered a heart-shaped locket in gold with leaves engraved upon it. She took in a breath. "It's gorgeous!"

"It reminded me of the day we were studying the clouds, and we said one looked heart-shaped."

She hoped she wasn't blushing, but her face did feel warm. "Yes. I remember."

"It's a locket for whatever picture you might want to put in it."

"I think I'll wait until I find just the right one."

* * * * *

Selene relaxed with Artie in the dining room after Christmas dinner.
Aunt Louisa had kept an eagle eye on them, so Selene didn't dare suggest
they retreat far from her view. Guilt pangs about keeping Hestia in town
visited her, but at least the stomach pain hadn't returned.

"Y'all put on quite a Christmas meal for us. I'm honored to be
included among your guests," Artie told Selene. He patted his stomach,
a satisfied expression on his face.

"Of course we wanted you here. I wouldn't have agreed to help host
this dinner otherwise. You have been a friend to me since I've been here,
a friend when no one outside of the family would be. Well, except Booth
and his family, but they're copacetic, too."

"What about Miss Olive?"

Selene didn't know how to answer. "Oh, she's nice in her way. But
you're the only man who's taken an interest in me lately—well, except for
the postman, but he's not as nice as you are."

Artie laughed.

"I am glad you're okay with spending time with me. I enjoy talking
with you, Selene. You're smart and witty. I can see why you kept your
friends entertained in New York. That's saying something when one
considers how sophisticated New York is."

His compliments made her feel shy. She hadn't heard such kind
words from a man in a long time, especially from a man who seemed to
want nothing from her that she wasn't ready to give. "I suppose that's one
way of looking at it."

He rose and retrieved a gift he had set beside the sideboard. "I brought you a gift to say Merry Christmas."

"Did you?" She felt her face redden. "I'm embarrassed. I didn't get you a thing."

"I think it is quite permissible for a gentleman to give a lady a Christmas gift without expecting anything in return, don't you?"

"Oh, but I do feel terrible."

"Please don't. I want you to have this." He handed her the present.

The gift was wrapped in white tissue paper and tied with a white bow. Judging from its rectangular shape and weight, a book awaited her. She opened it and discovered she was right. "It's a Bible!"

"I'm sure you already have a Bible in New York, but you said you'd been borrowing your aunt's Bible. I thought you might like to have your own copy for your use here in Maiden."

"Why, it's lovely." She ran her hands over the white leather cover then opened it. He had written in his own hand that he had given it to her for Christmas 1922. "I will always remember this day."

"How can you forget, with it written in India ink?" He chuckled.

"True." She opened the book to Psalms. The gold-edged pages felt luxurious. "This is a lovely Bible. You shouldn't have gone to such expense."

"I do have an ulterior motive. I hope you and I can read the Bible together this year. If we persist, we can be complete by January 1, 1924."

January 1924? That sounded so far into the future. Why was he talking about something so far away? Surely he didn't have plans for her.

"Not to brag, but I've read it once. I'd like to read it again, and it will be more fulfilling to read it along with you than by myself."

She swallowed. "But January 1924 is a long time away. I won't be here that long."

"I thought of that."

His matter-of-fact statement left her feeling surprisingly sad. "Oh."

"You may not be here in the flesh, but you can write me letters to tell me about your progress, can't you?"

"I suppose so." The idea didn't seem as fun as seeing him in person.

"Don't be sad. You'll be here through the month of April, at least. So we can read together a good part of the time."

"Children!" Aunt Louisa called them from the parlor. "Where are you? Come on in and be sociable."

"She must be worried we'll misbehave," Artie whispered.

If anyone else in Maiden had said that, Selene would have been insulted, but she knew Artie only wanted the best for her and was her friend. In another time and place, maybe they could have been more.

Lord, I have been such a fool.

"Selene!" Aunt Louisa's voice sounded irritated. Maybe she really was fearful she might be spooning with Artie.

"Coming!" She rose to answer her aunt's beckoning. Forgetting about the slick areas still on the floor, she hurried. The heel of her shoe slipped on a spot of wax, causing her foot to fly forward. Before she knew what happened, she had fallen on her rear.

"Selene!" Artie squatted beside her. Fear covered his face. "Are you okay?"

"I—I think so." How could she be so foolish, when she knew the floor in the little-used room was still slick?

Booth and Hestia ran into the dining room. "What happened?" Hestia spotted her cousin. "Selene!"

"I'll be fine," she said, even though she wasn't sure she told the truth.

Aunt Louisa and the Barringtons followed suit.

"Why are you on the floor?" Aunt Louisa looked pale.

"I slipped and fell."

"The baby!" Mrs. Barrington cried. "We must call Dr. Lattimore right away."

"As though he has nothing better to do on Christmas Day. I'll be fine." Selene had embarrassed herself enough without bothering the good doctor as well.

"I'll hear nothing of the sort," Aunt Louisa said. "Artie, help her get up so she can go to her room and get in bed."

"Yes, ma'am." He complied.

Selene felt a bit wobbly.

"Can you make it?" he asked.

"I think so."

"Let me carry you." Artie lifted her into his arms.

"Don't you fall, now," Aunt Louisa cautioned.

"I won't." Without another word, he carried her into the bedroom, with everyone following. Hestia went ahead of them and, with lightning speed, folded down the quilt, leaving the sheets for Selene's repose.

"I can't believe this happened," Selene wailed.

"I'm sure you'll be fine. Dr. Lattimore just needs to check you, that's all," Hestia assured her. "How do you feel? Are you in any pain?"

Selene stopped to consider the state of her body. "No."

"That's a good sign." Hestia breathed a sigh.

Booth intervened. "I'll fetch the doctor right now."

"He's probably at his daughter's house. You know where that is, don't you?" Aunt Louisa's face showed her concern.

"Emily Madison? I know the place."

"Yes. Hurry."

Selene didn't think Booth would ever get there with Dr. Lattimore. Artie stayed with her, holding her hand. Under different circumstances she might have thought him romantic, but not this time. He was a friend, consoling her.

"If only I hadn't waxed the floor." Hestia was wringing her hands.

Artie tried to console her. "You'd think it would have been okay to walk on by now."

"Yes, but we don't use the dining room every day, as we do the other rooms. That must be why it was still slick in there." Hestia hovered at the foot of Selene's bed. "Can I get you anything, Selene? Milk? Water?"

The last thing she wanted after a feast was more on her stomach. "I'm fine."

"A bromide?" Aunt Louisa offered her solution for everything.

"I'm not sick. I just fell." Selene tried not to sound irritated.

"I wish I hadn't asked Hestia to wax," Aunt Louisa lamented. "I should have known better than to ask her to make the floor slick when I knew I had a woman in the house in such a delicate condition."

"You have no business falling, either, Louisa." Mrs. Barrington's voice managed to be both kind and stern. "You certainly can't afford another break."

"I know it. No more waxing for this house ever again. Of course, if I hadn't been so insistent that she come into the parlor in a hurry, this wouldn't have happened."

"Now, now, Louisa," Mrs. Barrington consoled. "You can't blame yourself."

"No, Aunt Louisa. It won't do any good." Still, Selene wished her aunt hadn't beckoned her with such vehemence. Maybe then she truly wouldn't be in bed.

"Are you sure I can't get you anything?" Hestia plumped Selene's pillow. "Another pillow, perhaps?"

"No." Selene sounded vexed in spite of her best efforts. She felt foolish and hurt and wanted everyone to leave her alone.

"Y'all mean well, but I think Selene needs to rest," Artie said in a soft voice. "No disrespect intended."

Selene smiled. *How does he read my thoughts like that? No one else ever has.*

"Is that what you want, Selene? For us to leave you alone?" Aunt Louisa crossed her arms.

Hestia answered for her. "I think that's a good idea. There's been much too much commotion. Thank you for being so astute, Artie."

Everyone left, and Artie rose from his place beside her in a chair by the bed. "No." Selene's voice sounded sharp enough to stop him. "Not you. I don't want you to leave."

"You don't have to be nice. I'll leave, too."

"I'm not being nice. I'm being selfish to ask you to stay. Will you?"

He hesitated. "Well, if that's what you want."

"It's what I want. Wait with me while the doctor comes over. I don't know how long it will take. Do you mind?"

"No. I'll stay. I'm sure Booth will move as fast as he can. The doctor's daughter's house is only a few blocks from here."

"I hope he's finished dinner before Booth comes bounding in there. I'd feel so terrible if we interrupted, especially after we had such a nice celebration here."

"Yes, we did. I'm sorry you fell. I wish I had seen what was happening and could have caught you."

"No one could have caught me. It happened too fast. Artie, I'm scared. Petrified."

"I have a feeling you can guess what I do when I'm scared. I pray. Shall we pray together now?"

"Yes." Her voice was so soft it hardly registered.

"Heavenly Father, we don't know what You have in store for us, but we know You want what's best for us. We pray that it is Your will for Selene's baby to be safe and that Selene will return to full strength and vigor, Lord. We pray for those who feel responsible, that they will overcome their guilt and be able to forgive themselves. That includes me, Lord."

Selene squeezed his hand. "Please. It's not your fault. It's not anybody's fault."

"You are being very brave." He leaned over and embraced her. When he did, even though it was as a friend and not a beau, she felt more warmth from him than she ever felt from Ned. She realized for the first time that she had substituted a pale reflection of love for the type of love God wanted her to have in her life. She said a silent prayer of thanks for Artie's friendship.

There was a knock on the door. It was Dr. Lattimore. "I understand you took quite a fall."

"Yes."

Artie excused himself. Selene prayed the examination would be reassuring. She wanted the baby.

Chapter Sixteen
....

"Happy New Year!" Booth blew a horn to celebrate the beginning of the year 1923. "This will be the best year of our lives."

Hestia blew a horn, too. She wasn't sure she could agree with Booth. The year promised to be interesting, but it also possessed the potential for much heartbreak. Now that she'd been in Maiden awhile, she had become attached to the town and its people. The town felt more like home than Haw River.

Booth tapped her on the shoulder with his horn. "A penny for your thoughts."

"They're not worth a penny."

He nudged her. "What are you thinking about? Really?"

She hesitated. "Maiden. And Haw River."

"You want to go back, don't you?"

She looked into his blue eyes. "No. Not anymore."

* * * * *

Sitting up in bed, Selene placed her hand on her expanding belly. Since her fall, the doctor had insisted on complete bed rest. On the one hand, she welcomed the excuse not to do chores. On the other, her boredom had only increased with lack of mobility. At least she could anticipate the birth. The baby kicked and moved most days, and she felt love for the little life growing inside her. She wished she didn't have to give up her baby, even to a nice family. A family with a husband. A family with a father.

She read yet another letter from Flora. She skimmed over the news, skipping to the only part that mattered:

> *Ned and his wife have been scarce lately. They don't show up at any parties. I ran into her at Macy's the other day. Can you believe she's already in a family way? I'll bet that's the only reason he married her.*
> *The skunk.*

Hestia entered. "What's wrong, Selene? You look upset. Did Flora's letter vex you? If it did, I'll tell her to stop writing."

"No, don't do that. I have to keep up with the news if I hope to resume my life once I get back to New York." Though she said that, she noticed her stomach didn't jump with anticipation at the thought of returning to the city. Not like it used to.

"Artie's here."

One of the reasons why New York no longer seemed as appealing. "Oh?" She glanced at the clock on the nightstand table. "Oh. It's already seven? He's right on time."

"Are you up to seeing him?"

"Of course. I always am."

Since she and Artie had agreed to read the Bible together, Selene considered his visits the highlight of each evening. They talked about the passage they read that day. Artie had read many books and commentaries on the Bible, and he understood family lines better than she ever could. He also came prepared with maps and could show her locations of events. He made her readings come alive. Without him, she wasn't sure she could have stuck with it. They always left the door to her room open so Artie's lessons could be heard by Aunt Louisa and Hestia. Sometimes they would enter and listen to the lesson.

After Artie left that night, Selene took out her stationery.

Dear Flora:

Thank you for the news.

Artie and I are still studying the Bible. I know you think that's silly and I'm just doing it because I'm bored. I admit, it might have started that way. But now I really look forward to studying the Word. I think you should try it, too.

She doubted Flora would listen, but she could at least try.

* * * * *

On February 14 Hestia woke up depressed. At first she didn't know why, but she remembered all too soon. Not only was it Valentine's Day, but she should have been married today. She didn't long for Luther, but to be married. Then she realized all the more that marrying Luther would not have worked. She let out a sigh.

Selene rolled in the bed and sat up.

Hestia looked over at her sleepy-eyed cousin. "I'm sorry. I didn't mean to wake you."

"It's time to get up anyway. At least, getting up as much as is possible for me in this sorry state." Her belly grew larger each day. Even blankets and the quilt couldn't hide Selene's new shape. "Ouch!"

"Is that a pain?"

"Not this time. The baby kicked again. I wish he'd be more careful." Selene had gotten far enough along that everyone had taken to calling the baby *he* rather than *it*.

"Oh, he doesn't know better."

"I know, but that doesn't change the fact that it hurts." Selene rubbed her belly. "Things could have been so much different. I should be celebrating Valentine's Day with Ned now. We should be husband and wife, and he should be bringing me breakfast in bed."

"Somehow he doesn't sound like the type to bring anyone breakfast in bed."

Selene rolled her eyes. "I suppose not."

Hestia lifted her arms, stretching her body. "Just think. Only one more month and you can go back to New York."

"It might be a little more than that. The doctor isn't exactly sure."

"Is anyone ever exactly sure?" Hestia hugged her knees.

"Plus, I'll have to stay awhile and recover."

"That shouldn't take you too long. You're young and healthy."

"Some days I don't feel so young or healthy." Selene frowned. "And I'm not sure about New York anymore. There was a time when I wanted nothing more than to go back. I longed for it every day. But now, I don't know. Flora's letters have changed. They don't seem as friendly anymore."

"I know what you mean. I don't feel as much a part of Haw River as I once did. I don't miss it as much, either."

"I don't miss some of the things about New York now, either. My outlook has changed. I don't think I can go back to living the same way I did, now that I've been reading the Bible and seeing what it really has to say."

Hestia's heart warmed, but she had to caution her cousin. "I know you mean that, but do you think it will be easy to live this way once you go back to your old surroundings? Temptations await you in New York, temptations you don't have here. And there's no Aunt Louisa to hold you back."

"Or Hestia."

Hestia smiled. "I'm keeping you out of trouble, you think? How about Artie?"

"He helps. He does inspire me to do better. You know, when this happened, I was afraid no other man would ever look at me again. I'm not saying there's anything romantic with Artie and me." She stared ahead.

"I have a feeling you would like that if it happened."

"Don't tell anyone, least of all Artie. But yes. Yes, I would. And it's not because of the baby, but because of Artie. And who he is." She paused. "So what about you and Booth? Would you like him to be romantic with you?"

Hestia didn't answer right away. She remembered that day when they had looked up in the sky, lying on a cushion of raked leaves. She could have sworn Booth came within a snail's tooth of kissing her that day, and in her heart, she hoped another opportunity would arise. But nothing happened, so they simply remained friends.

"Well?" Selene prodded.

"I don't harbor any hopes, since I'm still supposed to go back to Haw River." Hestia couldn't help but think her imminent departure held Booth back from expressing any strong romantic feelings. Whenever she was near him, she sensed his love.

"Supposed to go back? You mean it's not definite any longer?"

"I'm sure Aunt Louisa would love me to stay with her. In fact, she'd love for both of us to stay indefinitely."

"You, maybe, but Aunt Lou thinks I'm a handful."

Hestia laughed. "I think you've changed quite a bit in actions and in heart."

"Yes, I have. So you think you'll end up being Aunt Louisa's companion?"

"I don't really think so. She's not in the position to require a full-time companion here at home, and she has no desire to travel, so I wouldn't be needed there. No, it's Haw River for me."

* * * * *

Later that day, the mail arrived. The idea depressed Hestia. She wouldn't be getting any Valentine's Day cards. She wished she could have cooked a meal for Booth, but since he hadn't made romantic moves toward her, she didn't want to ask him to dinner on Valentine's Day.

Aunt Louisa beat her to the door to gather the mail. She riffled through the stack.

Hestia couldn't resist teasing her aunt. "You seem anxious. Are you expecting greetings from a secret admirer?"

"Secret? I have many admirers, and some are not so secret." Aunt Louisa gave her a mischievous smile as she held up an envelope that obviously contained a card. "See?" She handed her the rest of the mail.

"I hope there's something in here for Selene."

"I'm not so sure I am. She needs to have her baby and then put all this behind her."

Hestia looked through the mail and took a couple of cards addressed to Selene. The feminine handwriting on both told they were from her friends, most likely sent out of compassion.

Hestia pulled out three cards for her. Her group had remembered her after all. She and her women friends sent each other Valentine's Day cards every year so no matter if they had beaux or not, they wouldn't be forgotten. The cards would be bittersweet this year. Surely they would include notes about how things should be so different today.

To her surprise, she noticed a card with no return address and handwriting she didn't recognize, addressed to her. "Wonder who sent this?"

Aunt Louisa looked as curious as Hestia. "Open it and find out."

She didn't have to be asked twice. Taking the silver letter opener from Aunt Louisa, she slit open the missive. Inside was a card with a charming couple on it, nostalgia from a bygone era. "Hoping a sweet lady has a sweet Valentine's Day." It was signed, "Will you be my valentine?"

Hestia looked for a signature. "He didn't sign his name."

"I reckon it's Booth, don't you?"

Hestia's heart jumped at the thought. "I don't know. I hadn't expected him to send me a card."

"Did you expect any men from Haw River to send you one?"

"No, and I don't recognize the handwriting. Can't say I've seen much of Booth's handwriting, though."

"All things considered, I'd say it's definitely Booth."

"Is that wishful thinking?" Hestia didn't want to admit Booth's love was her wish, too.

"Wishful thinking?"

"You do want me to stay here, don't you?"

"I could think of worse things." Aunt Louisa smiled.

"Well, unless the secret admirer makes himself known, I won't be able to give him an answer either way. Besides, it can't be Booth. Why would he put the card in the mail when he could just bring it over here and give it to me directly?"

Aunt Louisa's posture deflated. "That's true. Maybe it is someone from Haw River, then."

"Whoever it is, I hope he makes himself known very soon."

* * * * *

Booth felt nervous as he got ready to go to Miss Louisa's. Did Hestia know the card was from him? Maybe he should have put a return address on it. Maybe he should have just carried it over himself.

He had made a special trip to Lincolnton to buy an extravagant gift—a half-dozen red roses for Hestia. Maybe he shouldn't make such a bold gesture. She hadn't committed to staying in Maiden. Then again, she talked about Haw River less and less. He sniffed the roses, taking in their sweet scent. At least while she was here she could enjoy a nice Valentine's Day.

Feeling like an awkward teenager instead of a confident man, he took tentative steps onto the veranda and knocked on the front door. His hopes that Hestia would answer were realized when she appeared and invited him to step into the parlor. She looked lovely in a new fuchsia dress fashioned in a linear style. The bold color looked good on her. "You must be dressed for Valentine's Day."

She looked down at her frock. "I hadn't even thought of that, but you're right—I do look as though I dressed for the day." She smiled. "Do you like it? I ordered it out of the Wish Book."

"It does." He remembered his gift, which Hestia had been kind enough to pretend not to notice. "I brought you something." He handed her the roses.

"They're beautiful. You didn't have to, but I love them." She chose an especially pretty bloom and sniffed it with a dainty motion. She reminded him of a gentle portrait. "They smell wonderful. Thank you."

He couldn't wait to ask his next question. "Did you get any cards today?"

"You mean, any from someone who wouldn't sign his?"

He cleared his throat. "Did you get more than one?"

"Ah, that's my secret." She smiled coyly but turned serious. "No, just one that wasn't signed. The rest were from my women friends."

"I'm surprised I don't have competition." Though he joked, he felt relieved. "I feel silly. I've never asked a girl to be my valentine before. At least, not since I was in grade school. And she turned me down."

"Silly her."

"So what will it be? Will you be my valentine?"

She hesitated.

He drew close enough that he could inhale the scent of the perfume she'd gotten for Christmas. The scent always smelled nice on her. "I know the offer is only good for the next couple of months, but at least we will have a wonderful memory."

"I would like that. I would like that very much." She looked at the pine floor and back. "You know, your card made me realize something. I really and truly have gotten over Luther."

Even the mention of his name sent jealousy through Booth. "Was there a doubt?"

"No. And yes. You see, today was supposed to be our wedding day."

"Oh." His heart hurt for her.

"This was one of the hardest days of my life. And your card helped me get through it. Thank you."

Hestia didn't know it, but he'd thought often about that day they'd lain together in the leaves, looking at clouds floating in the sky. Often he'd thought about kissing her. If only Miss Olive hadn't stopped him, he would have kissed her then. He'd fantasized about kissing her on Valentine's Day, thinking the occasion would be perfect for a romantic gesture. But as soon as she said that was supposed to be her wedding day, the idea no longer felt right to him. He'd wait just a bit longer.

But if Haw River was her ultimate destination, perhaps it would be better if their lips never met. He bid her a good-bye much less loving than he'd planned, forcing himself to be content with her gratitude. Touching his arm, she looked at him with longing in her eyes. Yet he couldn't linger.

Leaving Miss Louisa's yard, his walk must have made him appear dejected, but he didn't care. He felt dejected. What should have been a superlative Valentine's Day had turned out to be a dud.

"Booth!" a male voice called.

Booth saw Artie in the distance. He waved and walked toward his friend. Though in no mood to talk to anyone, he couldn't very well change directions.

Artie was soon upon him. "What's the matter? You look like you lost your best friend."

"I'll be fine."

Booth felt grateful when Artie didn't press for details. "I don't mind telling you I'm nervous as a cat. I've decided to ask Selene to be my valentine."

"She's not available, Artie." Booth's sour mood made his warning sound harsh.

"That might be true, but not for the reason you're thinking. I can forgive her past, but I have to be sure she's right with the Lord. I can't be unequally yoked. At this point, I think if we joined our lives in marriage, we would be. I can't let that happen. I've made too many mistakes in my weak state already."

For Artie to brook the notion of marriage shocked Booth. "You– you're going to propose?"

"Not yet. I'll just tell her how I feel."

Booth had no doubt Selene would respond with warmth. If only he had been so lucky.

* * * * *

Sitting up in the bed that had become her prison, Selene looked at the card that arrived in the mail. She hadn't expected to receive any. Flora sent and signed one, and Mildred, another. Hers included a note:

Selene dear:

> *Still miss you terribly. Nothing is the same without you.*

> *I have to say, things here have calmed down since you left and Ned married that girl. We haven't been going to as many hooch parties. I'm not as impressed by the fellows there as I once was. Not that you'll find me in church, mind you, but I don't have the heart to go to the parties anymore. Flora's chasing after Ethan*

now, and you know what a creep he is. A charming creep, but a
creep. As for me, I'm keeping time with Timothy. He's a straight
arrow. I think maybe he won't mind a flapper even though he's
not as dapper as our usual fellows. Of course, if we wed, I won't be
much of a flapper any more. It will be a baby carriage for me, but
a respectable amount of time after our wedding day.

Oh, I wish we could be talking instead of me getting writer's
cramp from penning this long letter. When will you come home,
Selene? We need you.

Mildred

Her friend's plea consoled Selene, even as her eyes misted. The letter told her all the more how nothing would ever be the same. The carefree time of parties and fun had passed, and her friends were getting serious. She realized it was for the best. No need for them to find themselves in her position.

Hestia stuck her head in the door. "You have a visitor."

"Me?"

"I don't see anyone else in here. You'd better wipe those tears away. Artie won't want to see you like that. Did someone write something that upset you?"

She stared at the letter in her lap. "I—I miss my friends."

"You'll be going home soon enough. Just thank God for the friends you have here to get you through. Now dry those eyes."

"Okay. Give me a minute before you send him in, will you?"

"Of course."

Selene made certain her white bed jacket was buttoned to the top, and she wiped her eyes with the handkerchief she kept in her nightstand drawer.

After a few moments, Artie came in, bearing a single pink rose in a bud vase. "Happy Valentine's Day."

She gasped at the rose. "For me?"

He nodded. "Can I set it on the table beside you?"

"I'd like that."

"I would have gotten a full bouquet, but I knew you didn't have much room in here."

"It's perfect." Selene didn't exaggerate. She'd never seen a more beautiful flower.

"But why?"

He deflated. "Oh. I overstepped, didn't I?"

"No," she blurted. "I—I mean, I don't want you to give me this because you feel sorry for me."

"I wanted you to have this rose as a gift from me." He sat in the chair he always used when they studied together. "I don't feel sorry for you. I can see you've repented. I really can't see you going back to a fast life, even once you return to New York. And when you do, my prayers will follow you." He paused. "But feel sorry for you? No."

"Really?"

"Why are you so surprised? You're the new type of woman, a member of the first generation born after the year 1900. You've been granted the right to vote. You're the envy of the world, not a victim."

She took a moment to think about his words. He was right. If she didn't waste her life, she'd be a success. Still, she couldn't resist a wry comment. "And just look at me now."

"That's right. Just look at you now." He bent toward her and gave her a kiss on the lips. She hadn't kissed anyone since Ned. Artie's lips felt soft yet strong. His mood wasn't one of insistence but gentleness. So different from Ned. And so much better.

She hadn't expected him to kiss her—or that she'd be so moved by him. She didn't want him to break away, but when he did, she had a question. "What was that for?"

"To show you how fond I am of you. Are you sorry? If I offended you, I'll respect you enough never to do that again."

"Respect me?" No man had ever said such a thing to her.

"Yes. Respect you. I do have respect for you as a person, and as a woman."

She remembered Ned. He was the first man she'd ever loved. She never thought of herself as fast. Unlike some of her acquaintances, she hadn't enjoyed the attentions of several men. At first Ned had been sweet, attentive. Then his kisses became more urgent, and he became demanding. If only she hadn't felt she needed to prove her love for him. She wanted to blame her father, but she couldn't. She knew right from wrong, and she was paying dearly for compromising herself. Ned had even promised marriage, so she hadn't felt compromised. Only after he made sport of her and their secret engagement did she realize she had made the mistake of her life.

"I really mean it. I respect you, Selene." Artie's words made images of Ned dissolve.

"You won't believe this, but that's the most romantic thing anybody's ever said to me."

He didn't laugh as she expected. Instead, he gave her a serious look. "You know what? I believe you."

Selene thought about her past. "I don't deserve your respect. I don't deserve anyone's respect."

"Yes, you do. You've been very brave to leave your home to come here to wait out this pregnancy. I know you're not the first and you won't be the last girl in such a situation, but that was a brave thing to do. You have kept your head up even after the man you loved left you. And best of all, you have pursued a relationship with the Lord since you've been here."

"Because of you. Aunt Louisa and Hestia encourage me to read the Bible. Aunt Louisa preaches at me once in a while." She grinned. "But you took the time to sit with me and help me understand what the Bible really says. Thank you. But why did you kiss me?"

"Because, I—I love you."

Selene gasped. "How can you love me? I'm a fallen woman."

"I don't see you as a fallen woman. I see you as a beautiful woman. Don't let the fact that I'm not bold and brash fool you. I have never been a man of convention. I have never lived in fear of what others think. If anything, you should be questioning your judgment in being involved with me, a reformed drinker and gambler. What respectable woman would want to hitch herself to the likes of me?"

"Do you think you can't do any better than to be involved with me?"

"I know I can't do any better than to be involved with you."

She had meant to ask if he spent time with her because no respectable woman would have anything to do with him, but his answer told her something else: that he really wanted to keep company with her. That she was his first choice. She couldn't remember feeling more special. Tears flowed down her cheeks.

"Now, you're much too pretty to cry. Especially on Valentine's Day." He took his handkerchief from his trousers pocket and wiped away the tears.

Chapter Seventeen

....

Wanting to wake up to the fragrance and sight of the beautiful roses, Hestia took the flowers into her room. Booth's thoughtfulness had helped make this a better Valentine's Day than it could have been otherwise. She'd never forget his kindness.

She found her cousin sitting up in bed. "I thought you'd be asleep by now."

"I'm too excited to sleep." Selene cut her gaze to a single rose in a glass vase on her table.

"That's pretty." Hestia almost felt guilty that Booth had given her six roses. Though impossible to hide them, Hestia made no show as she set her vase of flowers on the vanity. "Did Artie bring it?"

Selene nodded. "You got quite a take. Booth, naturally?"

"Yes." She tried not to look self-satisfied as she studied her roses. If only Booth had kissed her and proclaimed his love, the night would have been perfect.

"Tell me something, Hestia."

"What?" Hestia climbed under the covers of her bed but remained upright, leaning against a soft down pillow propped against the oak headboard.

"How popular is Artie?"

Hestia hadn't been expecting that query. "How popular is Artie? What kind of silly question is that?"

"Oh, I was just wondering. I mean, is he popular with the ladies?"

"I haven't noticed. Why?"

"Well..." Selene hesitated. "It's just that he said he loves me. And he kissed me."

Hestia gasped and tried to fight her jealousy. Why couldn't Booth be as outspoken? "He did? How do you feel about that?"

"It was a shock, I can say that. I've been thinking about him. I don't understand why he likes me."

Hestia regretted that her cousin had to question why a man would be attracted to her. Truly her confidence was at a low level. "Haven't you looked at yourself lately? Even with the baby coming soon, you still have a spark, that certain something, that most women don't have. I think that's why he likes you."

Selene looked at her abdomen. "That certain something, huh?"

"You must have an attraction. I didn't get a proclamation of love tonight. Or a kiss."

Selene's eyebrows shot up and back. "I'm surprised, the way Booth moons all over you. He must like to move slowly."

"I think you're right." Hestia took comfort in Selene's observation even as she wished he'd move faster. She forced such an unladylike idea out of her mind.

"Do you think Artie just feels sorry for me?" Selene sounded pitiful.

"Haven't you learned anything from being in Bible study with him all this time? I'd be shocked if Artie would form a real relationship with someone out of pity. He's overcome a lot, and I think that discipline has made him unsympathetic to people he thinks are weak."

Selene thought for a moment. "I can see that."

"You're a strong woman, Selene. I think that's why he keeps coming here to see you. I know he'll be heartbroken when you go back to New York."

"You really think so?"

"I guarantee it." Hestia only wished Booth would be as sorry to see her go.

* * * * *

The next day, when Artie stopped by to talk about their Bible reading, he seemed a bit more animated than usual. Selene suspected he felt nervous.

She tried to calm him. "I hope you don't regret what you said last night."

"I don't. Do you?"

"No. I haven't felt so good in a long time. Because of you, I had the best Valentine's Day in memory." Not caring if Aunt Louisa would consider her too bold, she took his hand and squeezed it then let go. "You're a good man, Artie Rowland. Much better than I deserve. Because of Ned, and because of my condition, I hadn't thought of love. Now it's all I think about."

He gave her a smile of understanding, and Selene felt a sense of peace.

* * * * *

A week later when Artie came over for their in-depth Bible study, Selene wasn't tempted to apply face paint. Artie wouldn't judge her, but he wouldn't want her to wear it. She couldn't remember a time in years she hadn't applied face paint when getting ready to see a man she considered a beau. The freedom felt good. All the same, she took care to don her best bed jacket and to make her hair look as good as it could, considering its two-toned state.

Artie showed up on time as always, a smile on his face and a happy greeting on his lips. Ready to discuss Paul's missionary trips, he had maps in hand. Booth, Hestia, and even Aunt Louisa wanted to sit in on the lesson. Selene was sorry, because she enjoyed her relatively private time with Artie, even if it did involve discussing maps and missionaries.

Artie sat down with all of them. Selene almost felt as though she were holding court since they all had to bring their chairs around her bed. He showed them the apostle's journey and talked about how the prisoners, Barnabas and Paul, were released from their chains.

"They were freed much as we're released from the bondage of sin. Just as I was released from the chains of gambling and drinking," Artie said. "Bondage is such a tricky thing when it's sin, because it seems like fun. I always felt on top of the world when I was winning at the gambling tables, and I felt more confident, not so shy, when I drank to excess. But I realized that these were masks of power, pretend power, with sources from Satan. Now I gain my strength from God, not hooch and chasing easy money."

"I wish I hadn't touched hooch," Selene said. "I never want to see it or be anywhere around it again."

"That will be hard once you go back to New York, won't it?" Hestia's voice held no criticism or judgment.

"Yes, it will. My friends have slowed down some, but not entirely."

"You'll just have to keep away from parties when you go back. You'll have to drop the friends who insist you go to them." Artie's mouth formed a determined line.

"Drop my friends?"

Artie nodded. "I was forced to give up several of my friends when I changed. They didn't like the new me. They said I wasn't fun anymore. But Selene, for the sake of your spiritual and physical health, you've got to do the same thing I did. Find new friends."

"I dread that."

"No one said it would be easy. But do you want to be in bondage?"

"No. No, I don't."

"Then you'd better go to the Lord right now," Aunt Louisa said. "He's the only one who can help you."

Artie leaned toward her. "The Lord's the only One who could help me. He's the only One who can take away your sins and make you as bright as freshly fallen snow."

"I'd sure hate to go to heaven and wait for you only to find that you weren't coming there to be with me." Aunt Louisa's voice cracked.

"Really? You want to be with me in the afterlife?" Selene couldn't believe it. "I didn't think you wanted to be with me much even now."

"Heaven wouldn't be the same without you." A tear escaped from Aunt Louisa's eye, a sight Selene found shocking and touching. "I don't want you to be punished. Please come to the Lord."

Hestia put her arm around Aunt Louisa but looked at Selene. "Yes, please."

"I want you as my sister in Christ, too." Booth looked at her with sincerity in his eyes.

Selene felt overwhelmed by the love in the room. She knew everyone there was fond of her, but she hadn't realized the depth of their emotion. Unconditional love was new to her, too. Remembering Artie's words, she had no doubt many would drop her if she developed a relationship with Christ. Her father loved her as a daughter, but his selfish love was not without its familial expectations.

This group was different. Aunt Louisa had agreed to take her out of kindness. Booth owed her nothing, and Hestia had showed her compassion even in her shock over Selene's situation. And Artie—he had no reason to love her except for love itself. If anything, he had every reason not to love her. But he did. The love of these people showed her the love of Christ—selfless love.

At that moment, Selene knew she had grown up enough to distinguish genuine love from surface emotions. She wanted that love forever. "Then I will accept Christ. I really want to be with God, and with all of you, in eternity."

Artie regarded her with an unremitting but kind gaze. "You really mean that? Then profess your faith!"

"I do." At that moment, Selene realized how much she had changed since she arrived in Maiden. No longer was she the carefree flapper. Even her speech patterns had matured, involving less slang. She felt the Holy Spirit surrounding her with these newfound Christian friends.

She would be a mother. Nothing would ever change that. That very fact made her feel more like a part of the world that really mattered, not the society circle whose most important concern of any given day was where the next party would be. Her life had purpose. She was God's child now and would be bringing another soul into God's creation.

"I hadn't thought much about eternity before I came here, and especially before I started listening to your devotionals, Artie. But now I see how important it is. I'd hate to face death without knowing where I would end up." Selene didn't want to mention it to her friends, but the prospect of giving birth frightened her. She had no reason to believe she would die in childbirth, but sometimes, in spite of everyone's best efforts, the day they gave birth was the last day some women spent on the earth. At least now, she would see Jesus if God decided to take her at that time. Before, she didn't know for certain. Other than being baptized as an infant, she hadn't paid much attention to the Lord. Now she wanted to know Him. And with Artie's help, she could.

* * * * *

The next day at work, Artie stopped by Booth's office. Booth set aside his papers long enough to speak to his friend. "Last night was amazing, wasn't it, old man?"

"The best night for any Christian." Artie shut the door behind him. "Have you got a minute?"

"Always, for you. Is everything okay?"

Artie nodded. "It's about Selene."

Booth pointed to the empty wooden chair. "Have a seat."

"I'll stand. I'm too excited to sit. I have to tell someone, and I know you'll keep what I say in confidence."

"Sure thing." Booth wondered what Artie could possibly have to say.

Artie cleared his throat. "You see, last night had bigger implications for me than anyone realizes. I haven't told anyone else this, but I have an engagement ring for Selene."

Booth felt his mouth drop open much as a baby bird's. "An engagement ring?"

"I know that seems strange to most people, but not to me. You see, I became infatuated with Selene the first day I saw her. And that infatuation grew into love. But my wife must be a Christian." His voice took on a tone of awe. "And now she is."

Artie's love for Selene touched Booth's heart. "If you were any other fellow, I'd ask you if you were just trying to be her knight in shining armor, wanting to rescue her from her problem of being an unwed mother. But I can see you really love her for herself."

"Absolutely. The baby is only a gift, as far as I'm concerned."

"So why didn't you ask her last night?"

"You don't know how bad I wanted to do that. Yet I just didn't feel a leading from the Lord. The night was big enough for her—for all of us—without me adding such an important question. But I will ask her, in God's time."

Booth pondered Artie's confession. "I'm happy for you. I think she'll accept."

"I hope so. If she does, I'll be the happiest man alive."

* * * * *

Hestia rode toward Lincolnton, just over the Catawba County border in Lincoln County. She sat in the passenger seat of the roadster, with

Judith driving. "I hope I can find a decent hat this close to Easter," Hestia shouted over the roaring motor.

"Serves us right for waiting until the Friday before Easter," she shouted.

Thankfully, Hestia had tied the hat she already wore tightly enough that the wind wouldn't whip it off her head. The open air felt brisk, but the sun shone and with a spring wrap, she felt protected enough to enjoy invigoration without feeling chilled.

"Glad you could come out today," Judith yelled. "Daddy doesn't let me have the motorcar often."

Soon they arrived in town and Judith found a place to park. Hestia rejoiced in the chance to speak in a normal volume.

"I can't wait to see the new hats. I hope I can find something to match my new dress."

Judith jumped from behind the steering wheel. "I love what you did with your aunt's dress pattern. You inspired me to try a linear number, too."

"I can't wait to see it. We'll be the most stylish women in church." Hestia got out of the Studebaker and shut the door. "Do you think Peter will notice?"

She blushed. "I hope so. He sent me a card for Valentine's Day, you know."

"That's making progress, I'd say."

"I'm glad I took you up on your suggestion to invite him to our Thanksgiving dinner. I couldn't believe he accepted." The two women walked past a pharmacy.

"And why wouldn't he? He's getting the prettiest girl in town."

They stopped in front of a milliner's shop and admired the window display. "Look at how close to the head the new styles are."

"For shorter hair." Judith's voice told of her mixed emotions. She touched her wavy locks.

In empathy and feeling adrift herself, Hestia patted her own hair, which was pinned into a chignon. "Sometimes I wonder if Selene is right. Am I behind the times?"

"We're behind the times together." Judith peered not at the hats, but at her reflection in the window. "Once you go back to Haw River, I wonder if we'll be behind the times alone in our respective towns."

"Maybe the new styles are starting to gain acceptance. They wouldn't be displaying these hats if no one was buying them." Hestia noticed a brown hat trimmed with white rickrack. She didn't favor it for spring. Instead, she preferred the pink one with a crystal rhinestone and perky yellow feather. "I have noticed more of the girls our age getting their hair bobbed. Respectable girls, at that."

"Maybe fashion has gotten to the point that if you get a bob it doesn't have to mean you drink bathtub gin."

"We certainly don't have to wear Ox Blood lipstick," Hestia pointed out.

"Or dye our hair."

"Let's go in." Hestia just had to try on the pink hat.

As they entered, Hestia noticed a buxom woman of short stature giving her image in the mirror a critical eye. "I don't know if this is really me or not."

A tall saleswoman surveyed a broad-brimmed hat overburdened with an array of wax fruit—bananas, grapes, apples, and pears. "Oh, but it is, Mrs. Williams. It's even more beautiful than the hat I fashioned for you last year. I worked on it for so long, making it just as you said you wanted."

Mrs. Williams cut her glance to Judith. "What do you think, my dear girl?"

Judith looked like an ill-prepared student. "Uh, I don't know. What do you think, Hestia?"

Hestia did her best to resist giving Judith a dirty look. The customer tilted her head in doubt, while the saleswoman's clasped hands and hopeful expression told her that Hestia could make or break the sale. Why did she have to be stuck in the middle? The hat overwhelmed the woman, and the fact that she was voluptuous and wearing fruit made her look as though she couldn't go anywhere without food. Hestia pictured her plucking a banana off her head and eating it in the middle of worship service. The image amused her so much it took all her discipline to hold back a giggle.

"Don't you think it's beautiful?" The saleswoman's eyes widened. "I spent all night on it, fastening the fruit in place, just so it would be ready in time for Easter Sunday."

"This is the hat you ordered?" Hestia looked at Mrs. Williams.

She examined herself. "Yes, it is made to my specifications."

Hestia searched for what to say. "I think it shows a remarkable degree of talent. And the colors are very nice."

Mrs. Williams's expression lightened. "Yes, they are. I'll take it."

"Thank you!" The saleswoman's posture relaxed and she threw Hestia a grateful look. "I'll be right with you girls."

"No hurry," Judith said. "We'll just browse."

Hestia looked at every hat in the store. Mrs. Williams's was notable for being the only one sporting a broad brim. All the others were fashioned in the new style, made to fit close to the head. A white hat with white roses struck her, but she decided it looked too much like a bride.

A bride. Something she wouldn't be anytime soon. She swallowed.

"Look at this one." Judith pointed to a felt hat. "Don't you love the color?"

"I think the beige would look very well with your hair, but I would look sick in it."

"Well, if you wouldn't look sick in it, would you like it?"

Hestia studied the hat, with its cream-colored ribbon and orange rose. "Yes, I would."

A green hat caught Hestia's eye, but upon closer inspection she realized the hue wouldn't do a thing for the shimmering pink dress she had sewn for herself. If she bought a hat from this milliner, it would be the pink one with the rhinestone and yellow feather or nothing.

The bell on the door tinkled, signaling the exit of Mrs. Williams. The saleswoman approached them. "Thank you for encouraging Mrs. Williams for me. She does the same thing every year—orders an elaborate hat no one else would want. Then when she sees it, she acts as though it's the most hideous thing ever. Honestly, she's a trial. Oh, I don't suppose I should say that. I'm sorry."

Hestia realized that frustration had overtaken the woman's better judgment. But who didn't have a bad day? "You did a wonderful job with it."

"I can't say I'd wear it, though." Judith giggled.

Hestia elbowed her in the rib. "Judith!"

"That's okay. I wouldn't wear it, either." The saleswoman picked up the pink hat Hestia had been admiring. "Now this is my favorite."

"Is it?"

"Yes, and I think it would look lovely on you." She handed it to Hestia. "Try it and see how it looks."

Hestia happily complied. Only, the hat didn't fit well over her hair.

"Do you like it?"

"Yes, but..."

"It's made for shorter hair." Judith's voice sounded with regret.

"It's true that a lot of the girls are getting bobs." The saleswoman nodded.

Hestia looked at her more closely and noticed she didn't have a bob, but then again, girlhood had passed her by long ago.

"A lot of the girls?" Judith tilted her head.

"Yes." The woman nodded. "Just about every one of them coming in here now has a bob. I think they're taking the plunge for Easter."

"Let me try on the beige hat." Judith reached for it.

"That is a good choice for you. It will look well with your dark hair."

"That's what I told her," Hestia said.

Judith tried on the beige hat. Indeed, it did look well with the color of her hair, but like Hestia, she sported too much of a mane for the hat to look right. She set it down. "I don't think I should take it."

"Oh, but it's lovely on you." The saleswoman's voice sounded only a tad less pleading than it had when she spoke to Mrs. Williams. "I have an idea. Why don't you set your hair in a low bun so it won't get in the way of your hat? I think that will work just fine."

Judith brightened. "That is an idea. What do you think, Hestia?"

Hestia visualized Judith wearing a low bun with her new hat. "I think that just might work."

"All right. I'll take it."

"And the pink one for you?" The saleswoman pointed to it.

Looking at the hat, Hestia hesitated.

"Oh, come on," Judith prodded. "You can wear your hair in a low bun, too. We'll look wonderful together in church."

"I don't know...."

The saleswoman went for the kill. "Don't wait too long. Two other women have already been in here eying that hat, and Easter Sunday is only two days away."

"She's right," Judith pointed out. "If you wait, it's liable to be gone when you get back."

Hestia couldn't remember ever seeing a lovelier hat. "I'll take it."

Chapter Eighteen

....

Selene thumbed through one of Hestia's copies of *National Geographic*.
Expecting no one, she ignored the knock on the front door, so when
Artie entered her room a few moments later, she registered mild surprise.

"Your aunt said you were awake and wouldn't mind seeing me."

Selene set aside the periodical. "I never mind seeing you, Artie."

Always the gentleman, he asked after her and they exchanged
pleasantries. Pulling a chair up next to her bed so he could sit beside her,
Artie wasted little time in changing the subject. "Finally."

His one-word observation piqued her interest. "Finally what?"

He took in a breath and hesitated. She'd never seen him appear
nervous in the past, but he rubbed his hand on his thigh and didn't seem
to realize what he was doing.

"Are you okay?"

"I think so. It's just that, I've been waiting to ask you something,
and now that's it's been over a month since you accepted the Lord and
I can see you growing closer to Him each day, I think I finally can."
At that moment, she noticed his eyes appeared especially green. He
wasn't matinee-idol handsome, but his face was pleasant to behold. She
imagined his features would age well.

"What is it, Artie?"

"Now, I don't want you to answer right away. I know you're used to
the big city, and Maiden isn't a big city by any stretch of the imagination.
But I have a house and a job here, and I've made it my home." He cleared
his throat. "And I guess Miss Olive, and maybe some other people, have
been more than happy to tell you that a lot of folks around here don't
want much to do with me."

She remembered the first day Miss Olive realized Artie was visiting their house and how she had told Aunt Louisa that she shouldn't let Hestia or her have anything to do with him. The same day, Hestia realized Selene was in a family way. She cringed at the memory. "I'll be honest. She did say something about your past. But who am I to criticize? You're a good man today. That's the Artie I know…" Should she say it? "…and love."

"You have just made me very happy. Very happy." He swallowed, obviously overcome with emotion. He took a moment to recover his composure. "I'm trying to be a good man. Some people, especially people at my church, realize that. Even they had doubts at first. They took me into their fold because of Granny. Out of respect for her, they got to know me. I've finally lived down my past, as least as far as they're concerned. But I might never live it down with some of the people here in town." A thoughtful look, as though he pictured some of those people in his mind, crossed his face, but then he shrugged. "I'll just have to live with that."

"I'm sorry. Are you telling me this because you think I'll have trouble when I go back to New York? Because if you are, I appreciate it, but I know I won't be as popular as I once was." She tried to send him a cheerful smile, but she knew the halfhearted crooked grin she made hardly fit the bill. "I'll have to live it down, as you say."

"It sounds as though you've got a hard row to hoe after this wherever you end up."

"Don't try to make me feel any better."

"I'm sorry. I'm making a big mess of this, aren't I?"

"A big mess of what?" Whatever it was, she wished he'd get to the point.

"The question I have for you. I just don't want you to think everything would be—copacetic—as you say, if you married me."

Selene was glad she hadn't been holding one of Aunt Louisa's prized china figurines, because if she had, it would have dropped out of her hands and shattered into a million pieces. "Wha–what did you say?"

"I said, if you married me."

"Marry you? Are you sure?" Her heart beat so hard she could feel it in her ears. That such a man would ask her to marry him, after everything, amazed her.

"I am."

"What about the baby?"

"I have prayed about this and thought about it every night. If you want to know the truth, the thought that you could be the one for me crossed my mind when we first met, but I had to get to know you better first. I want to be a husband to you and a father to your baby. But at first I wasn't sure you wanted to keep the baby. I was always told you planned to give him up for adoption."

"That–that's still the plan." Selene wished she could keep her tears from falling.

"I'm sorry. The last thing I want is to upset you. Forgive me." He patted her hand.

She concentrated on the bed post, unwilling to look him in the eye. "You haven't done anything wrong. I just wish things were different."

"I know. And things can be different, largely because I can see you really do love your baby." He took in a breath. "I think I have reached a place in my life where I can offer the woman I have grown to love a good home. I'll admit, I didn't think I'd fall for a woman who already had a child on the way, but my feelings for you are undeniable."

Tears streamed down her cheeks. "No one has ever made me such an unselfish offer."

"Please don't say anything now. I'll return for my answer in a day or two. What I am proposing is a name for your baby, yes, but together we'll have to overcome many obstacles. We might not be welcomed into every home in Maiden, but I have a feeling your aunt Louisa and Booth will stand behind us, and I know the people at my church will support us."

"Don't forget Hestia."

"Of course she'd love you through everything if she were to stay here, but isn't she going back to Haw River soon?"

The thought left Selene feeling depressed. But after the baby arrived, she couldn't depend on Hestia any longer. She would be in neither Maiden nor New York. "Yes, she'll be leaving."

"If you decide to accept my proposal, we'll invite her to visit often. I promise." He squeezed her hand. "Good night, Selene. I'll see you again soon."

"Okay." She wished he didn't have to go. But he did. She had much to contemplate. She knew she had made the right decision about the Lord. She could only hope her next decision would be the right one.

* * * * *

Later, after Judith dropped her off at the house, Hestia carried in her packages with pride. Not only had she bought the hat, but she had splurged on a pair of satin shoes with rosettes attached. Maybe she shouldn't have made such bold moves, but she had been impulsive. Impulse wasn't something she allowed herself often. She'd blame it on the spring air.

She went into her bedroom, where of course Selene waited. "Oh, there you are. I have news." Parted lips and wide eyes showed more optimism than Hestia had seen from Selene since her arrival.

"What is it?"

"You'll never guess."

She paused, wondering if she should verbalize her thought. "Um, you want to keep the baby."

"I do, but that's not my news." She looked down at the quilt covering her body. "Although this would give me a chance to keep the baby."

"Huh?"

"Artie came to see me today."

"That's nice. Did you discuss your latest Bible reading?"

"Oh, you! Can't you figure it out? Artie asked me to marry him."

Hestia gasped. "Marry him? Did you tell Aunt Louisa?"

"Not yet. I wanted you to know first."

"What did you say?"

"I haven't said anything yet. His offer's tempting. Very tempting." Selene looked down at her midsection. "I have come to love Artie over these past months, but…"

"You don't want to stay in Maiden."

"That's not it."

Hestia knew her face registered shock. "It isn't?"

"I can't say I thought I'd settle here, but because of Artie, this town has much more to offer than I ever thought it could. And I want to keep the baby, Hestia. Is that so wrong?"

Hestia considered how no one thought living with distant relatives would be ideal for the child. "No, it's not. But what if the baby looks like Ned? Will you still love him?"

Selene rubbed her abdomen. "Yes. Yes, I would. I forgave Ned long ago. But I hate to think of the sacrifice Artie would be making to marry me. Everyone will know the truth about the baby."

"All three of you would face some gossip, no doubt. But I also think people will have enough common sense not to blame the baby. And even though the baby would be getting a legitimate name belatedly, he'll never remember anyone else as his father. Before you know it, the whole situation will be ancient history. You'll seem like any other married couple."

"You really think so?"

"It will take time, but I think so." Hestia pondered the man who asked Selene to be his wife. "I admire Artie."

"I do, too. I think I could make him a good wife. I'd really try."

"I know you would. Anybody who can change as much as you have while you've been here can do most anything."

Selene's sigh sounded her contentment, a peace that she had resolved her quandary.

"Let's call in Aunt Louisa. She needs to know that Artie proposed."

"No." Selene shook her head. "I'm not ready to tell her yet."

Hestia understood that their aunt could be intimidating, so she didn't press. Instead, she started unpacking her goods.

"Did you have fun shopping with Judith?"

"Yes. At first I thought you might resent me for getting out of the house, but I'd say your afternoon was much more exciting than mine."

"Oh, do let me live vicariously through you. Show me what you got."

"You really want to see?" Hestia's voice sounded her excitement.

"I wouldn't ask if I didn't."

Hestia showed her the shoes then the hat.

"You can't wear your new hat without getting all that hair out of the way."

Hestia sighed. "I'm wearing it in a low bun."

"A low bun? If you do that, you'll not only be a Mrs. Grundy, but you'll look like one, too."

Hestia didn't want to admit it, but Selene was right. "Maybe I should send it back."

"Did I hear the term Mrs. Grundy?" Aunt Louisa asked, entering the room. "Selene, I must insist that you stop using such derogatory terms."

"I'm sorry, Aunt Louisa."

Their aunt eyed Hestia wearing the pink hat. "That is quite flashy."

"Is it too much?"

Aunt Louisa studied the feather. "I don't suppose so for a young woman like you. But you have too much hair for it."

"That's what I was telling her." Selene sighed. "I can't believe my hair has grown out so much. I can almost cut all the color out of it. I'm not used to looking so mousy, though."

"I don't think you look mousy at all," Aunt Louisa said.

"That's what you'd say. I am in desperate need of a new bob. Won't you try to cut it for me, Hestia?"

Hestia didn't blame Selene for wanting a new haircut, as hers had grown shaggy, but Hestia lacked confidence with scissors. "Oh, I don't know. I haven't cut very much hair. Scissors don't touch mine."

"It's nothing. Why, Flora and I cut each other's the first time we got our bobs."

"I'm pretty handy with scissors," Aunt Louisa said. "Why don't you let me do it?"

"You?" Selene placed her hand on her chest. "Handy with scissors? Why, I can't imagine you ever cut hair."

"I did indeed. Why, for a time, I ran a beauty parlor out of this house."

"You know, I seem to remember Papa mentioning that." Hestia thought it best not to remind Aunt Louisa she had closed up shop long before The Great War.

"I haven't forgotten how to cut hair. Granted, we never chopped ours as much as you do now, but I could trim a straight line for the ladies who wanted to keep their hair from getting that ragged look."

Hestia thought about how the end of her hair had taken on the unflattering shape of a sloppy letter *v*. "I could use a trim myself."

"Well, we have our work cut out for us this afternoon, don't we?" Louisa winked. "Don't you like my joke?"

"I suppose that is funny." Hestia chuckled, and Selene shook her head.

Filled with a sense of purpose, Aunt Louisa brightened. "Let me go fetch my scissors."

Eager to get her hair freshly bobbed, Selene shifted her considerable weight and sat on the edge of the bed.

Aunt Louisa returned with the scissors and studied her charge. "Hmm. I'm not sure I should trim your hair dry, Selene. Do you feel well enough to walk over to the sink to have your hair washed? I think the weather is warm enough that washing it won't endanger you with prospects of a cold."

"Copacetic!" She started to get out of bed.

"Be careful!" Taking her arm, Hestia led Selene to the kitchen. The two women shampooed Selene's frayed hair until it squeaked.

"I think she can sit in the chair here long enough to have her hair cut," Aunt Louisa said.

"Do you feel up to it, Selene?"

"Oh, yes." Selene looked happier than Hestia had seen her in a long while. "I want to look nice for Artie."

Hestia watched as her aunt, with more skill than she knew the older woman possessed, snipped Selene's hair into a neat line.

"Oh, let me see," Selene said after Aunt Louisa was satisfied.

"Here's a mirror." Hestia gave Selene a silver mirror.

Selene held it up and regarded her reflection. "I almost look like myself again."

"I thought you might like it. I admit, it took me some time to get used to the new style, but it can be right flattering on some of you younger women." Aunt Louisa touched Selene's hair. "You look much better with your natural hair color than you did when you first came here, with your hair that frightful white."

"I liked being a bright blond." Selene grimaced at her reflection. "I think my natural color is dull."

"I think it's a fine color. A dark blond with natural luster." Aunt Louisa nodded once.

"Tell it to Sweeney." Selene looked at Hestia. "How about you, dear cousin? Why don't you get your hair trimmed?"

"I said I would. Do you mind, Aunt Louisa, since you've got the scissors out anyway?"

"I'll be happy to oblige."

"Will you let me stay and watch?" Selene asked. "I'm feeling fine, and I promise not to move from this seat."

"Well, I don't suppose Dr. Lattimore will mind too much. You've been so good." Aunt Louisa smiled.

For Selene's sake, Hestia made haste to wash her hair. It took longer to cleanse than Selene had taken with hers, since Hestia's fell to her waist, but eventually she was ready.

Aunt Louisa held the scissors. "How much do you want me to take off?"

Selene studied Hestia's hair "How about three feet?"

"Three feet?" Hestia took a seat in a chair. "Don't you mean three inches?"

"No. I mean three feet."

"Selene!"

"Oh, come on. Isn't it time for your hair to match your new dresses? Think about your Easter bonnet."

Hestia remembered the array of hats in Lincolnton. "I know. I've been torn. The newer styles do lend themselves to shorter hair."

"Of course they do. Long hair is nice for little girls, but with the new fashions, all the stylish women—not just flappers—will be wearing their hair short, especially now that spring is just around the corner."

"You think so?" Hestia realized Selene's sentiments reflected what the milliner said.

"I know so." Selene pointed her finger at Hestia. "I may not get out much, but I haven't forgotten everything about the world."

"What do you think, Aunt Louisa? I don't want people to think

I'm a…" She looked at Selene and felt chagrined.

"You can say it." Selene rolled her eyes. "Flapper."

Hestia cleared her throat. "Judith said she was thinking about getting her hair bobbed."

"Really?" Aunt Louisa seemed surprised. "Do you think she'll do it?"

"Usually when Judith entertains a notion enough to mention it, she goes ahead with it. Why, I wouldn't be surprised to see her with a bob on Easter Sunday."

"She'll have one if she plans to wear a new cloche hat."

Hestia thought about the pink hat with the rhinestone. "Okay. You can bob it. If you don't mind, Aunt Louisa."

"What will your father say?"

"I'll take full responsibility. And I'm the one who'll have to live with him, not you."

"Let me save your hair for you," Aunt Louisa said. "You'll want to remember it." With a piece of twine she tied Hestia's hair near the nape of her neck, then braided the rest and tied if off again.

"Are you ready?"

"I'm ready." Hestia took in a deep breath. Selene's eyes widened.

"Here goes." Aunt Louisa took her scissors and with a quick but careful motion cut off the braid. "There it is. Your hair. You can keep it forever."

Hestia studied the braid. Was that her hair? Hair that had been a part of her for so long, part of her identity, her crowning glory? And now it was gone, in the name of fashion. Reaching around, she touched the small of her back. No hair. Raising her hand close to her ear, she felt the bottom of her newly short hair. Her long hair. It was gone. Gone forever.

"Oh!" She started to sob.

Aunt Louisa set the braid on the table and embraced Hestia. "There, there. If you don't like your new style, you can always grow it back."

"That's right." Clearly Selene wanted to encourage Hestia all she could. "It'll grow back."

"How many years will that take?" Hestia sobbed.

"Well, it's gone now, and I can't glue it back on." Having spent her quotient of sympathy, Aunt Louisa got down to business. "Now let me finish it off so it'll swing the same as Selene's. Now don't you like the way Selene's looks?"

Hestia sniffled and studied her cousin in her fresh bob. She nodded. "I just hope Booth likes it."

"He will."

"And if he doesn't, plenty of others will think it's the bee's knees." Selene tapped her hand on the table for emphasis.

Aunt Louisa trimmed Hestia's hair, adding flattering bangs since those, too, were the style. "Now take a look. What do you think?"

Accepting the mirror, Hestia obeyed. "Who is that?"

Selene let out a low whistle. "With a little lip paint, you could pass muster in New York."

"I'm not aiming for that, but I hope no one in Maiden is too shocked."

"The fact that I not only allowed you to bob your hair but that I did the bobbing myself may shock some people." Aunt Louisa tilted her head, admiring her handiwork. "Most don't remember me when I was a young thing. I cut quite a fine figure, if I do say so myself. But with your natural looks and modest dress, I believe we are striking an appropriate appearance for you. Modern, but not too daring. And your conduct shall continue to honor God."

"Yes, ma'am." Still, her heart pitter-pattered. What would Booth say when he picked her up to go to Easter services?

"You're so lucky you get to go on Sunday." Selene rested her chin in her hand and sighed. "I wish I could put on a new dress and go out."

"Your time to go out again will come." Hestia hoped her words comforted her cousin, even though she could hardly speculate when an outing would be possible. She noted Selene's large midsection. She looked as though she had the watermelon that had won the blue ribbon at the county fair attached to her.

Aunt Louisa spoke up. "I think the baby might be here sooner than you think."

Hestia swallowed. That would mean Selene would say good-bye to her baby forever. Even though she wasn't the mother, Hestia had become attached to the thought of the baby, over the months. How could Selene give up the baby? She prayed for Selene to have courage when the time came. She didn't think she could give up her baby if she were in Selene's place.

Hestia thought about her father and his detached attitude toward his patients. She had always thought him a bit hard-hearted for lack of emotion. Now, for the first time, she understood him. She didn't think she could have a relationship with people on such an intimate level and not become involved. Maybe she wasn't cut out for medicine after all.

A tear escaped her eye. Let them think she still mourned for her long hair.

Chapter Nineteen

....

On Saturday night, Hestia's dream about floating on a ship with her deceased grandmother was interrupted when Selene shook her. She tried to ignore her cousin, but Selene kept shaking her. "Go away."

"I can't go away. I'm covered in water."

Hestia bolted upright. "Your water broke?"

"Is that what you call it?" Hestia had never seen Selene so pale. "I'm scared."

Hestia's feet hit the chilly floor. "Get back in bed. Your time has come."

"My time." A look of understanding crossed her features. "The baby will be here soon."

"I hope so. Let me get the doctor." She made haste to change into her street clothes.

Aunt Louisa entered. "I heard you girls stirring. What's going on in here? It's after midnight."

Selene let out a groan of pain.

"I think her time has come." Hestia's voice betrayed her anxiousness.

"Oh!" Aunt Louisa nodded. "I'll get everything ready."

"I told Selene I'd notify the doctor." Hestia made a move to retrieve her sweater.

"The doctor? Oh, no, we don't need him," Aunt Louisa protested. "I'm delivering this baby."

"You?" Selene asked. "I don't mean any disrespect, but you're not a doctor. Or a midwife."

"I know, but I have assisted at births."

Selene let out another groan. "Hestia?"

"I've never assisted in a birth."

Aunt Louisa wagged her finger at Selene. "I wouldn't let her even if she had. She's a delicate maiden, and she shall not be exposed to the rigors of childbirth."

"But I'll never learn about medicine if I never help with anything," Hestia wailed.

"I'm sorry to disappoint you both, but Selene and I will be going it alone."

"No. Please. I want twilight sleep." Selene regarded Hestia with wide eyes.

"I don't remember promising such a dangerous thing." Aunt Louisa scowled. "Besides, the pain of childbirth is part of the natural process of new life. It will be over before you know it."

"At least your generation had chloroform." Selene looked pale.

"Chloroform has its dangers. I think you should have a natural delivery."

"I'm a modern woman, and I want modern medicine. Get the doctor so he can administer twilight sleep. If you don't, I'll never forgive you."

Aunt Louisa turned to Hestia. "Does your father use twilight sleep?"

"Yes, but I've never seen what happens with it. The only thing I know is she'll have to be tied to the bed."

"Tied to the bed?" Selene's mouth dropped open.

"It's for your own safety. You might start thrashing around and hurt yourself while you're under the influence of the medication." Hestia tried to remember if they had enough twine to tie Selene.

"Oh. Well, I want it anyway."

"Those suffragettes and their ideas," Aunt Louisa muttered. "They've ruined the world. First they insist that women should get involved in the filthy business of voting, and now they want to take away the beauty of natural childbirth."

"I don't care about voting." Selene's tone took on a sharp edge. "I care about twilight sleep. Get the doctor."

Aunt Louisa crossed her arms. "I'm having nothing of the sort. You'll have your baby the natural way, just as my mother gave birth to me."

Selene clutched her midsection. "Please!"

Hestia felt sorry for Selene, but there was no arguing with Aunt Louisa once she made up her mind. She rushed to Selene's side and held her hand. "Oh, do be brave, dear one. All shall be well. I'll pray for you."

"You go on and do that." Aunt Louisa's voice matched Selene's in sharpness. "But try to get some rest, too. Lay down on my bed."

Not in the mood to lie down, Hestia went to the back stoop. At least since she could pray, she didn't feel helpless. She hated to admit, even to herself, that part of her was glad her aunt had insisted she couldn't help. Papa's skill at practicing medicine made his profession seem, if not easy, at least calm. Listening to Selene's screams rattled Hestia. She hated herself for her emotion.

The Easter moon lit the sky enough so that she could see Miss Olive's house. If the neighbor had been awake, she surely would have ventured over by now for a cup of flour.

The whistle of a passing train seemed to sing its sympathy for Selene. The familiar noise comforted Hestia.

She looked in the opposite direction at the Barringtons'. If only Booth could be with her to console her. The thought of her cousin lying in labor, experiencing such pain, without even the benefit of old-fashioned chloroform, vexed her. She wished Papa were here. He'd no doubt convince his sister of the error of not having any mercy on her young charge. If Hestia didn't know better, she'd think her aunt was deliberately punishing Selene for being wicked, by making her suffer without aid. But it was her aunt's old-fashioned attitude and stubbornness about progress—Hestia's new bob notwithstanding— that stood in the way of mercy.

The hands on the clock seemed to move slowly. Hestia knew she needed to sleep if she hoped to look fresh for Easter services, but anticipation and anxiety kept her awake. Hestia stayed on the back stoop all night, unwilling to go inside and hear the full force of her cousin's agony.

Finally, as the sun dawned, Aunt Louisa stepped out onto the stoop. Hestia had grabbed a few winks of sleep as she sat upright in a wicker chair, but she felt as though she hadn't shut her eyes in a month.

Sweat beaded Aunt Louisa's forehead. "The baby's here."

Hestia felt suddenly awake. "How's Selene?"

"Glad it's over."

"What is it? A boy or a girl?"

"A girl. But it doesn't matter. The baby isn't ours."

A literal stab of pain shot through her heart. "I want to see her anyway."

"I don't suppose I can keep you from seeing her, but don't get attached."

Hestia went into the room she and Selene had shared these many months. "How are you, Selene?"

She nodded. "Tired."

"Will you let me see the baby?"

Selene didn't look as though she wanted to give her up, but she did. "Aunt Louisa says I can't hold her long. She didn't want me to be with her at all. She'll be sending a telegram to my cousin, and she'll come here as fast as she can to get her." A teardrop fell on Selene's cheek.

Holding the baby, Hestia gave her a little kiss on the forehead. She opened her eyes and yawned then shut them again. The blond-haired newborn resembled the Myatts. "You don't want to give her up, do you?"

Selene shook her head. Silent tears fell with full force. "I thought I wanted to, but I don't."

Hestia spoke softly. "Let's pray."

"I'd like that." Selene bowed her head.

"Heavenly Father, Selene has a big decision to make. Lord, is it Thy will for her to keep the baby? You know she has an offer of marriage from someone who loves her. Is this Thy will, Father? Please let us know. We all want what's best for Selene, Artie, and most of all, the baby. In Jesus' precious name, amen."

"Amen. Thank you." Hestia handed the baby back to Selene.

"That was hardly the most eloquent prayer on record, but it was the most heartfelt."

"I want to do what's right."

"Do you really love Artie? I mean, enough to make him the wife he deserves? There's so much to being a good wife. You haven't witnessed that, growing up most of your life without a mother. I see my mother support my father every day, in ways both big and small. It's in how she speaks to him with love and respect and in the little things she does for him. The big things, too. She makes him a happy home. That's what Artie will want from you. That's not too much to ask. Any man worthy to be your husband deserves that."

"My mother spent most of her days being pampered."

Hestia recalled Selene's immaculate mother and believed she spent many hours on her appearance. "That's not the kind of life you'll find here. Artie has a good job, but you won't be a lady of leisure. You'll need to be a good housekeeper, a good cook, and tend to the baby. No doubt he'll want another child one day, too. All of this will be easier if you really love him."

"I do. I've told him so. I—I just never thought it could come to anything."

"Well. I think he's right, though. This has been a big night for you. You need to think about it."

Selene studied her baby. "I will. Long and hard. I have more time to think than you do. Booth is due here to pick you up for Easter services in a couple of hours."

"So soon?" Hestia gasped. "It's hard to believe Easter is already here, isn't it? I'd better get going."

After Hestia completed her toilette, she looked at herself in the vanity mirror. The Easter bonnet, with its rhinestone and yellow feather, made her presence jaunty. Now that she had her hair bobbed, the hat looked stylish and correct, not as though she were trying to stuff too much hair underneath it. She still didn't recognize herself right away with the new style, but it had already started to grow on her. Her hair might be short, but she was still the same person. Booth had told her he would think she looked beautiful no matter what. She only hoped he meant it.

She liked the new dress she'd sewn for Easter. Following the basic pattern Aunt Louisa had used to make her Christmas dress, she added embellishments so it looked different. The light color looked good on her and was in the spirit of Easter.

Selene admired Hestia. "You look swell."

"I'm not so sure, tired as I am, but thanks for saying so."

"I wish I could go with you, but I'd say I'm occupied today." Selene's smile was that of a serene mother.

Hestia felt proud of her cousin. "You've come a long way. When you first got here, church was the last place you wanted to go."

"If I marry Artie, I'll be going every Sunday, and Wednesdays, too."

Hestia found the image of the little family appealing. "I wonder what he'll say when he sees the baby?"

"I hope he likes her."

"She's so sweet. How can he not?" They heard a knock on the front door. "That must be Booth."

Aunt Louisa had already answered the door by the time Hestia got to it. Indeed, their visitor was Booth, but Artie was with him.

As she always did, Hestia looked beyond him so she could wave at his parents, who were usually waiting in the automobile. On this morning, she didn't see them. "Where are your parents?"

"Mother got called to go early this morning to help decorate because Mrs. Carpenter is ill. I already took them to church."

Hestia noted Artie's presence. "Nice to see you, too, Artie."

"Morning. Since it's Easter I thought I'd say good morning to Selene before I went to my church," Artie said.

Artie didn't notice Hestia, but she saw Booth standing with his jaw slackened. "Hestia? What happened? You look different."

She recalled her new bob and touched the yellow feather. "Do you like my new Easter bonnet?"

"Uh, it's more than that. Your hair. Where is it?"

"Oh. My hair. I—I had Aunt Louisa cut it off into a bob." She felt her heart quicken with nervousness. "Do you like it?"

"Like it?" Booth studied her. "I—I love it!"

"You do?"

He grinned. "You sound surprised."

"That's because I am surprised. I wasn't sure if you'd like it or not."

"If you had asked me yesterday if I'd like it, I would have said I didn't know. But now that I see you with short hair, I like it just fine," Booth assured her.

"I know no one cares what I think," Artie interjected, "but it looks nice. What about Selene? I'd imagine she thinks it's swell."

"Yes, she does. And speaking of my cousin, I have a bigger—and much more important—surprise than my hair. Selene had her baby last night. She arrived at dawn."

Artie beamed. "A girl! I want to see her. And Selene, too. Selene's okay, isn't she?"

Hestia nodded.

"I wish y'all had gotten me so I could have been here when she was born," Artie lamented.

"I—I didn't think of that. I'm sorry. If it makes you feel any better, you're the first two people outside the family who know," Hestia consoled him.

"I've got to see them both. Excuse me." Artie shot past Hestia and headed toward the bedroom.

"You'd better ask Aunt Louisa if it's okay," Hestia called after him.

"I'm sure Miss Louisa has the door barred." Booth joked but didn't sound entirely happy. Hestia had a feeling that was because the baby's arrival meant she wouldn't be staying in Maiden.

"We have a few minutes. Why don't you stop in and say hello to Selene and the new arrival? She won't be here much longer."

"You're going to feel sorry to see the baby go, aren't you?"

"I didn't think I'd care, but I do."

Hestia and Booth knocked on Selene's door even though it was open. Hestia saw Artie looking at the baby as though she were his own. If Hestia didn't know better, she'd swear they were modeling for a talcum powder ad in a periodical. Hestia entered, with Booth following. "She's beautiful, isn't she?"

"Yes, she is." Artie looked at the blond-haired bundle then at Selene.

Hestia and Booth kept their distance but could still see the new baby. "She's a pretty baby. As pretty as babies can be, anyway." He nudged Hestia. "We'd better go. Artie, aren't you due to go to preaching soon?"

"Yes, but if it's all the same to Selene here, I'm staying with her and the baby. This is celebration enough for me."

"I'd like that." Selene smiled, glowing.

Hestia and Booth bid them good-bye and went into the parlor. They nearly ran over Aunt Louisa, who still wore her housedress. "I can see you have no plans to go with us today."

"I'm tired as it is, and I think I've got my work cut out for me here."

Hestia didn't feel so fresh herself, since she hadn't slept much all night. "Do you want me to stay home and cook so you can rest?"

"No. I'm too wound up to sleep." Aunt Louisa nodded toward the kitchen. "I've got the ham in already for dinner. We can eat a little earlier than we'd planned. I'm sure we'll be ready once all the excitement dies down."

"Guess it's just you and me, kiddo," Booth teased Hestia.

"What a thing to call her!" Aunt Louisa chastised. "If you start treating her like a flapper, I'll make her grow out her hair."

"He's just joking, Aunt Louisa." Hestia patted her aunt's bony shoulder. "I couldn't be a flapper if my life depended on it."

"It just might." Aunt Louisa cut her glance to the room where Selene, Artie, and the baby were. "I've got to tend to them. They're getting much too attached to that baby, and it's not theirs."

"She can change her mind."

"Change her mind!" Aunt Louisa acted as though such a turn of heart would spell the end of the world. "But she's being adopted."

"Yes, and though that was generous of your relatives, I get the impression the cousins like the idea of more money. They can never love the baby as Selene can. Maybe all of this is God's plan, Aunt Louisa. Maybe the little girl should be with her mother, and with a man who really loves her mother. And her. Can't you see the look in Artie's eyes? He's in love with them both. I don't think Selene should give up the baby."

Aunt Louisa let out a harrumph. "What's the matter, have you gotten into Selene's stash of cheap novels? This is real life, not a fantasy."

"I don't know, Aunt Louisa. Having a good man declare his love for you is the stuff of fantasy, but it's happened to Selene." As soon as she uttered the sentence, Hestia realized she wished a good man would declare his love for her. What was stopping Booth? Not wanting to appear eager or bold, Hestia refused to look in his direction.

"Uh, we'd better go," Booth prodded.

"I'll say you'd better go." Aunt Louisa's stern expression told them she'd brook no excuses. "A good worship service is what Hestia needs to get silly stars out of her eyes once and for all." Aunt Louisa peered out the window. "Where are your parents?"

"They're already at church."

Booth took Hestia by the arm as they descended the front steps. They were too immersed in their own thoughts to talk much about the day or what had happened. They didn't speculate about the sermon, because no matter where one attended church on Easter Sunday, the resurrection miracle would be the topic. Though predictable, each year the message proved welcome. It was the greatest story ever told.

* * * * *

Later, Booth pulled the automobile onto a patch of grass by the church. The lot was jammed by the Easter crush of automobiles.

Hestia meditated on the stained-glass windows. "Selene missed so much growing up, only hearing the sermons on Easter and Christmas. I think now that she's met Artie, she can understand why it's good to think about the Lord every day, not just twice a year."

"Amen to that." His smile looked bittersweet.

Hestia heard the sound of a nearby automobile door shut. Judith and her family emerged from the Nash Roadster. Hestia waved and waited for Judith to come closer. "Hey, you!"

"Hey, yourself."

"Judith! You bobbed your hair!"

Judith looked at Hestia and gasped in return. "And you did the same thing!"

"You look wonderful!" They complimented each other in near unison. Like schoolgirls, they giggled.

Hestia admired Judith's new look. "I'm so glad we decided not to wear our hair in low buns."

"Me, too. It's a new era, Hestia."

"I'm not sure how I feel about it." Mr. Unsworth didn't bother to conceal his distress. "Come along, now, or we'll be late. It's crowded today."

Mrs. Unsworth nodded. "It's always crowded on Easter Sunday."

"Do you like Judith's hair, Mrs. Unsworth?" Hestia couldn't resist asking.

"Of course. I'm the one who bobbed it!" She winked.

Hestia touched Judith's arm and whispered in her ear, "Selene had her baby. A girl."

Judith gasped. "Mother! Selene had her baby."

"The end of an ordeal for everyone," the older woman commented.

Judith touched Hestia's arm. "Try to stay here in Maiden as long as you can. I can't go around with this new style all alone!"

Hestia nodded. While Judith may have joked about the style, she knew her sentiment about Hestia's imminent departure was sincere. Again, Hestia felt pain in her heart. Haw River had its appeal, but Maiden's charms had embraced her. She felt more at home here than she had anywhere else. She fought back tears that threatened.

Hestia was glad to discover that several of the younger women had chosen this point in time to get bobs. Seeing them confirmed that she had made the right decision. They were all stylish women. Shrieks, gasps, and flattery flew through the church. Some adults looked askance while others nodded knowingly.

"See?" Hestia said to Judith. "You won't have to face the world alone with your new style after all."

"I'm a little disappointed."

"Why?"

"I was secretly hoping to be a trendsetter."

Hestia laughed. She'd miss Judith.

After the service, where they sang the most popular Easter hymns including Hestia's favorite, "Up from the Grave He Arose," the congregants left in a collective, joyous mood. Only Hestia felt a bit down.

"What's the matter?" Booth said on the way to the automobile. "Didn't you enjoy the service, especially the singing?"

"Yes. Didn't you hear me singing as loudly as I could? Hope I wasn't too off-key."

He laughed. "Never."

"I was tired when we left this morning, but church invigorated me."

"I'm sure you had quite a night."

"Yes. One reason I came here to visit was to learn more about medicine, but I really learned more about myself. I don't think my nerves can take seeing people suffer, even if I can help them." Hestia hated admitting defeat.

"But what did you think medicine would be like? You know people suffer."

"I realize now how much Papa sheltered me. I saw very little beyond the occasional scraped knee and high fever."

"You've been with family members. It would be different with strangers."

"Maybe, but I'm not so sure. I hate seeing anyone in distress." She looked beyond him to the sun. "I'll miss this place." She decided to make a bold move. "And, most especially, you."

"We're ready, Booth." Normally Hestia didn't mind hearing Mrs. Barrington's cheerful voice, but it grated on her at that moment. What would Booth have said if they hadn't been interrupted?

Booth and Hestia talked about anything but her impending departure as they went back to Aunt Louisa's. She didn't want to think about it, and she had a feeling Booth didn't, either.

Chapter Twenty

....

"So shall we tell her?" Artie wanted to know.

"I don't see any reason to delay," Selene answered. She looked at the baby. "What do you think, Easter? Is it time to tell Aunt Louisa?" Easter didn't respond except to look at her mother. Selene couldn't believe the beauty of her newborn. Dressed in a white bonnet and gown, wrapped in a white blanket, she appeared as though she had just left the side of God's throne. "Who does she look like?"

"You," he answered. "But I never knew her real father."

"She doesn't look a bit like him."

"What if she does when she gets older? Will that upset you?"

"No, because I already love her too much." Selene looked at Artie. "Would you mind terribly if she ends up not looking much like me?"

"No, because like you, I already love her. I want to be a good father to her."

"You will be. As far as I'm concerned, you will be her real father. And that's what the world will know, too."

"Yes. I understand about that. I understand more than you know."

Selene wanted to know what he meant, but Aunt Louisa entered. "Enough admiring the baby. I told you not to get attached to her."

Artie rose. "Selene and I have news for you."

Selene froze and was grateful that Artie didn't seem to mind breaking the news.

"Yes?"

"Not to be disrespectful, Miss Louisa, but we won't be giving her up for adoption. I plan to marry Selene in a private ceremony as soon as she's well enough to stand."

Suddenly unsteady, Aunt Louisa sat on the bed. "Marriage? Artie, I know you mean well, but you shouldn't be so impulsive."

"Impulse isn't ruling me. I've prayed long and hard about this decision. My joy over making Selene my wife, and being a father to the baby, knows no bounds."

"You think you can marry here in Maiden?" Aunt Louisa didn't need to elaborate.

"I'm sure my pastor will marry us."

Aunt Louisa looked as though she was trying to absorb the news. "I thought you had feelings for Selene, but I had no idea you'd act upon them. And Selene, you said yes?"

Selene nodded.

Artie looked into Selene's eyes and then at the baby. "Easter will be my daughter."

"Easter?"

Selene nodded. "That's what we named her. Easter Hestia Louisa Rowland. Isn't that a beautiful name?"

"Easter...Louisa?" A hint of a blush rose to the elder woman's cheeks. "Now, don't give your child my name to cater to me, hoping I'll change my mind."

Selene smiled. "You and Hestia have been here for me this whole time. You both deserve to be honored. But I wanted to honor God by naming her Easter, especially since He sent her on Easter Sunday. And Easter is what she shall be called."

Artie touched Easter's cheek. "I feel sorry for the relative who'll be losing her."

Aunt Louisa's next statements surprised Selene. "I think it's for the best that won't be happening. She was only taking the baby as a favor to the family and because your father planned to provide for the baby. I'll venture she'll be relieved. It's my brother I'm worried about now. He hadn't planned for you to keep the baby. He thinks you'll be back on the train to New York in a few weeks. I doubt he's ready to admit to his mistresses that he's a grandfather now. Albeit a young one."

"I'm sure he'll deny being a grandfather if he thinks he can get away with it." Selene's voice displayed a touch of bitterness. "He's fine in New York without me. He made that clear enough with all the postcards he sent from around the world."

"He sent those out of love," Aunt Louisa argued.

"Yes, he does love me, in his way. But he has his own life, and that's the way it should be. I won't be his problem. I'll be here in Maiden, with Artie. I think when Father sees the situation, he'll agree it's a blessing from God."

"He'll blame me for not taking better care of you." Selene could tell by the way Aunt Louisa blew out her breath that she felt resignation rather than anger, bitterness, or fear of reprisal from her brother.

"Not taking better care of me?" Selene chuckled. "I'd say we couldn't have created a better outcome if we tried."

"Maybe in some quarters people would feel that way. But no one ever anticipated you would live here forever. I have no doubt your father has someone in mind for you to wed."

"Oh, he mentioned a prospective beau now and again, but I have a mind of my own. And my mind says that Artie Rowland is the one for me." She extended her hand and touched his. "If this hadn't happened, I wouldn't have come to Maiden for an extended stay—or even come to Maiden at all, and I never would have met Artie. I have to think that this baby is part of God's plan."

"As do I." Aunt Louisa wiped a tear.

"You ladies won't have an argument from me." Artie gazed at Selene before turning his attention to the older woman. "Please know, Miss Louisa, that I really love Selene. I want to be a good husband to her and a good father to her baby."

"You're a bachelor. You really want a ready-made family?"

"I hadn't planned on it, I'll admit. But when I met Selene, I loved her right away. Only I couldn't be unequally yoked. When she accepted Christ as her personal Savior, I knew she had changed. Like Selene, my present is different because of God. He gave me many second chances, and I want to be part of Selene's second chance. I want to give her the best life I can. I feel certain my friends will accept us and Easter. Don't you worry. I'll take care of them both, gladly."

Selene saw Aunt Louisa's eyes mist. "I think you owe it to Selene and her father to ask his permission."

"Let's wire him and have him visit us. I want him to see his granddaughter." Selene cuddled her baby.

Aunt Louisa looked Artie straight in the eye. "If you can take the hardened flapper who came here a few months ago and turn her into a loving mother, who am I to stand in your way? I'll do everything I can to help you, son."

* * * * *

Hestia sat beside Booth in the Model T as he parked it in the Barrington driveway. His parents disembarked. Mrs. Barrington had mentioned she bought a ham that would take all afternoon to bake. That left Booth time to visit with Hestia. At least, she hoped.

"I don't want to keep you from lunch."

"A nap is more like it, but I'm too excited to sleep." Hestia yawned.

"You'd think you were the one who just had a baby."

Hestia started walking to her aunt's house, with Booth beside her. "I feel as though I did, in a way. I shared a room for months with Selene, remember? She didn't hold back on telling me everything she was feeling."

"Soon you'll be back in Haw River, with a room all to yourself, I assume."

She remembered her home. The teddy bear from her youth still occupied a special place on her bed. "Yes, I have my own room. Lavender and white."

"I can picture you in a lavender-and-white room. You miss home, don't you?"

"Yes, there's a lot of it I miss. I always thought I'd stay in Haw River forever, helping Papa in his office until I married Luther. But you know how that went."

"You already know what I think of Luther."

Hestia had long ago forgiven Luther, thanks in large part to Booth. "I'll always be grateful to you for helping me see that I can have a happy life without him. It's peculiar how I've been gone so long that my friends' letters don't mean so much to me. At first I felt as though I was in the center of everything, but now when they write, I feel as though I'm reading about someone else's life, an outsider watching from afar."

"They don't mean it that way, do they?"

"Of course not. They can't help it. That's just the way life is, I'm finding. It's all my fault. I told them I'd be gone three weeks at most, and I ended up being away several months without so much as visiting at Christmas." By this time they had reached the veranda. Since they'd just left church, neither had any desire to sit, so they stood near the door.

"I'm glad you stayed here for Christmas. It wouldn't have been the same without you. It won't be the same without you. Nothing will. You have no idea how much you have added to my life, Hestia."

She remembered the smell of the cedar tree and how handsome he had looked that night. "May–maybe I can arrange to stay a couple of extra weeks."

"Do you mean that? You really want to stay? Or do you just feel sorry for me?" He grinned in the lopsided way she loved.

"I want to stay."

"Then stay forever."

"Forever? I love Aunt Louisa dearly and I know she thinks the world of me, but I can't expect her to let me stay with her forever. She's much too independent."

"And so are you. You deserve your own home."

What was he saying? "I—I don't have my own home here."

"But you can, with someone who loves you. Me."

"You? You love me?" Her heart beat with such ferocity she could hardly speak.

"You couldn't tell?"

"You could have told me, you know."

"I wanted to so very much, but I knew you'd be sacrificing your life to move here to be with me. It didn't seem fair to ask somehow." He took her hands in his. "I've saved up some money, and I can find us a house. It won't be the biggest or grandest in town, but I'm sure I can find something for us somewhere. Somewhere you can be happy—as my wife."

"Your wife!"

"Yes. My wife. Would you like to be Mrs. Booth Barrington?"

"I–I'm surprised!"

"Are you really?"

"Well…yes! I didn't think you'd ask me. Are you certain?"

"I've never been more certain."

"Neither have I." Unable to restrain herself, she jumped up and down. "Yes! I'll marry you. Ever since we laid in the leaves together, I knew I loved you."

"You don't know how much I wanted to kiss you that day. How much I want to kiss you now."

"What's stopping you?"

He drew her closely into his arms, and she felt a joy she didn't think possible. His kiss, the kiss she had wanted forever, proved even sweeter than she could have imagined.

"Mercy!"

They turned to see Miss Olive wearing her most outraged expression.

"Sorry, Miss Olive," Booth told her. "You can't protest us now. We're getting married!"

"Married! When?"

Booth paused, but only for a second. "New Year's Day 1924."

"What does your aunt say, Hestia? And has your father given his permission?"

"He will, I have no doubt. And so will Aunt Louisa." She looked into Booth's sparkling blue eyes. "New Year's Day 1924 is perfect. Just perfect."

"So that's what all the commotion is over here." Miss Olive's tone sounded satisfied, as though she had been instrumental in solving a monumental mystery.

"Not exactly." Hestia shared her account of the previous night's events.

"So the baby's here." Miss Olive tsked. "What a shame to have such circumstances of birth. I'll go in and see if there's anything I can do to help."

Booth squeezed Hestia's hand as the neighbor disappeared. "There's nothing like Miss Olive to dampen a mood, is there?"

Hestia chuckled. "She doesn't mean any harm. I want to tell them the good news, but I don't want to rub our happiness in Selene's face. She must feel terrible about giving up the baby."

"At least Artie is here to console her."

"Yes, he has been a great comfort to her. Come on, let's go in." Holding hands, they entered the parlor but noticed that everyone seemed to be hovering in Selene's room. Alarm shot through Hestia. "I hope the baby's okay."

"There you are," Miss Olive said. "Already celebrating their engagement with a little too much vigor, if you ask me."

"Engagement?" Aunt Louisa asked. Selene and Artie looked surprised by the news as well. "When did this happen?"

"Just now," Booth said. "Well, I've been thinking of asking Hestia for some time, but I hadn't gotten up the nerve. With the baby being born and the reality of Hestia returning to Haw River upon me, I knew I had to tell her how I really felt about her." He looked into her eyes.

"I think you knew all along how I feel about you," Hestia told him.

Selene beamed. "So you're staying here in Maiden?"

Hestia nodded. "Yes. I hope I can stay here with Aunt Louisa during my engagement. We hope to wed on New Year's Day. Do you think you can put up with me that much longer, Aunt Louisa?"

The older woman smiled. "I would be happy to have you here as long as you want to stay."

"This is a dream come true!" Selene cried. "Artie and I are planning to marry as soon as we can, and I'll be living in Maiden, too. We'll raise Easter together."

"Easter? What a beautiful name."

"Easter Hestia Louisa Rowland," Selene said.

When Hestia heard her name, tears flowed. She ran to Selene and embraced her. "That's so beautiful of you to do. Thank you."

"I want you to be my maid of honor at my ceremony, even though it won't be much." Selene squeezed her hand.

"Of course. I would be thrilled. And it's not the ceremony that matters, but the marriage."

"True."

"Booth, will you stand up for me?" Artie asked.

"I'd be insulted if you didn't ask, old man."

Hestia looked at Artie. "I'm so glad you and Selene decided to wed. Selene has proven she deserves a second chance, and she couldn't have found a better man for her."

"Coming from you, that's quite a compliment." Hestia could see by the misty look in his eyes that Artie was moved. "I was about to tell Selene more about second chances when we got sidetracked."

"Oh?" Selene asked.

"Yes. Very few people know this, but I was adopted."

A collective gasp filled the room.

"It's true." Artie nodded. "For a while, I felt terrible about it, even though I shouldn't have. My adoptive family showed me nothing but love and patience, and what did I do about it? I indulged in bitterness and resentment and the type of life that brought me and everyone around me nothing but pain and heartache. But I mended my ways, just as I see that Selene has mended hers. Only Selene is much smarter than I ever was. She got on the right track at a very young age. It took me a few years." He looked at Selene, love coloring his eyes. "Your child deserves a home with her mother. If you'd been ambivalent about this baby, I wouldn't have taken such a leap. But you've been wanting to keep her for quite some time, and most especially now that you've seen her."

"Yes," Selene admitted with no hesitation.

"And now you can. Both of you will live with a man who loves you. Easter, as the best father I can be. And you, Selene, as the best husband I can ever hope to be."

"I love you," Selene declared.

The collective gasp changed to a collective sigh.

"When I came here, I was miserable and didn't know it," Selene said. "But love found me in Maiden, North Carolina."

"I knew I was miserable when I arrived." Hestia remembered her heartbreak and recognized her gratitude that she would never again feel put-aside. She had the love and devotion of a good man. A man she would love forever. "I never expected love to find me in Maiden. But it did." She looked at Booth. His eyes sparkled with the joy of realized love.

Want a peek into local American life—past and present?
The *Love Finds You*™ series published by Summerside Press
features real towns and combines travel, romance,
and faith in one irresistible package!

The novels in the series—uniquely titled after American towns with unusual but intriguing names—inspire romance and fun. Each fictional story draws on the compelling history or the unique character of a real place. Stories center on romances kindled in small towns, old loves lost and found again on the high plains, and new loves discovered at exciting vacation getaways. Summerside Press plans to publish at least one novel set in each of the 50 states. Be sure to catch them all!

NOW AVAILABLE IN STORES

Love Finds You in Miracle, Kentucky by Andrea Boeshaar
ISBN: 978-1-934770-37-5

Love Finds You in Snowball, Arkansas by Sandra D. Bricker
ISBN: 978-1-934770-45-0

Love Finds You in Romeo, Colorado by Gwen Ford Faulkenberry
ISBN: 978-1-934770-46-7

Love Finds You in Valentine, Nebraska by Irene Brand
ISBN: 978-1-934770-38-2

Love Finds You in Humble, Texas by Anita Higman
ISBN: 978-1-934770-61-0

Love Finds You in Last Chance, California by Miralee Ferrell
ISBN: 978-1-934770-39-9

Love Finds You in Paradise, Pennsylvania by Loree Lough
ISBN: 978-1-934770-66-5

COMING IN JUNE

Love Finds You in Treasure Island, Florida by Debby Mayne
ISBN: 978-1-934770-80-1

Love Finds You in Liberty, Indiana by Melanie Dobson
ISBN: 978-1-934770-74-0

summerside
PRESS